PRAISE FOR Still the One

Fans of Susan May Warren's Christiansen family novels will fall head over heels for Rachel D. Russell's charming debut. With its likable romantic duo and cast of familiar supporting characters, *Still the One* is a worthy addition to Warren's beloved Deep Haven collection.

— CARLA LAUREANO, RITA® AWARD-WINNING
AUTHOR OF *FIVE DAYS IN SKYE* AND *THE
SATURDAY NIGHT SUPPER CLUB*

A new story set in Deep Haven? Yes, please! *Still the One* captured my attention from its opening pages. I adored wounded Cole right off the bat (heart eyes for days!) and found myself relating to heroine Megan. Weaving together heart-tugging romance and small-town charm, debut author Rachel D. Russell is sure to win readers with this hope-filled story.

— MELISSA TAGG, CHRISTY AWARD-WINNING
AUTHOR OF THE MAPLE VALLEY AND WALKER
FAMILY SERIES

A debut author to watch, Rachel D. Russell has crafted a story packed with genuine emotion, irresistible characters, sizzling chemistry, and well-deserved second chances. The path to love is not easy for long-separated childhood friends Cole and Megan, but the hope and healing they each offer and find along the way will fill the reader's heart to overflowing. Fans of Susan May Warren's Deep Haven and Christiansen Family series will welcome the opportunity to spend time with old friends, but even readers new to Deep Haven will feel like they're coming home.

— BETHANY TURNER, AWARD-WINNING AUTHOR
OF *HADLEY BECKETT'S NEXT DISH*

With a sincere and engaging voice, Russell's debut novel explores issues of abandonment, rejection, and the struggle to forgive in this perfectly paced romance readers everywhere will adore. *Still the One* skillfully weaves a fresh take on second-chance love in a setting as familiar as your own hometown.

— NICOLE DEESE, AWARD-WINNING AUTHOR OF
A NEW SHADE OF SUMMER AND *BEFORE I
CALLED YOU MINE*

With cameo appearances from popular Deep Haven characters and the introduction of fabulous new characters, Rachel D. Russell's *Still the One* is the perfect addition to the Deep Haven Collection.

— NICOLE COOK, INKWELL INSPIRATIONS

STILL THE ONE

A DEEP HAVEN NOVEL

SUSAN MAY WARREN
RACHEL D. RUSSELL

sunrise
PUBLISHING

A NOTE FROM SUSIE MAY

Dear friends,

I have this problem. When I finish a great book by a favorite author, I immediately search for the next one by that author. And if there isn't a "next" one, I read through that author's backlist.

And when I'm done with that, I go in search of an author that is similar to them. Or one who writes about similar places or characters.

And therein lies the problem. I struggle to find authors that are like the ones I love. I'm not alone. Over the years, I've received countless letters from readers who want more of the best-selling, award-winning Deep Haven stories. Like me, they love to escape into this tiny community on the North Shore of Minnesota.

So I thought...what if I found authors who wrote like me, who also loved Deep Haven, and might want to write a story in that world? And what if they were new-to-market authors who simply needed a little mentoring, and then an introduction to readers?

I was so thrilled when this story by Rachel D. Russell came

across my desk. Not only does she have a vibrant, compelling voice, but her story about a broken former Army Ranger who comes "home" to Deep Haven to find his first love (sorta) waiting for him captured my heart.

You'll find this story about a wedding planner who recruits this former soldier into her world to be a charming, funny, cozy, and delightful read. (And be ready to cry. It's just that good.) Yes, like any good editor, I worked with Rachel to help her bring Cole and Megan's story to life, but the story and voice are hers, and I know you'll love it as much as I do.

Welcome back to Deep Haven! Enjoy!

XO,

Susie May

For my husband, Brian, always my hero

&

For my mom, always my encourager

CHAPTER 1

*A*nything had to be better than returning to Deep Haven. Enemy fire. Jumping into hostile territory. Twelve months of MREs. Even cleaning the pit toilets in a remote desert outpost.

Anything but having to face the one person who'd destroyed his life.

Cole Barrett turned up the defrost fan, his grip tight on the steering wheel.

The clouds hung low over Lake Superior, passing cars whipping up a cocktail of snow and ice against his windshield as he traveled north on Highway 61. And now, because the rental company had loaned out the Ford Explorer he'd reserved, he was stuck in a ridiculous Dodge Grand Caravan and thirty minutes behind schedule for his meeting with Deep Haven real estate agent Nathan Decker.

In forty-eight hours, the deal would be done. He'd have his grandfather's house cleared out and listed for sale, and hopefully, he'd also hear from the U.S. Marshals Service for an interview. And, really, it couldn't happen fast enough.

He eased his foot off the gas when hazard lights materialized through the snowy January haze. As he drew closer, he spotted a woman standing on the berm of plowed snow that bordered the highway, her Subaru pitched into the ditch.

She wore her blue knit cap pulled down low, and wisps of blonde hair snapped around her forehead as they escaped the scarf wound halfway up her face.

From the angle of her car, the quick math told him she'd hit a patch of ice and spun off the road, burying her front end in the snow.

Cole glanced at the clock and groaned. Yet another delay. Yeah, well, he couldn't just leave her there. There was no way she'd get out without assistance, and considering how hard it was to get a text through to Nathan up the road in Deep Haven, he didn't figure she had any help on the way. He slowed, pulling onto the shoulder ahead of her.

Slush splattered on his boots and he tugged his black leather jacket closed against the icy Minnesota gale that sliced through the fabric of his shirt. From the looks of the slope of the ditch, if she'd slid a foot farther, her front bumper would have embedded into the berm and he'd need more than his bare hands to dig her out.

As it were, the right leverage and his brute strength might get them both on their way in a jiffy.

"Hey!" She'd scrambled down the snowbank as he approached. "Thanks!"

She opened a passenger side door and dug through a box, chucking a bundle of blue flowers out of it.

"Are you okay?"

She looked over her shoulder at him. He couldn't help but think that she resembled a miniature Stay Puft Marshmallow Man in her thick, gray down coat and wrappings, only her hazel eyes visible. She pulled her scarf away from her mouth to speak.

"I'm fine, if you include the fact I'm super late and—oh, never mind." She turned around, holding the empty box. "You know, my day started out pretty spectacular. Blue skies, happy bride. I'm not sure how it took this plunge into the abyss of terrible."

"You too, huh?"

"You can't even imagine." She pulled apart the box. Clearly, this wasn't her first off-road excursion.

"Let's see what we can do." He circled the car, dropping to his knees to scrape the ice and snow out from under the tire. The cold seeped through his denim and bit at his hands. "I don't think it will take too much to get you back on the road. You're not jammed in deep." He looked at the swirl of tracks leading to her tires. "I don't see any icy patches. Did you swerve to avoid a deer?"

She shook her head. "I wish. It was a lunch accident."

He frowned but didn't know how to follow up. He took the cardboard and wedged it under her tire. "Okay, put it in reverse and I'll rock it, and let's see if we can get some traction. Once you get up on the road, get it in drive and keep going. Okay?"

She nodded beneath her layers. "Got it. Thank you for stopping." She looked up at him, let out a long breath. "It's a little embarrassing when a minivan outmaneuvers the four-wheel drive."

"You're welcome. And, it's not mine." Heat rose in his face and he suddenly felt the need to defend himself. "The rental company messed up."

"Oh?" For the first time he got a smile. She leaned to look past him at the van. "I don't know, though. I think it makes a real statement."

The kind of statement he might have liked, if his life hadn't derailed. Yet another thing he could thank his ex-wife for.

She climbed back inside her car and started it up, waited for a break in traffic. He put his shoulder against the front bumper and pushed. It didn't take much to regain traction. He nearly fell as her car rolled back onto the pavement. She put her window down. "Thanks!"

"No problem!" He found his feet, waved, and jogged back to the van, his jeans wet and chunks of ice clinging to his boots. Perfect. Now he'd be late, hungry, and cold.

Her lights had nearly disappeared before he got back on the road, heading toward the inevitable.

The radio offered little comfort when the only clear station came through with Tim McGraw's "Live Like You Were Dying." All that did was take him back in time, to summers on the North Shore.

He wished he could still love Deep Haven. Walking along the pebbled shore. Racing to World's Best Donuts after school. Fireworks over the harbor.

I love summer. He could hear his best friend, Megan Carter, see her long hair pulled back into some sort of fancy braid. Her toes barely holding on to her bright pink flip-flops. The contagious enthusiasm almost made him believe the impossible. She'd flopped down on the dock next to him, smelling like sunshine and summer, giving him a red licorice rope and a smile. *Do you have to go home?*

He tightened his grip on the steering wheel. Yeah, even his good memories of Deep Haven could choke him with sadness, which was exactly why he liked to keep moving forward. Make a plan. Get things done. Find a new challenge.

Because, for the first time in his adult life, he had an open plate with nothing on it. No responsibilities. Nowhere to be.

No one to belong to.

Freedom. At least that's how he planned on looking at it. He felt sure Rebecca saw it that way.

Today was the beginning of a fresh start, one that didn't include the Army telling him where to be and what to do. Or him disappointing a wife he barely knew.

Time to take control of his life. Starting with the sale of

Grandpa's house. The man had never lived with much. Well, except whiskey. Most items could be hauled out for donation. Cole doubted he'd find anything of value in the old Victorian on Third Avenue West.

He pulled into the parking lot of the Java Cup and got out. Across the street, the harbor glistened, calm and frozen, the sky overcast and hinting at another storm. A gust caught his collar and he pulled it up as he hustled into the coffee shop. The bold aroma of fresh brew, the sound of coffee grinders, and the low conversation of a few locals brought him back to the small-town aura. During the summertime, the place tripled in size. At the height of winter, only a few hardy locals braved the weather to venture out for coffee.

All his hopes for a meal faded when he was met with a tray of stale donuts. Tomorrow he'd swing by earlier.

"Cole Barrett?" A man waved from a nearby table, standing to extend a hand. Silver peppered his brown hair, and he wore a gray fleece jacket, the name Decker Real Estate embroidered on the breast.

"Yes, sir." Cole shook his hand.

"Nathan Decker. You're the only guy who's walked through the door in the past hour that I didn't recognize. I was starting to wonder if you'd make it."

Oh, yes. Small-town life.

"Sorry. I hope you got my message. There was a problem in Duluth with my rental car and, anyway, my apologies. It isn't like me to miss an appointment."

"I'm in a bit of a rush now to meet my wife, but I did put together all the paperwork. Have a seat." He held out a folder and slid back into the chair across from Cole. "Go over it and sign where I marked. My business card is inside."

Cole opened the folder. "Thanks. How long do you think it'll take to sell?"

Nathan paused, as if measuring his words, and Cole's chest tightened. He looked up. What had his grandfather done now?

"There's a tenant in the garage apartment and she's claiming she signed a six-month lease. She's refusing to leave."

"What?" Nathan would have had less impact with a right hook.

"I didn't realize it until yesterday."

Cole closed the folder, spread his hand on top. Took a breath. "I'm not planning on sticking around, Nathan. I need to sell the house to cover my grandfather's care."

Nathan raised a brow, waited while the woman behind the counter carried over two tall coffees and slid one in front of each of them, along with a donut for Cole. "Thank you, Marie." Nathan lifted his cup, swirling it in a circular motion, as if to stir the contents. He turned back to Cole. "I figured you'd be ready for something hot to drink after your long drive."

"Ma'am." Cole gave her a polite nod and took a sip, letting the hot liquid warm him. "What is this?"

"It's called a Megan. Very popular around here. Chocolate and caramel latte."

The name stirred inside him, but he dismissed it. "It's good. Thanks. I had forgotten how cold it gets here."

Nathan set his drink down and leaned back in the chair. "So, you haven't seen your grandfather yet?" His voice didn't hold judgment, just a gentle prodding curiosity.

"No." And he had zero intention of adding him to his itinerary.

"My understanding is his Alzheimer's is fairly advanced."

Cole shrugged and rubbed his hand across the smooth-planed wood table. "My memory's still good." Like the memory of cowering in the corner. A child at the mercy of a monster. Maybe justice was finally being served.

Nathan's eyes stayed on him.

Fine. "Let's just say that after my parents died, living with my grandfather wasn't an ideal situation. It was a dark year."

"That's right. You lived here for a year after your folks died," Nathan said, giving a nod to two women who passed the table on their way out.

"Yeah. I was twelve. Just starting seventh grade."

"You must have made a few friends."

"A few. I'm not sure anyone will remember me." And frankly, he didn't even know if Megan was still around. "My family used to come here every summer when I was growing up."

For the second time, Megan walked into his brain and sat down. *I was hoping I'd see you back here. The summer isn't the same without you.*

And his life hadn't been the same without her. But that was long ago, and he'd been a child. She'd probably left town after high school, following her big dreams.

Nathan tugged a business card from his wallet and handed it to Cole. "This is the number of the care center. I used to volunteer there. They're good people. Trustworthy."

Cole appreciated Nathan's kindness, but the last person he was worried about was his grandfather. He shoved the card into his pocket. He still wasn't sure why his grandfather had named him as Power of Attorney.

"So, what am I going to do about this tenant?"

"I don't know what you can do, but it's Friday. Maybe let it settle over the weekend."

"Maybe I can talk to her. Tell her my situation..."

"Good luck. She's pretty stubborn." His phone buzzed. "I need to go before my wife comes looking for me. Tonight's our anniversary."

A wife. Waiting for him. Cole had to stop what-iffing about what a family might be like. Rebecca had destroyed all those hopes.

Laughter erupted from a group of teens huddled over their phones in the corner nook.

Nathan scribbled a few notes. "I'll get started on the listing. I'm sorry this is going to take longer than you intended. These go to your grandfather's house." He slid a set of keys across the table. "I'm not sure what condition the house is in. I haven't been inside. Will you be staying there?"

"I guess." Cole had planned this as a pass-through stop. An unwelcome requirement in his life, like a root canal.

"Or I could call the Christiansens at Evergreen Resort and see if they have a room available." Nathan stood, waited for an answer.

Cole remembered the Christiansen family. Big. Rowdy. And tight. If he'd ever had another real family, he'd have wanted it to be like them. He'd witnessed more than one skirmish between the young brothers, but he'd also shared a few dinners around their table. No matter what, they stuck together.

"That won't be necessary." He'd make his own plans. Besides, they were heading into the weekend and Cole knew exactly where the Christiansen clan would be at zero-nine-hundred on Sunday. If he was going to have a sitrep with God, it would be on his own terms.

"Okay. Let's connect early next week."

"Sure. Thanks again." Cole shook his hand before Nathan headed out the door, holding it open for a boy, about ten. He wore a blue jacket that looked a little big for him and carried a stack of tickets in his ungloved hand. Cole took the last bite of stale donut and watched the boy march to the counter. What he lacked in stature, he made up for in purpose.

"Hi, Marie, we're selling raffle tickets for the Huskies peewee hockey team. I thought you might be interested." The boy wore athletic pants and worn athletic shoes, his dark hair peeking out from his knit hat.

"Hockey, huh?"

"Yes, ma'am." The boy smiled. "We're hoping to attend the Peewee Meltdown in Minneapolis."

"Unfortunately, Grayson already came by." She leaned forward, her elbows on the counter. "I bought nine, and Bill and Kathy took the rest."

"Man, he's beat me to every shop in town. Are you sure none of you don't want more?"

"I'm sorry, Josh." She grabbed a towel and wiped down the counter. "Good luck."

The boy's shoulders fell. He held a stack of raffle tickets in his hand—it didn't look like he'd sold any.

And Cole knew exactly how that felt—to want something only to have it vanish in your hands. His chest tightened. "Hey— did you say something about a hockey raffle?"

The kid turned. "Yeah. They're two dollars each or three for five. The raffle is next Friday and the grand prize is a jersey signed by the Blue Ox team. The *entire* team."

Cole rubbed a hand across his two-day stubble. "What position do you play?"

"Mostly wing."

"Nice. You must have quick hands."

He gave a shy grin. "My coach says so. You played?"

"A long time ago." One of the Cougars' junior league MVPs. Until a car wreck robbed him of everything he loved. He nodded toward the tickets. "How many have you sold?"

"Three." The boy eyed the busy table of teenagers, dropped his voice, and wrinkled his nose. "To my mom."

Ouch. Cole remembered the days his mom would have done the same thing. "How many do you have left?"

"Twenty-two."

Cole drew his wallet from his jeans. "In that case, I'll take twelve."

"Really?" The boy's mouth fell open.

"Absolutely." Cole held a crisp twenty out to the boy who

began a slow, deliberate count of the red tickets. Cole wouldn't be around for the drawing, but the kid didn't need to know that.

The boy handed Cole the tickets in exchange for the cash. "Thank you, sir."

"You're welcome—Josh, is it?"

"Yeah." He tugged his hat down over his ears. Cole spotted a missing front tooth—hopefully not from a hockey stick. "I need to get going. I have to catch my ride."

"Sure. Thanks for the raffle tickets."

The boy grinned. "See ya around." He waved and ran out the door.

Cole stood, tossed his empty cup in the trash, and stuffed the bright stubs into his pocket. At least the boy wouldn't come in last.

He snagged up the keys.

It seemed most prudent to park around the block and walk. Do a little recon to find out if the tenant was home.

Not a whole lot had changed on Third Avenue West. The Art Colony-slash-former church building still took up most of the block, although it had gotten a fresh coat of white paint. And the Congregational church across the street still hosted bingo night on Wednesday, along with dinner. Next door to his grandfather's house, the red cabin had been turned into a B&B.

As for the old homestead, it looked, well…yes, he'd say yes to the first buyer that came along. The front porch of the two-story Victorian sagged, a few shingles hung catawampus on the roof, and plastic flapped from the windows, a pitiful attempt at winterizing from bygone years. Yellow paint peeled from the ratty siding as if the house was shedding.

The place embodied every brutal memory he held, and then some, of his last year in Deep Haven.

Next to the old Victorian, however, a newer garage had been built, two stories, fresh paint—and he'd bet it was where his unruly tenant lived.

Perfect. *She's pretty stubborn.* Nathan's words rattled around his head, and he took a breath, not sure where to start.

The sight of a woman walking down the sidewalk caught his attention. She held a large box of ribbons in her arms, the wind toying with a few. She wore a long, gray winter dress coat over a floral skirt. It flapped against the tall brown boots that hit just below her knees. Behind the load she carried, her blonde, shoulder-length hair blew across her face.

She neared, her foot slipping on a patch of ice. "Oh!" She righted herself, but the sudden movement tossed blue flowers, bows, and a three-ring binder into the snow, the ribbons skittering away like mice.

He grabbed a couple, ran after a few more, and found himself chasing ribbons down the street.

"Thank you," she said as he returned holding the runaway ribbons. She stood to face him, pushing tangles of hair from her face. Then, a wave of recognition seemed to wash over her. "Hi again." A slight smile lit her face. "Hey. Are you here for the wedding?"

The wedding—wait. It was the woman from the side of the road.

Huh. She looked better without the massive parka. She was pretty, those eyes again reaching out to him, and something warm in them cut through the chill of the day. "Hi. Again. Uh, no. Definitely not here for a wedding."

"Right. I'm a wedding coordinator. These are decorations for tonight," she added, reaching for the ribbons he held. "This is so not my day." He piled them into her box as she tried to hold them down. "Lucky you—you get to save me twice."

Yes, lucky him. And he couldn't help but smile back. Because she was smiling at him as if she wasn't kidding. As if he actually might be her hero, and he hadn't had a woman—including his wife—look at him like that in so long, well, he didn't realize how much he hungered for it.

Silly. She was just some stranger…

And then he spotted her binder and read the laminated name badge stuck to the cover.

MEGAN CARTER

Megan. *Carter?*

He looked up, studied her for a moment. No way.

He stilled, a hitch catching his breath. What were the chances…

She shook the snow off the ribbons and placed them back into the box. "I really appreciate this. You've been my hero today." Her voice reached in, winding itself around the soft, raw places he kept secured. It was fuller than it used to be, the alto tones richer, but yeah, it still had the power to send his heart skittering.

And wow, she'd gotten pretty. Prettier. Even the gray skies couldn't dampen the bright gold of her eyes or the pink blush of her lips. He couldn't believe he hadn't recognized her on the road.

He held out her folder to her and swallowed, his tongue sticking to the roof of his pasty mouth, taking in her petite, feminine form. The curves. The smile on her face.

Megan Carter, all grown up, was a knockout.

It all was just enough to cause him to fumble, the contents of Nathan's folder spilling onto the sidewalk.

She bent to get it, like he'd done with her folder, and her gaze paused on the listing agreement.

As she picked it up, she looked at the agreement. Then at Cole.

Her warm smile faded.

"Cole *Barrett?*" Her hand trembled as she held out the papers.

He must have nodded because the spark, the warmth in her eyes vanished, and a chilly breeze rushed in.

"So you're the one who's trying to ruin my life."

Megan sat in the back of the reception hall after her final pre-wedding walk-through. The day could not end soon enough.

It had started as a stellar day.

Good thing she was adept at keeping a lid on all the thoughts a wedding planner should never say. Like when the flowers went MIA, the florist claiming that Megan gave her the wrong date—not—and she'd had to make a forty-mile run to Lutsen.

Or when the bride's mother announced that the pew bows were all wrong, even though they were exactly what she'd ordered. Megan had smiled, piled all twenty-six bows back into the box, and told her she had blue silk flowers at her apartment and could make them up before the evening ceremony.

Megan had known she'd make it work, though, because that's what she did. Created Perfect Days for starry-eyed brides. And her current bride, Shelly Anderson, was counting on her to pull off this wedding without allergic reactions, absent musicians, or runaway ring bearers. Which had only actually happened once, so odds were in her favor on that one. She wasn't beyond instituting a leash law for wedding party members under the age of four. Or over seventy-five, regardless of the number of legs.

Yeah. Anyone who thought the business of happily-ever-after was glamorous had never had to crawl under the third row of seats to clean up an unwanted wedding gift left by the current bride's Pekingese. Her stomach had contracted, the involuntary clenching causing a series of unladylike gags.

She hoped the two windows she'd left open would air the place out without bringing the temperature to just south of frigid.

Despite her oh-so-spectacular day, she'd had everything under control until that call from Nathan Decker had spun her off the road.

No, the insides of a stale peanut butter sandwich dropping onto her lap had spun her off the road, landing her car into the drift with a puff of snow. Note to self—don't brake while trying to hang up and retrieve lunch.

You need to move. The owner wants to sell. Nathan's words had hung in her brain as she climbed up on the berm to assess her predicament. No grace period, no taking into account that she'd made the apartment over the garage her home.

No thoughts about the nine-year-old boy who needed stability. Just...out.

She'd been fuming so hard she was nearly rude to the good Samaritan who'd rescued her—and yes, she'd noticed how easily he'd tackled pushing her Subaru from the ditch (hello, muscles). It had consumed her brain all the way back to Deep Haven where she'd parked out front, piled all the ribbons and flowers into one box, and climbed the interior stairs to her garage apartment.

Her apartment. And no matter what Nathan said, she wasn't going to budge. Not now, not when her dream of owning the Black Spruce B&B was so close. There was no way Katie James would extend her purchase agreement again. If she didn't come up with the rest of the down payment within the next sixty days, she'd have to say goodbye to all the plans she'd made for herself and Josh. All her ambitions to convert the B&B into a wedding venue.

It couldn't happen.

Once inside, she'd peeled off the layers, unwound her scarf, and began the process of perfecting the pew bows before grabbing her phone.

She was still annoyed, she knew it, and had schooled her voice when Ivy Christiansen picked up on the second ring. If anyone knew a good lawyer, it had to be the assistant county attorney.

"Hey," Ivy had said.

"Hi. Sorry to bug you, but I have two questions. Would you be able to pick up Josh from practice? I need to finish these bows for the wedding and get them down the street."

Good thing Ivy was a to-the-point gal too. "Sure. Tiger's down at the rink helping coach the Huskies."

Megan had tugged a piece of ribbon from the spool and wrapped it around another set of blue flowers. "Thanks. Okay, second. I need a lawyer. A really good one because Nathan Decker left me a message that I'm being evicted and Mr. Barrett's house is being sold."

"What? By whom?"

"I'm assuming it's Mr. Barrett's daughter and her son. The woman has hardly shown her face over the years. Packed him away in that nursing home faster than you can say, 'I want my inheritance.' Terrible. Practically selling his house out from underneath him."

"I don't think he's coming home, Megs. Poor man has Alzheimer's."

"Yes, well, you better believe I called Nathan right back and told him I had a six-month lease signed two months ago and *my* math says I'm not budging for four more months." She wasn't going to let Josh pay for the choices she'd made. He deserved more, so much more, and she was going to give it to him.

"Do you have a copy of the lease?"

"Somewhere. I wasn't expecting to have to prove I could live in my own apartment."

"Calm down."

Yes, probably. "I'm just...I'm so close to buying the Black Spruce. If only hockey camp didn't need that stupid down payment. Three *thousand* dollars! He'd better be getting golden skates and learn to shoot like Owen Christiansen for that kind of cash."

Ivy had laughed. "He is skating with Jace Jacobsen, although I could still get him to sit down with Josh for free—"

"No. We don't need any handouts. It's just...I want him to feel like all the other boys. Get all the things. Camp. Gear. And attend the tournament."

"You're an amazing mom, Megs."

She'd held up the bow. "Yeah, well, I'm scraping my piggy bank for pennies here, and moving in the middle of winter...I can't afford that. Besides, where would I even move?"

Silence, because Ivy knew the dismal answer. There simply weren't cheap places to rent in a community of high-end vacation rentals.

Although, the tourist town was amazing for the wedding business.

"We're not going to let you get evicted. Yes, look up your contract. And I'll call one of my legal contacts and get back to you as soon as possible."

"Thanks. I really appreciate it." Megan had glanced at the weather, wishing it would cooperate. Her apartment window faced the harbor, the frozen water gray and dismal against a pewter sky. Was it too much to hope for an early spring?

"No problem. You have the Anderson wedding tonight?"

"Yeah. My schedule for the next three weeks is completely nuts. But that's a good thing because there's a lull after Valentine's Day. I spent the entire morning running errands for Mrs. Anderson after she decided the decorations were all wrong. I'm almost done changing those. And then I skidded into the ditch coming back from Lutsen."

"Oh, no! What happened?"

"I was driving back on Highway 61 and Josh's lunch box was on the seat with remnants of PB and J. Okay, really, it was mostly just the crust. And it was stale. But—"

"You ate *what*?"

"Yes. The crust, and a glob of old jam fell on my lap just as I was hanging up with Nathan, and then, I don't know, I think I slammed on my brakes, hit a slick spot, and ended up in the ditch."

"Are you okay?"

"I'm fine, but then this guy stopped." A guy. She hadn't even gotten his name. He'd been nearly a foot taller than her, his shoulders broad, and dark hair clipped short. Bright blue eyes that took in everything and a jagged scar running from his left temple down to his jawline, interrupting the brown stubble. He'd looked like a warrior, even in jeans and hiking boots.

A warrior—and a hero.

"A guy? You said that like there's a little more to it than some everyday guy."

"Well..." All the men Megan usually met were getting married, but if she were honest, he still hadn't struck her as any kind of everyday joe.

Ivy had let out a long, "Mmmhmmm?"

"No. I mean, he was cute and I was very relieved he stopped, but I'll never see him again. And, don't take this wrong, but he kind of reminded me of Josh's dad—who left me another hang-up, by the way."

"Oh."

"Yeah. I don't know why, but ever since middle school, I've been mush for blue eyes and dark hair." No, she knew exactly why. She'd blame it on her summertime friend, Cole. She could always count on his family to spend summers in Deep Haven and it'd been so easy as kids. Carefree. When he moved to town after his parents' deaths, it was the best year of her childhood. Then, he was gone. And though Trevor had blue eyes and dark hair, he'd turned out to be nothing like Cole. "It's no big deal. I just have to deal with this apartment situation. My wedding schedule. Josh's hockey camp." And a thousand other things.

"You're not calling Trevor back?"

"No. Definitely not."

Megan had heard voices in the background over the phone

before Ivy responded. "I gotta go. Mom duties call. Josh can eat with us and we'll drop him by around eight-thirty."

"Thanks, Ivy. You're the best." Megan had disconnected and finished attaching the last of the blue flowers to the bows, gathering them into a box.

For all the fantasies she orchestrated with the brides-to-be, when it came to her own dreams, her failures could fill an entire wedding chapel. In fact, they would likely fill an entire cathedral, reception hall, and even a honeymoon suite. Not that she'd ever been in one of those.

After she'd finished the bows, Megan had changed into her clothes for the wedding, opting for her bright floral dress and tall boots. She liked to keep her makeup simple and decided to leave her hair down.

The walk to the Art Colony was only half a block and she'd still have time to get all the bows hung before the bridal party arrived.

Most of the sidewalk had been cleared, with only a few slick spots. Maybe it was the wind or maybe her distracted thoughts, but somehow, she had managed to lose traction, her foot sliding out and causing her to flail to catch her balance.

Every last bow with its perfect blue flowers had flown into the air.

They'd scattered like a flock of house sparrows fluttering through the sky.

Out of the corner of her eye, she'd spotted a stranger on the sidewalk grabbing them before they were swept away.

"Thank you." She'd looked up at him. Stilled.

The warrior-hero, back in action. Right here on her sidewalk. Huh. She'd smiled. "Hey. Are you here for the wedding?"

He'd given her a soft look. Something slow and sweet, and her stomach had done a crazy little flip-flop.

"Hi. Again. Uh, no. Definitely not here for a wedding."

"Right. I'm a wedding coordinator. These decorations are for tonight," she'd said, feeling like her wedding question merited an explanation. "This is so not my day." She'd reached for the ribbons he was holding, and he'd piled them into the box. "Lucky you—you get to save me twice."

He'd stooped to pick up her binder—gallant of him—and then paused. Held on to it while she finished picking up the last two bows and tapped the snow away.

She'd reached for the binder.

Why was he staring?

"I really appreciate this. You've been my hero today."

He'd handed the binder back, but in the jostle, his file folder fell open, the documents fluttering to the sidewalk. She'd reached to grab the paperwork and sucked in a breath, her hand stilling. There, in tidy print on a real estate agreement in her hand...COLE BARRETT.

No. She'd looked at the listing address. No. No... Everything inside her had frozen.

And maybe it shouldn't really matter, but somewhere deep in her heart...well, this was *not* how she'd wanted to meet Cole Barrett again.

He was supposed to be pining for her.

Not showing up to wreck her life.

"Cole *Barrett?*" She'd snatched the folder away, and lost any hope of keeping a lid on her words. "So you're the one who's trying to ruin my life."

If he thought he could walk out of her life fifteen years ago and then come back and take everything from her—

Her eyes had burned.

No. She'd shaken her head.

She was so done crying over Cole Barrett. She'd grabbed her box and walked away, not daring to look back.

Now, two hours later, she was still trembling. But she had to shake it off. Shake him off.

Because she had a wedding.

Megan stood up, took one last look at the reception hall.

Showtime.

At least she'd managed her pre-wedding prep with focus. Shelly Anderson was going to have a happily-ever-after today no matter what. With blue flowers and bows. With the gorgeous floral displays Claire Atwood had delivered. Witnessed by eighty close friends and family, and Elsa, her incontinent Pekingese.

Because if Megan couldn't have the happy ending, then someone around here should.

CHAPTER 2

*C*old, stale air wrapped around Cole when he stepped into his grandfather's house, and a sharp mustiness stung his nose. He flipped the light switch. Nothing. It figured. He'd had to practically pry the door open to get inside.

He dropped his green rucksack on the floor and let Megan's words drive into him. *So you're the one who's trying to ruin my life.* Yeah, returning to Deep Haven had been a gross tactical error. He pressed his palms to his temples, let the jumble in his head settle. This was supposed to be fast. In and out.

The hurt in her eyes, the accusation. He knew what betrayal felt like. And all he could do was watch her walk away, taking with her the only good pieces of his entire day.

Think. He was a seasoned Ranger, skilled in tactics and strategies. He could figure out how he'd get this wreck of a house sold. And what was Megan doing here?

He grabbed his phone to illuminate the room, but the darkness swallowed the light. With a tug, the curtains opened and a gray pallor was cast across the room. The sight of Grandpa's recliner in the corner gave him pause. Ratty and worn, but sitting exactly where it always had.

Exactly where he'd been the night the social worker brought Cole to Deep Haven after the car wreck. He'd just known Grandpa would be able to dull the ache in his heart. Ease the pain. That they'd have good times again, like his summer visits. But as soon as he'd entered with his suitcase and backpack, he knew everything had changed. The joy was gone from Grandpa's eyes and he spent more evenings with his whiskey than with Cole.

And when he reached his tipping point...

Cole swallowed and set his jaw. He'd never understand how a man could lash out at a child. Maybe grief could actually break someone, the loss of losing his only son two years after losing his wife to cancer. But even the broken must answer for the choices they made.

A knock at the door jolted him back to the present.

He tugged it open, bracing himself for another barrage from Megan.

A dark-haired man stood in the doorway, a ragged beard covering half his face.

"Can I help you?"

"Casper Christiansen." He held out a hand.

Casper Christiansen. Really? Last time he saw Casper, they were slapping the puck around on the frozen rink near the school. And they'd both been twelve. Casper stood there in a heavy green parka, snow sticking to his hat and determination in his eyes. Clearly this wasn't intended to be a social call.

Still, Casper was an old friend. An ally. And Cole was feeling pretty desperate for one of those. "Casper? Geez, did you never start shaving?" He shook the offered hand. "Cole Barrett."

It took a second, but Casper grinned and nodded. "You're *kidding!* Cole Barrett. Wow. Good to see you." He laughed and pulled Cole into a man hug, smacking him on the back before releasing him. "It's been forever."

"I never would have recognized you." Cole shook his head

and smiled. "Come on in." He stepped aside for Casper, lifting and pressing the door shut behind him.

Casper slid his knit cap off his head. "When I heard some guy was trying to evict Megan, I was expecting it to be Lorraine Barrett's son. I've never met him, but I didn't think it would be you."

Ouch. "Thanks for that. But, no. My aunt has decided to take a hands-off approach since she convinced my grandfather to go into care—that's always been her SOP." One of only two other blood relatives—the woman who'd refused to take him in. She and her son had never reached out to Cole. Yeah, Cole had little use for her either.

"And my cousin's too busy chasing his next big thing to bother." He tried another light switch. Nothing. "I'd offer you coffee, but I don't even know if there's a functioning coffee pot in the place." He gestured to the couch. "Do I want to know how you found out about the house sale?"

Casper looked down at the faded couch. "It's okay, I can stand. I happened to be with Darek when his wife, Ivy, told him."

Great. "And she heard...?"

"Megan called looking for a lawyer. Ivy's the assistant county attorney."

Cole held up his hands. "Hey, man, I had no idea it was her."

"And her son."

Yeah, the day just kept getting better and better. Now he was the cad not only forcing her out of the apartment, but she had a son. A *son*. That news stirred the nausea in his gut. He still hadn't eaten anything except the stale donut. Maybe that was a good thing.

"You okay?"

"Nathan didn't say there was a whole family."

"It's just Megan and her son." Casper smoothed his hand

over his beard. "She's a single mom." He paused. "The dad isn't really involved. Lives in the city."

Cole wanted to ask. Wanted to know more. But it really wasn't his business because she was right. He'd left town and moved on, only letting the childhood memories kick around in the back of his mind when the world grew still around him.

"What about you? Is that your minivan out front? Wife? Kids?"

"No. It's compliments of Duluth Auto Rental. It was supposed to be an SUV." That van. He needed to ditch it ASAP. It had gone from a ridiculous mix-up to a large-scale reminder of the failures in his life. "Divorced," he said, staring at the family portrait on the bookshelf. His parents flanked him on both sides, all smiles, standing beside his team's hockey trophy. They made it all seem so easy.

Casper gave him a nod. "I'm sorry to hear that."

"It was for the best." Because he wouldn't stay married to a woman he couldn't trust. *Please, Cole. I'm sorry. Let's work this out —get counseling.* He'd discarded Rebecca's pleas and served her the divorce papers as soon as he'd returned from deployment. He shrugged his shoulders. "I've moved on."

"So—you're trying to sell *this* place?" Casper's incredulous tone was impossible to miss.

"I know. It's a bit of a fixer. It doesn't look like my grandfather has touched anything since I was a kid. I haven't even made it through the whole place." Cole led Casper through the living room to the kitchen. He tried the faucet. Nothing. "Apparently, there are plumbing issues too." He turned the handle back. "My aunt must have had the city shut off the water."

"I suggest you fix the lighting too. Buyers tend to like modern conveniences."

"You're full of helpful tips, aren't you? I always thought Darek was the know-it-all." Cole doubled back to the first-floor half bath that sat off the short hallway between the living room and kitchen. He pulled open the door and surveyed the interior. Ugh. "Why did anyone ever use peach-colored sinks and toilets?" He closed the door.

"That is one of the great mysteries of interior design, I'm sure. At least it isn't a black toilet. I've seen those." Casper leaned against the wall next to the stairs. "And you're getting some heat. It's at least fifty-five in here."

"Almost tropical." Cole paused at the thermostat on the wall. The indicator hung near the fifty-degree mark.

"And you're selling now? You're not sticking around?"

"The money will pay for Grandpa's memory care and no, I can't stick around." Cole shook his head as he took in the entirety of the first floor. "I guess I'd better take a look upstairs."

Each step groaned under their weight as they climbed to the second floor.

Cole swallowed and veered away from his old bedroom facing the backyard, instead turning to his grandfather's bedroom at the front of the house. A quilt lay at the foot of the tidy bed, careful folds highlighting the craftsmanship.

"At least these rooms don't need major work." He ran his fingers across the perfect stitching on the quilt. *This pattern is called a wedding ring.* He remembered watching his grandmother work on it, mesmerized by her ability to create uniformity as her needle pressed in and out of the fabric, again and again. *I take all these pieces that don't seem to belong anywhere and bring them together.*

Casper shoved his hands into his pockets. "So, when you leave here, where are you heading next?"

"I'm waiting on a job interview with the U.S. Marshals Service and, once I'm hired, I won't be around to deal with this." When his grandfather's caseworker had called about the care facility, Cole didn't understand why he'd been named on the Power of Attorney. And maybe part of him resented the need to step in and deal with the affairs of the very man who hadn't been there for him.

"That's not your everyday career path."

"I've been serving in the Army for seven years as a Ranger. Was looking to get out because..." He paused, choosing his words. Because he couldn't watch more soldiers' lives risked for the media sound bites they might make. Doomed missions soldiers were being sent on to meet someone's political agenda with little chance of success. "It's kind of a long story, but my buddy from the Rangers and I made plans to work for the U.S. Marshals Service together. He's already been hired, and I got sidelined in the process to come take care of this mess." He gestured toward the house. "He's already working in DC, so the plan is that I'd work out of that office, too."

"Sounds like a good job for you. Not too much of a change of pace, huh?"

Cole laughed. "Yeah. What about you? What have you been up to?" He led the way back down the stairs.

"Married. I have a beautiful daughter. Another baby on the way. Did some adventuring before I discovered a treasure right here in Deep Haven." Casper reclaimed his spot against the stair wall. "I still love archaeology, but my family is my focus. I'm able to help around town." He looked out the window. "We're supposed to have a storm coming in. I help make sure the city plows are ready to go. Was just finishing up when I saw the van out front."

Cole nodded. It made sense that a man like Casper would settle down and raise his family here. After all, he had roots. "And your parents?"

"They're semiretired. Letting Darek head up the resort. I help out here and there." Casper paused, his mind in apparent thought. "I'm heading back to my place for dinner. Why don't you join us? You can stay with us until you get this place squared away."

"I've slept in much worse." Cole toed his boot against a loose floorboard at the base of the stairs. "I really don't want to impose. I'm not sticking around."

"Dude, no. I'm not letting you stay here. You don't even have running water. We're supposed to have a snowstorm tonight, and while fifty-five degrees may keep your pipes from freezing, you're going to appreciate someplace warmer. Grab your gear and follow me."

And there went his plan to steer clear of any Christiansens.

Ten minutes later when Cole followed Casper into his lakeside bungalow just down the road, garlic and oregano filled the air. Cole's stomach betrayed him with a low rumble.

The bungalow felt warm. Homey. Bright orange flames crackled in the stone fireplace, the sweet scents of cedar and pine filling the space and blending with the smells from the kitchen.

"Raina is in the kitchen," Casper said. "C'mon."

Cole followed him through the house to the kitchen at the back. A woman stood at the counter slicing garlic bread, her long, dark hair pulled back.

A blue-eyed girl with curly dark hair stood on a chair next to her, helping.

Oh, Casper had definitely married up.

"Get everything in town covered?" She leaned in to give Casper a kiss. "And you brought company." She smiled, her hand against the curve of her abdomen.

"I did, as best as could be done. Cole Barrett, my wife, Raina, and our daughter, Layla."

"Ma'am." He nodded to her.

Raina turned from the cutting board to the oven and grabbed a potholder. "The new villain of Deep Haven?"

"Pardon?" Did she say *villain*?

"I spoke with Megan a little while ago. She mentioned some

trouble with the apartment." She popped open the oven, slid a casserole dish out, and set it on a trivet.

"Oh." Cole was definitely behind enemy lines. "I didn't realize—" He stared at the lasagna. He couldn't even remember the last time he'd had homemade lasagna. Cheese bubbled across the top, lightly golden.

She raised a hand. "It's okay." Her soft laughter filled the space, warm and bright. "I'm giving you a hard time." Raina winked. "Mostly. I'm sure it'll all get figured out."

She pulled a serving spoon from the drawer. "Affordable rentals are hard to come by around here, especially this time of year." Raina wiped her fingers on a towel. "But, it's nice to meet you. We're glad to have you join us." She began slicing the pan of lasagna. "Dinner's ready. Why don't you two wash up?"

He had the distinct feeling he knew exactly what Raina's idea of "figured out" would look like. And it didn't include a For Sale sign in the front yard of his grandfather's house. But how hard could it really be to find another rental?

When Cole sat down at the table, he paused while Casper reached out, slid his fingers into Raina's, and said a blessing over their meal. Even thanked God for bringing Cole back to town and allowing them to share their home.

The gesture rubbed a raw spot in Cole's chest that only got worse as they talked over dinner and shared with him what each of the Christiansens had been up to. It wasn't unlike meals with his parents, and Cole blinked away a little heat in his vision when Casper lifted Layla into his arms. The small hands curling around her father's neck, her face buried against his neck.

"Daddy, will you read me a story?"

"Of course." He turned to Cole. "Make yourself at home."

Raina began clearing the table.

Cole got up, grabbed a couple dirty plates. "Please, let me wash. It's the least I can do."

She gave him a gentle smile. "I never argue with a man who begs to wash dishes. The scrub pad is next to the sink."

He set to work on the smaller cooking bowls first while Raina began drying. "Thank you for dinner. That was amazing. I don't even remember the last time I had a real, home-cooked meal, let alone lasagna that good."

"You're welcome. I've been perfecting my lasagna for quite a few years." She lifted another bowl from the rack. "That must be hard. Always being on the move. Being away from home."

Maybe it was. If he ever stopped long enough to think about it. If he had a true home, he might miss it, perhaps. He'd forgotten what it felt like, maybe. "I've been on the move for as long as I can remember. When I left Deep Haven, I went into foster care in Duluth."

"And then into the Army?"

"Yes, ma'am."

"Megan said she knew you," Raina offered, placing measuring cups back into the cupboard.

"Yeah. We lost touch when I moved." He thought of the woman on the road. The woman whose day had gone amok. What had she said? *The abyss of terrible.* And the truth began soaking into his bones, leaving him cold. It was *him*. He was the one, exactly like she'd said on the sidewalk, who'd ruined her day and, somehow, possibly her life.

Not the impression he wanted to leave on the girl who'd, once upon a time, helped him through the worst year of his life.

"That happens." Raina paused, set a cutting board back into place, and turned to him. "It's funny, sometimes, how God brings us full circle, when we're ready."

Cole was pretty sure God had nothing to do with it—at least not a God he wanted anything to do with. So he let her words hang in the air with a noncommittal nod. Pressed away the lingering thought.

She finished drying the last dish. "Thanks for your help. Let me show you to your room so you can get settled."

He followed her back toward the front of the house to the guest bedroom, the exhaustion of the day pressing in on him. The sooner he put Deep Haven in his rearview mirror, the better. He wasn't sure how he'd accomplish that task, but maybe, just maybe, things would be clearer in the morning.

Megan had been chewing on uncertainty for hours, and it hadn't been very satisfying. Ever since returning from the Anderson wedding, she'd been thumbing through her account statements on the dining room table again. No matter how she crunched the numbers, they didn't improve. She was still short four thousand dollars for the Black Spruce.

Snowflakes blew against the window with a light tapping. She slid out of her chair and looked across the snowy yard. Darkness filled the Barrett house, like any other night since she'd moved in. She tried to shove down the niggling curiosity of where Cole might have gone. Because she really didn't care. Wouldn't care. *Couldn't* care.

She closed her eyes and leaned her forehead against the cold pane of glass. How was it that the one time she met a guy who came to her rescue, who showed up like a real-life hero, he turned out to be the worst thing that could possibly happen to her?

Still, maybe she hadn't been fair to him. Cole hadn't seemed to know she lived next door, based on the way he stared at her. But he didn't bother coming after her when she'd practically fled to the Art Colony either. Just stood there on the sidewalk like the specter of doom.

Her pale orange tabby pressed against her legs, talking to her with soft meows until she scooped him up, snuggled his fur against her face.

"Puck, you are the silliest cat."

In the light of the street lamp, she spotted Ivy's Tahoe pull up. Josh climbed out, waving goodbye before he tromped through the fresh snow to the downstairs entry. His footsteps bounded up the interior steps, echoing in the garage's open first floor until he burst through the second-story apartment door, red-cheeked, grinning.

"Mom. You wouldn't believe what I did at Tiger's house after practice." He began shrugging out of his coat and kicking off his shoes.

She smiled, his enthusiasm filling her heart. "What?"

"We went up to the lodge and I got to ride on one of the snowmobiles!"

"You did?" She tamped down the burgeoning panic. It was one thing to snow tube. But snowmobiling? She took a deep breath. Lots of kids went snowmobiling, right? She snagged him into a hug, pressing her nose into his soft, short hair. "I sure hope you wore a helmet. And a seat belt."

He wrinkled his nose. "They don't have seat belts, Safety Mom."

She laughed at the nickname. "I know. I was kidding. Mostly." She forced herself to release him. "It's my job to worry about you and keep you safe."

"But, yes, Tiger's grandpa wouldn't let us ride without a helmet. Tiger and I got to follow him to check on one of their cabins."

"Excellent."

"And I sold twelve tickets when Ivy let me run into the Java Cup."

"Marie bought that many? That's fantastic."

"No, some guy did." He grabbed the jug of orange juice from the refrigerator and poured a tall glass. "He told me he used to play hockey. And then, it was weird, because I thought I saw him at Mr. Barrett's house when Tiger's mom brought me by to grab my gear bag."

"The guy who bought your tickets was at Mr. Barrett's house today?"

"Yeah. I'm pretty sure it was him."

"Was he tall, with brown hair? Wearing a black leather jacket?"

"Yeah. Why?" He downed the entire glass of juice.

Cole had bought half of Josh's tickets. Huh. That sounded more like the boy she'd known. The one looking out for others. Like the man who helped her out of the ditch. Not the one evicting her.

"His name is Cole. He's Mr. Barrett's grandson." She'd leave out the part about him wanting to force them from their apartment. "I actually knew him when we were kids."

"You did?"

"You know how our old house, well, Grandma and Grandpa's, is behind us?" She pointed in the direction of the back fence line.

"Yeah."

"When I was your age, he used to come visit his grandpa here every summer." She paused, letting the memories warm her. Like when she talked about someday being a wedding planner and Cole had teased her about happily-ever-afters. He'd stood there, in his T-shirt and shorts, while she extolled the virtues of holy matrimony.

How would you pick who you'd marry? Her question, and maybe she'd been probing a little.

He'd smiled, lain down under her makeshift arbor in the grass, and looked up at her with those crazy-blue eyes. *Well, if you're someone who wants to get married.* He'd wrinkled his nose. *You know, it's for old people. But my dad said he just knew. Knew my mom was the one.* He shrugged, tossed a daisy in the air. *So, I guess you know.*

And in that moment, under the summer sky with the heart of an eleven-year-old girl, she'd wondered what that would be like. To be the one.

Some things hadn't changed that much.

Cole had shown up four months later with his belongings jammed into a small suitcase to live with his grandpa. She'd felt a little ashamed because she'd been so happy to have him come to stay. He'd lost both his parents and the life he'd known and she was excited to have him there.

Megan blinked away tears and took a deep breath, tried not to let her own family heartache seep in. Her sister, Lillian, had needed her parents' attention and, really, Megan understood that. Even if their absence in her own life stung.

Pediatric heart conditions were tough to navigate. For parents. For siblings.

How Megan had needed a friend.

She looked at her son. "Anyway, since we were the same age and lived so close, we'd hang out together."

"That's cool." Josh sat down with Puck on the couch. The cat promptly began kneading his leg.

"It was."

"How come I've never seen him before?"

Yeah. Good question. Where had he been all these years?

"I don't know." But she'd find out. And maybe if she could just make Cole understand how important the Black Spruce B&B purchase was, find a way to stay long enough to make it all happen, everything would be okay. "How about a game of cards tonight?"

"I don't know. I beat you pretty good last night." Josh shot her a wicked grin, a gap where his right canine would be.

"I'm up for a rematch." She snagged the cards from the book-shelf and grabbed two mugs of hot cocoa from the kitchen.

"See if you can beat me this time." Puck jumped down from Josh's lap and wandered to the food dish.

"You didn't tell me how practice went today."

"Good. Coach says I've improved my speed coming across the ice. He thinks I'm good enough to start in the tournament."

"Wow—that's excellent!" See, she knew using the money from her bed and breakfast savings for the hockey camp had been worthwhile. It wasn't every day a kid got to skate with Jace Jacobsen and Blue Ox players.

"I hope you're ready to be beat at both UNO and War."

She began dealing the cards. "You think you're a match for me?"

"Mom, you're always too nice. You never want to play your Draw Four cards. Or change the color." He grew serious. "I think you should really try to play to win."

Laughter bubbled inside her and she sat down next to him, drew him close, squeezing him into another hug.

"Mom." He tried to brace against her and push her away, even though a smile curled the corners of his lips.

"You're not too old for hugs from your mom. I promise not to do it at the rink."

"Or at school."

"Or at school." She released him.

He slid to the opposite end of the couch to face her and set to work organizing his cards. The two-bedroom apartment didn't leave room for extras, but Megan found on a dark winter night that cards and hot cocoa were all they needed.

An hour later, Josh looked at her, his blue eyes more sleepy than bright. "One more round?"

"Buddy, I think it's time for you to get ready for bed. I have another wedding tomorrow and I'll need your help. Especially if it keeps snowing. Pray the snow stops."

"Just one more game?"

"How about instead I make pancakes before you head out to

shovel snow tomorrow? I think I can even pay you for your time." She gave him a wink.

"Yes, please." He smiled.

"Deal. Time for you to get ready for bed."

Fifteen minutes later, she took one last look out the window. The main house remained dark. Over the last hour with Josh, the knot in her stomach had unfurled. She probably could have handled her encounter with Cole better. Maybe not gone quite so much on the defense. Not actually accused him of *ruining her life.*

Ugh. Did she really say that? She wasn't usually one for the dramatic.

It only made sense that, at some point, the house would need to be sold. With Edgar Barrett in memory care, it would stand vacant. Forgotten.

A little like her. Maybe even a reminder of everything she'd never have because of broken promises.

But she had Josh. And though being a single mom was difficult, there was nothing she wouldn't do for him. Like building her own wedding planning business here in Deep Haven. And going above and beyond for her brides. Maybe sometimes too far beyond—like driving to Lutsen right before a snowstorm.

She groaned, slipping into her own bed. That train of thought took her right back to the would-be stranger on the highway, whose regrettable good looks had occupied a few too many thoughts until she'd realized who he was and, worse, why he was here.

Apparently, not to tell her that she was *the one,* but to kick her out onto the street.

Her phone buzzed on the nightstand and she read Ivy's message. Let the full force of it wheedle into her.

Who is the landlord on the lease? Lorraine Barrett didn't have POA.

Oh. No.

Megan buried her face under her covers and tried not to cry. She didn't even bother to take another look at the crumpled document she'd dug out of the kitchen drawer with Lorraine's signature. Because without a proper Power of Attorney, her lease was a useless piece of paper. Cole could challenge it. And she would lose.

Everything.

CHAPTER 3

Of course they were buried.

Snow fell, deep and white and unwelcome in the dim light of Saturday morning.

It was usually sixty degrees in January at Fort Benning. Cole grimaced. He was afraid to look at what the thermometer hanging outside said.

He sat down on Casper's couch and took a long drink of coffee, plotting the day ahead. Megan would understand why she had to move out, once he explained it to her. He'd convince her that moving now was the best thing for everyone. It didn't need to ruin her life—whatever that meant for her.

"Hey. You're up early." Casper came down the stairs dressed more for dog sledding than a Saturday by the fire.

"Good morning. Army habit." The clock said seven. Usually he'd be done with a three-mile run and his workout by now. "I need to do a full inventory of repairs for my grandfather's place."

"I'm heading over to Deep Haven Community Church to clear snow." Casper disappeared into the kitchen and returned with a cup of coffee. "If you're up for it, I could use some help clearing the lot and a few other places around town. The guy who usually helps me is down with the flu. The church lot will need it for a wedding today and there are a few other driveways I like to make sure are clear for elderly residents."

"Sure. I'd be glad to help." He kneaded his hand against his chest. He also had to speak to Megan.

"You'll need to suit up better than that." Casper gave a nod to Cole's jeans and T-shirt. "My guess is you don't have a real coat in that duffel of yours?"

Cole laughed. "Probably not by Arctic standards. In Georgia, we consider forty degrees absolutely frigid."

Casper shook his head. "Yeah. That's practically summer. Let me grab you some warmer gear."

Deep Haven had changed little during Cole's absence. Based on the snow-dusted letterboard, the VFW still hosted local bands. Wild Harbor Trading Post had a sale on outdoor gear, and donuts remained the delight of anyone walking into World's Best, despite the new cupcake offerings on the board.

By nine-thirty, they'd plowed the church lot and several streets. Casper had sent Cole to shovel out Edith Draper's driveway before they reconvened at the truck parked near the Art Colony. The elderly woman had been so grateful, she'd tried to drag Cole inside for homemade soup.

"You live this way?" Cole leaned against the truck. The work had heated his body but the chill still nipped at his cheeks.

"Come on, you grew up a Minnesota boy. You had to have participated in at least one polar plunge."

Cole laughed, his breath crystallizing in the air. "I think my only polar plunge was thanks to a dare from Owen."

"That sounds about right."

The smell of wood stoves permeated the crisp air, and bright morning light glistened like thousands of diamonds across the snowy yards. Down the street, a large, shapeless mass sat in the driveway where Megan's car should be. The least he could do was dig her out before explaining to her why she needed to let go of the lease and move out. Cole grabbed the shovel. "Mind if I hold on to this for a bit?"

Casper looked at the house, then the car, a twitch of a smile at the corner of his lips. "Not at all. I can pick you up later. If not, Darek could when he swings through after practice. Thanks for your help."

"Sure. Thanks for letting me crash at your place."

Casper gave him a nod. "Stay as long as you need." He opened his truck door.

Every muscle in Cole's body would be screaming at him in another couple hours, but the work felt good. Far better than sitting around, waiting. He started digging out the walkway, sweat leaving cool streaks down his back, and mentally rehearsed his next conversation with Megan. Her last words still gnawed at his mind. Ruin her life?

She'd have to understand, right? He couldn't stay. The house needed to be sold. It was just a tiny rental above a garage. Certainly there were other rentals in town.

He'd finished the walkway and half the driveway when he heard boots tromping toward him. A boy rounded the corner of the garage, carrying a snow shovel. He wore a familiar oversized blue jacket and knit cap with a lock of dark hair sticking out from under it.

The boy's eyes widened. "Hey—what are you doing here?"

The kid from the Java Cup. Jake? James? Oh, yeah. Josh.

The boy set his shovel blade into the snow and snugged his gloves down over his wrists.

Cole blinked, let the realization settle in his mind. Josh, coming to shovel his driveway. Josh, Megan's...son?

"Thought I'd be helpful and shovel the driveway."

Josh surveyed the completed work. "My mom sent me out to do it."

"Your mom—Megan?" he asked, somehow driven to clarify what he already knew.

"Yeah." Josh eyed him with not a little suspicion and dug his shovel into the snow. "Is Mr. Barrett your grandpa?" He flicked a scoopful of powder into the yard.

Oh. Well. "He is." He studied the boy with fresh eyes. He could see her in the curve of Josh's nose, the fierce determination in the set of his jaw, the intensity of his gaze.

"I heard my mom tell someone you're going to sell the house and we'd have to move."

It was hard not to like a kid who was willing to be direct. Maybe even a little ruthless.

"I do have plans to sell the house."

The boy nodded. Taking it like a man more than twice his age, and suddenly Cole felt uncomfortable.

"I won't have to get rid of Puck, will I? He's my cat. Actually, he's still a kitten, sorta. I rescued him from down by the ice rink and no one ever claimed him. So, he's mine now."

"I see." Cole had nothing except for the memory of leaving his dog with a new family when he deployed the first time. And as he drove away, realizing he'd never be able to have him back.

Josh kept working, shoveling the mounds of snow without complaint.

Cole paused between scoops. "How long have you lived in Deep Haven?"

"Pretty much my whole life." Josh dropped his shovel, tugged his hat over his ears. "We lived with my grandparents until they moved away a few months ago."

"And you like hockey?"

"I love hockey." He dug his shovel back in and tossed another load. "We have a tournament coming up. And I'm going to attend a camp with members of the Blue Ox. Even Jace Jacobsen." Pride swelled in his voice.

"J-Hammer? Wow." Cole smiled at his enthusiasm. "Lots

going on for you. Sounds like you have a lot of support for your hockey."

"My mom never misses a game."

Cole glanced over as he dug in his shovel, looked for any sign of disappointment. But Josh kept digging, with no mention of his dad. Like the fact that his dad maybe had nothing to do with him didn't hurt. Didn't leave a vacancy. But Cole knew that couldn't be entirely true. He'd been that boy, looking to his dad, the hero. Knew how it had defined the man he would become. And the void when he was gone.

"I lost my parents when I was twelve."

Josh nodded, kept working.

"It was hard, sometimes, not having them around." Cole finished another section and began the next. "It sounds like your mom is pretty amazing." Which didn't surprise him in the least because she'd always been the person who put everyone else first.

Megan came around the corner, bundled in her Stay Puft gray parka, a hat with a thick white pompom, boots, and carrying a fabric tote bag. She blinked behind her blue scarf, unable to hide her surprise.

"Oh." She looked from Josh to Cole. Her breath frosted in the icy air.

"We're almost done digging you out," Cole offered, hoping she'd accept his peace offering, though, by the looks of it, she was planning to hike to her destination.

She still looked back and forth between him and Josh, finally asking, "What are you doing here?" She still had the same furrow between her brows when she was frustrated.

He laughed at her question. Like mother, like son. "Technically, I sort of live here. Though, not exactly, since it isn't quite inhabitable. Yet."

Megan raised a brow and shook her head as if trying to sort through his words. Then, "I see you've met my son, Josh." Her features softened, a smile lighting her face when she looked at Josh. It was the same way his mother used to look at him. The look that told him she'd do anything for him.

It put a strange lump in his throat. "A couple times now, actually."

"So I hear. The tickets?"

Right. That. Cole shrugged it off. "I couldn't pass up a chance to support youth hockey."

Josh leaned his shovel against the garage. "Do I still get paid for shoveling the driveway?"

Cole smiled. "You can have my share."

Megan laughed. It was a sweet, light sound that shook something loose in his core. "I think that can be arranged." She looked at Cole and chewed her lower lip, finally asking, "Do you have a couple minutes?"

"Yes, ma'am." Because he really didn't want to tell her that he had no choice but to evict her—*them*—in front of Josh either.

She turned to Josh. "I'll be right back, okay? We're going to run this around the corner. When you're done, head back upstairs. I left the kettle warm for hot cocoa."

"Okay."

"Can I carry that for you?" Cole reached for the tote bag she carried.

"I've got it. I just need to drop it off at the church. There's a wedding scheduled for today."

"Please. Let me carry it for you." He reached for it, letting the gentle pull of his hands convince her to release it.

"Okay. Fine. Thank you." She led them down the sidewalk toward Deep Haven Community Church and let out a long breath. "I'm sorry about how I reacted yesterday."

He waited for an excuse, but none followed. "I'm sorry you got the news the way you did. If I'd known there was a tenant—and if I'd known it was you—I would have come by in person."

She stopped walking and turned on him, her bright golden-brown eyes searching his, several snowflakes landing on her long lashes. "Where have you been all these years?" The question, charged with confusion, caused him to pause. He wasn't one to look back with regret.

He shrugged. "Foster care first. Then the Army."

He didn't miss the way her eyes shifted to his scar. *Don't ask.*

"You're in a big hurry to get out of here."

"It isn't personal. I have a job—well, I hope to have a job with the U.S. Marshals Service soon."

She looked up at him, tilted her head as if calculating something. Nodded. "Yeah. I always thought you'd set out to help others." Her words were quiet, reflective. He could see something sad and lost in her eyes before she turned away and continued walking with careful steps down the sidewalk. And he wanted to ask her what she'd been doing all these years too, but maybe he didn't have the right to ask. He was the one who owed her.

"What did you do in the Army?"

"I was a Ranger."

"Aren't those the guys who jump out of airplanes?"

The incredulous light in her eyes made him laugh. "Yes, sometimes."

"Wow. That's crazy. Thank you for shoveling the driveway. I'm not sure that really stacks up to Ranger duty. Were you the one who did the street too?"

"Yes, ma'am. You're welcome." And what else could he say? That it was the least he could do since he still needed her to move out? "Casper tapped my driving skills—I can handle more than a minivan on ice."

"Is that what you learned in the Army? Advanced minivan maneuvers?"

He smirked. She hadn't lost her sense of humor. "Something like that."

"And now you want to be a Deputy U.S. Marshal? Why?"

"I made plans with my friend, David, before we discharged. It's something we both felt would allow us to continue our service stateside. Work together."

She paused. Gave a little nod.

"What about your parents? Your sister?"

She lifted a shoulder. "They all moved to Florida last fall. Sold the house." She kicked her feet in the snow. "Lillian's going to school down there."

"And her heart condition?"

"She's been stable for several years. And they're close to a heart center."

They arrived at the church, stomped the snow off their boots.

Cole followed her inside and down the hallway. She flipped on the light to a classroom and slipped off her hat and scarf.

He needed to talk to her. Tell her why he had to sell the house. "Hey, Megan?"

"You can put that over there." She pointed to the long table and he set the bag down. Her phone began ringing and she checked the number. "Sorry. I need to take this—"

She answered it and stepped out into the hallway. As she paced outside the door, resignation threaded her voice. "Absolutely... Yes, I understand you can't do that... Sure. I'll get it to you as soon as possible. Thank you." She hung up and blew out a long breath when she came back into the room.

"Everything okay?"

Her shoulders sagged. "I hope it will be."

"What's going on?"

"It's the Black Spruce. I'm trying to buy it."

"The bed and breakfast next door? Isn't it vacant?"

"Yes. The owners moved to California and need to sell. I signed a purchase agreement and if I don't come up with the rest of the down payment by the end of March, then it will be void and it will go on the market. And some out-of-town management company is dying to snatch it up and turn it into another expensive rental."

Right. Maybe this wasn't the best time for the conversation. The one where he explained to her the five reasons she had to agree to break the lease and move out.

"I'd better get back to Josh."

"I was just starting to thaw."

She tucked her hair back into her scarf and wound it back around her neck before snugging on her hat and stepping out into the freezing air. "Oh, come on, Ranger, don't be such a pansy."

"Ranger?" Somehow, the teasing lilt in her voice unraveled him a little, as if she'd somehow sneaked inside a barricade he had forgotten he'd built.

"It isn't that cold." She stooped down and tossed a scoop of snow at him.

He ducked. "Hey!"

"Surely you experienced worse in the Army."

"Not by choice. And you'd better be careful who you pick a snowball fight with." He leaned down, scooped up a ball of snow and began shaping it, careful not to pack it too hard.

"Did they teach you that at the Ranger academy too? Was that a class?"

"Funny. No. And it's the Ranger Assessment and Selection Program." He pitched the snowball at her, aiming for her well-padded shoulder. She didn't even flinch when it shattered down her arm.

"My son throws harder than that." Her eyes lit with challenge, her breath rising in a puff from her pink lips.

"I wasn't trying to hurt you." The words hung in the air between them. He'd meant the snowball, but more than that. No, he'd never wanted to hurt her. She blinked, looked away, and pointed to the trees, heavy beneath their white burden. "It's usually subzero in January and February, so this is actually

SUSAN MAY WARREN & RACHEL D. RUSSELL

rather pleasant. I'd say we're hitting twenty degrees today." She held out a finger as if taking the temperature and wind direction.

"You say 'subzero' like it's normal. Can I tell you, it isn't normal?"

"Around here it is." She began walking back toward her apartment, her feet squeaking in the cold snow.

"You don't have to live like this. There are warmer places." Warmer. Brighter. So many other places. He caught back up to her, shoving his hands in his pockets, his chin down into the neck of his jacket.

"I like it here." She narrowed her eyes. "And you used to too."

"To be fair, most of the time I spent here was in the summer. I only endured one winter here. Way more ice and snow here than in Minneapolis."

"Endured?" She quirked an eyebrow at him, took a step forward to challenge him. "I remember the Christiansens taking us to Honeymoon Bluff. And dragging my sled to the top again and again with you. You know you loved it just as much as I did."

"I loved going fast."

She was so close, her sweet floral scent tugged at him. Distracted him.

"You loved all of it. Screaming down the hill. Crashing at the bottom. Lying in the snow and staring at the blue sky. And not going home until you were so cold you couldn't feel your toes."

Because he hadn't wanted to go home. He'd wanted to stay on that hillside with her forever. Carefree. Drinking in the joy of her shrieks and laughter.

Not face the drunken abuse of his grandfather. He swallowed, turned away. Pressed down the twist in his gut.

"There's another big snowstorm moving in. See?" She pointed toward the low-hanging clouds, heavy with moisture, in the distance. "Which could be bad news for my wedding travelers, but lucky for you. It's warmer than typical."

He wasn't feeling lucky. Snow had already begun falling again, a thick layer covering the road and driveway where he'd plowed and shoveled. And he still hadn't explained to her why she had to agree to move out.

If he wasn't careful, he'd be stuck in Deep Haven until the spring thaw.

∼

Megan woke the next morning with a devastating realization. Her wedding was in big trouble, and worse, not even God was on her side.

The depth of snow outside the apartment door was a clear sign to Megan that God had, in fact, completely forgotten about her. That the prayers she'd lifted in the sleepy darkness the night before, begging God for favor, asking Him to help her make this wedding happen, hadn't been heard. Or worse, He'd given her a resounding no.

She pulled open the exterior garage door, kicking the snow away with her boots. This was what she got for teasing Cole about the weather. She closed the door and tried the interior garage light switch again. Still no power, and snow continued to fall from the steel-gray sky.

Don't panic. Maybe the church had power. She climbed the stairs back to the apartment and began bundling herself in layers. She grabbed a flashlight from the kitchen drawer and shoved it into her pocket.

"I'm ready to go." Josh wrapped his scarf around his neck.

"Perfect." She scooped up Puck and set him on the couch. "We'll be back, buddy. You stay here where it's warm and cozy." The orange tabby began kneading a blanket, circling to hibernate through the storm. Smart cat. It was a tempting prospect if there weren't I-do's on the line.

Snow blew across their path as they worked their way through the deep drifts and clung to the trees along the street. She snugged her collar closed and stopped next to Josh. Listened to the soft pattering of flakes falling around them.

A stillness hung over the morning, a peacefulness she longed to hold on to. Snow made the whole world new.

"This is the best," Josh said, opening his mouth to the snowfall.

She forced a smile. "All right, Frosty, we'd better keep moving." They plodded their way down the block and around the corner to Deep Haven Community Church.

Casper Christiansen's truck and Pastor Dan Matthews's SUV were parked in the church lot. Another SUV was parked along the entry curb, and several sets of fading footprints followed the sidewalk to the church door. The snow around the entry had already been cleared, with fresh snow readily filling back in. She pulled the door open, holding it for Josh to tromp in ahead of her.

"Pastor Dan?" she called down the dim hallway. "Hello?"

"I'm in here."

She followed his voice around the corner to the conference room. He stood over the large table and his gray eyes looked up from the box of batteries and blankets in front of him. The floor-to-ceiling windows behind him cast bright reflected light across the room, creating a halo on his brown hair.

"The whole town's out of power." He finished loading another stack of fleece throws into the box.

"That's what I was afraid of," Megan answered.

"I'm going to make rounds around town to ensure we don't have any elderly who are homebound without any means to keep warm. Your bride-to-be is somewhere here, too, in a bit of a panic."

"Alexa's here?"

"Yeah. She's distressed, as I'm sure you can imagine."

"I bet." It wasn't too unusual for brides-to-be on their wedding day, but Megan figured it had more to do with the two feet of fresh snow outside than the nuptials.

He frowned. "I'm not sure how long it will take to get the power back—if anyone can even make it here safely for the wedding."

"Can I play out front?" Josh stood in the doorway, adventure lighting his eyes.

"Sure, sweetie, be careful and look out for cars."

Dan rubbed his jaw. "I'm hoping it doesn't take long to repair the lines. I'd hate to have to cancel tomorrow's church service, too."

"Yeah, I don't want to have to wear my snowsuit to the service." She grinned. "You know I would, though."

He laughed.

The exterior door clattered closed, and the low tones of tenor voices echoed down the hall. Casper Christiansen walked in, followed by Cole.

Snow still clung to their hats and jackets. The bulk of Casper's winter coat only added to his hockey-player size. He tugged heavy gloves from his hands and brushed the snow from his brown beard.

Cole had traded his leather jacket for a thick ski jacket. His days-old scruff, knit hat, and Gore-Tex pants made him look like he was ready for a backwoods rescue.

Huh. The last time she spoke to Raina, she and Casper were clearly on her side. Cole had the maddening ability to unsettle her every time he approached. His blue eyes locked on to hers and he gave her a tentative smile. Like he wasn't quite sure where he stood with her.

Good. He shouldn't be. Sure, he might have engaged in a snowball fight, but the man was still *evicting* her.

He pulled his knit cap from his head and scrubbed a hand over his hair. She was pretty sure his high-and-tight would not suffer the effects of hat hair.

Casper set his gloves down on the table. "Bad news. One of the white spruce behind the church has knocked down the power lines. It's going to take a while to get them repaired."

Megan closed her eyes and slumped against the wall. "How long will that take to fix? We have a wedding here tonight."

"I don't know. The electrical crews can't get into town yet because there's so much snow to plow."

Cole stepped forward. "Who's in charge of getting the outlying roads plowed?"

"Public Works, but we don't have a strong contingency plan for this type of situation. We're too isolated, with too few people to get it done."

"Hey—I have the floral delivery." Claire Atwood appeared, bringing with her a whirl of frigid air from outside. Her dark hair fell in waves around her face and her baby bump was already starting to show. She held a large arrangement of snapdragons, peonies, and roses in shades of lavender and pink. "I'm worried if we don't get these inside fast, I'll lose them to the cold."

"They're beautiful!" Megan touched one of the soft blooms, such a striking contrast to the deep winter surrounding them.

"Where should I put them? I have three more arrangements to bring in," Claire said.

"I can take that one for you." Cole lifted the arrangement from Claire's arms and followed Megan to the sanctuary. "Where should I put it?"

"Let me get my layout sketch." Megan tugged a binder from her bag and pulled her notes out. She placed them on the top of the piano so they could both study the plan. "Okay, it looks like that one is supposed to go on the altar."

Alexa Berg entered the sanctuary wearing her Uggs, anorak,

and red-rimmed eyes. She hung up her cell. "Jason's family is stuck in Duluth. They aren't going to make it." She shook her head.

Megan blinked. "What? Why are they back in Duluth?"

"They had an issue with two of the tuxedoes, so they kept their rooms there and drove back after rehearsal." Alexa squeezed her eyes shut.

"Oh no."

"My groom isn't going to make it in time to marry me." Her shoulders drooped.

In reality, getting married didn't require power, or even guests, but it did require a groom. And, ideally, everyone who had taken the time to RSVP. Light and heat would be a definite bonus.

"What are we going to do? We have the flowers. The cake is already in the refrigerator." Alexa wiped tears from her eyes.

"Hey—it's okay." Megan wrapped her in an embrace. "We're going to figure this out."

"Even if the power's back on, I need a groom to marry!" She let out a small cry of frustration. "It sounds like the roads are going to be a mess all day."

Megan released her, tugged her phone from her pocket, and began scrolling through her calendar. There had to be some way to make it work.

Alexa blew her nose and blotted her eyes. "Can we move it to Monday night? There's supposed to be a break in the weather Monday morning. Then everyone could be here for an evening wedding."

It wasn't an easy solution. Megan shook her head. "That's the Martin Luther King Jr. holiday. I'm already booked for a wedding at the Art Colony that night."

Alexa gestured toward Cole, who had placed the flowers behind the altar. "Can't your assistant do it?"

"My assistant?" Megan processed Alexa's request. "Cole?"

"Yeah. I mean, how hard is it? I just have to walk down the aisle. You've already done most of the hard stuff." She looked back at Megan. "Please?"

Right. All the hard stuff was already done. Every bride probably thought that until the day of her wedding. "No, he's not—"

"Do what?" Cole stood back to look at the flowers, then shifted the vase to center it.

Megan turned from the bride's expectant gaze toward Cole. He'd adjusted the flowers like it was an ordinary thing for him to do.

Alexa was about the last on the list of easy brides, but, *maybe*? Just maybe. "One moment." She lifted a finger to Alexa then turned to Cole. "I need to talk to you."

Confusion creased his brow. "Yes, ma'am."

She led him out the back of the sanctuary and down the hall a short way before turning to face him. She crossed her arms, hoping he wouldn't see her hands shaking. "How would you like a job? Okay, not a job—I can't pay you." She grimaced. "I need your help."

"What kind of help?"

"I need an assistant to pull off a second wedding Monday night."

He raised an eyebrow. "Like, as a wedding coordinator?" He paused, skepticism in his eyes.

She made a face, nodded.

"Oh, no. *No*." He held up his hand. "Megan. I'm not a frilly stuff kind of guy."

And maybe it was his immediate dismissal that irked her. Not that she had a right to demand his help, but...he *was* trying to uproot her entire life. She schooled her voice. "It's not hard, Ranger. You've jumped out of planes, right? Planned assaults?"

He stared at her, his eyes wide. "I don't think that should be used against me."

"Okay, look at it this way. You want me out of the apartment.

I need to procure the Black Spruce—and we can't move toward either goal without this wedding happening." She paused, letting her words hit their mark.

By his expression, she had his attention. "I'm already booked. This one is set up—on the wedding day, there isn't that much to do. You just make sure everyone and everything is where it needs to be when it needs to be there." Not exactly true—especially with a bride like Alexa. But Megan did have all her i's dotted. This *could* be easy.

"I really don't think I'm cut out for wedding coordination."

She gave him a look. "You can sneak into enemy territory and take out a target, and yet you can't tell a groom where to stand his ground and the bride when to deploy?"

He drew his brows together and shook his head. "What are we talking about here? Give me the specifics."

The tone of her voice rose an octave toward desperate. "I'll have it all decorated. You just make sure everyone walks down the aisle at the right time. I'll take care of all the arrangements. I just need someone to be here. I'll go to my wedding at the Art Colony. Make sure the caterer is set up. Then I'll come back here and help Alexa get dressed. And then, I'll need to run back over to the Art Colony to ensure the musicians are set and have everything they need and get the ceremony underway. But I need someone here when I'm gone. Someone to be my eyes and ears."

He leaned against the wall, his shoulders dropping. "So, I just need to hang out and make sure things keep moving along? We'd call that overwatch."

"Yes." She tried to give him an encouraging smile. "It can't be that different from running an op, right? You have a plan, you execute the plan. You have contingencies and if something comes up, you utilize the contingency plan—but the mission objective remains." See? She could speak his language.

"A wedding and an op are hardly the same thing."

"You can do this, Ranger. I just need you to show up."

She braced herself for his answer, fighting the reminder kicking around in her mind. No one ever showed up for her.

"This will help you get moved out sooner than later?" He scrubbed at his whiskers, looking down at her with those blue eyes. The ones that felt like they could see right through her. See all her heart laid bare. Every loss. Every unspoken dream.

"Yes." She hoped it wasn't a bluff. Hoped he wouldn't call her on it.

"Okay. Yes, I'll do it." He held up a finger. "But you'd better not put any pictures of me on the internet."

"Really?" She tried to keep the surprise from her voice.

"Yes—but I'm serious. No social media. The last thing I need is for the guys to see me toting flowers and cakes and whatever else around."

She held up her right hand. "I do so solemnly swear to hold your reputation as an Army Ranger in highest regard."

"I said I was serious." He tilted his head, pinched his lips together.

"Fine. No social media."

Cole gave her a slow nod, not a little apprehension in his eyes. "Okay."

"Thank you. I'd better let Alexa know we can do it so we can get started rescheduling everyone."

Casper approached from the back of the church and hung up his phone. "They finally got two plows through to clear the main roads. The linemen are on their way to start repairs." His gaze went to Megan, back to Cole. "Do you have time to help me clear the lot here again?"

"Sure." He let out a long breath. "So, we'll have to catch up later to discuss everything?"

"Yeah. That would be good."

Cole disappeared with Casper, and Megan punched in Claire's phone number.

"Hey—we have a change of plans due to the weather. Will these flowers last until Monday?"

"Sure, I'll swing by to pick them up and get them back into refrigeration. I might have to swap out a few of the more delicate blooms, but that's no problem."

"You're a rock star. Thank you."

Alexa took the news with elated squeals. "You are the best. I can't believe I have to wait to get married, but thank you for making it work."

Megan hoped they could actually pull it off.

They spent the next hour at the church, calling every guest, vendor, and bridal party member to update them on the change from Saturday to Monday. Each one had graciously agreed, relieved that they didn't have to try to venture out for the event or face cancelling their participation. Megan disconnected her last call.

"Whew. Glad that's done."

Alexa nodded. "Me too. I'm going to head back to my parents' place and get some sleep. I was up all night worrying about it and watching the snow pile up. I'll talk to you later."

"Sounds good." Megan headed back down the hall toward the church office. Josh came running through the front doors, ruddy cheeks and watering eyes. "Mom! You have to come see the snow tunnel I built. Cole pushed a ton of snow into a pile and it's perfect."

She tugged her gloves on and followed him outside. Cole stood triumphant at the top of a snow berm, arms stretched high in the air, his knit hat coated in snowflakes.

What in the world?

A snowball shattered across the front of her coat.

What? An *ambush*. And her own son had used himself as bait.

She scooped up a handful of snow, pressing it into a tight ball and lobbing it toward the mountain of snow and the pink-cheeked Cole. It fell short and she ducked down to grab another handful.

That's when she saw Josh's allegiance. He climbed the mountain of snow behind Cole, filling his mittens with snow, mischief in his eyes and a beaming grin on his lips.

It was two against one.

Megan stopped, frozen. Struck still with the realization that asking Cole to help was the biggest mistake she could have made.

She'd invited the enemy into her world. Her private, safe world.

Josh's snowball hit her square in the face.

CHAPTER 4

*C*ole hadn't been this sore since Ranger School. Apparently, being on snowplow patrol had its costs.

After spending the first three hours of his Sunday morning clearing the church parking lot with Casper and then piling branches that had snapped from the weight of the snow, Cole was ready for a long winter nap. At least the crews had managed to get the power restored.

He collapsed on the sofa, ready to hibernate when Casper came down dressed for Sunday service and headed into the kitchen.

He returned moments later with two cups of coffee and handed one to Cole before sitting down in the armchair.

"Thanks." Cole let the cup warm his hands. "So, you said there isn't a real contingency plan for assistance when there are power outages or weather events? That seems a bit...disorganized—no offense—but, I mean, what if there'd been an emergency? What if we were dealing with a critical injury yesterday morning?"

"It's an issue here." Casper took a drink. "I think there's never been anyone with the capacity and skills to spearhead

57

SUSAN MAY WARREN & RACHEL D. RUSSELL

putting it all together—all the different crews, the volunteers available, the training, the equipment." He raised a brow. "Does that offend your Ranger sensibilities?"

Cole rubbed his jaw. "It kind of does. What about other emergency services? Search and rescue? Water rescue?"

"I wish I could tell you we've got it all covered. We don't. We're a small town on the edge of a lot of wilderness."

"It's hard to imagine leaving all that to chance and luck."

Casper nodded. "There've been a few close calls." He set his mug down.

The words settled over Cole. But Deep Haven wasn't his problem.

Still, he couldn't help himself. "The town really needs a specialized team. The snowplows are one thing, but they're just one piece of the puzzle. Emergencies happen year-round."

"I agree. We had a forest fire years ago—destroyed the cabins at Evergreen. Something as basic as evacuation notifications were challenging."

Cole chewed the inside of his cheek. Nope. Not his problem.

"You heading to the service?" Casper broke the silence that had fallen over them.

Cole shook his head. No way. He needed to steer clear of Miss Megan Carter, who was sure to be front and center this morning. What was he thinking, getting into a snowball fight with her? And why did he feel like he'd done something wrong?

Maybe the way she called to Josh, demanded they head home, a little edge to her voice. Barely mumbling goodbye. And he should know better because Rebecca had taught him the fickle nature of a woman. That any woman—even, or maybe especially, a Christian woman—couldn't be trusted with his heart.

Not that his heart was at risk. No, not at all. So what that when she smiled, it unraveled him a bit. So what that when she stood close to him, the smell of roses made him want to lean in to it. So what that when she called him Ranger with a soft, husky tease in her voice, it gave a little tug on his heart.

Nope, no risk at all.

Casper pressed his lips together and gave him a nod. "Are you going to stop by and see your grandfather?"

Again, "No, sir."

Casper gave him a look.

Cole shook his head. "I can't."

Casper leaned forward, looked down into his clasped hands. "My dad once told me I was my own worst enemy."

Cole frowned. "Is that what you're telling me?"

"I know things were hard after your parents died. I saw how your grandpa changed, even as kids. We all could tell." Casper glanced up the stairs and then leaned in, lowered his voice and met Cole's eyes. "Listen, I know all about holding on to anger. Trust me—when I found out what Owen had done—" He paused, as if sorting out his next words. "Layla is my daughter, but biologically, she's Owen's."

Owen? Casper's younger brother? He blinked hard, trying to suppress his real reaction. Not the direction he'd expected the conversation to go. Cole swallowed. Waited.

"It was before we'd met. A mistake on both sides. And it took a lot for me to get through it. Really, it took God for me—and Raina—to get through it. To even heal my relationship with Owen. But because we did, Raina and Layla and I have an incredible life together. I would have missed all the blessings God had for me if I'd held on to my anger, no matter how I justified it. No matter how righteous I felt."

Cole set down his cup. God didn't have any blessings for him. He'd allowed his parents to die, sending Cole to his grandpa's. Everything had spiraled wrong from there. But he'd pulled his life together by himself. Joined the Army. Found his place. And he'd keep doing exactly that with the U.S. Marshals

Service. He didn't need help getting through it because he'd planned on keeping it far behind him.

"I know it's hard." And the earnest tone in Casper's voice said maybe he really did know how hard it would be. "But it's possible."

Layla scampered down the stairs and tackled Casper from behind. "I'm ready, Daddy." She wore a pink dress with tights, and she kicked her fluffy boots in the air.

Raina came down the stairs shortly after. "I tried to get her to opt for something a little warmer, but she insisted the pink dress is what a stylish kindergartner would wear."

"Then we'd better bundle you up because let me tell you, there's a lot of snow out there and it's still coming down."

They stood at the door and snugged on their coats. Casper put his hand on the doorknob. "We'll see you later." He paused. "Really, though, please think about what I said."

Cole shrugged. "Sure. I'll think about it. Thanks."

Casper gave him a nod and they headed out the door to the sounds of Layla's small voice describing exactly how many snow angels she thought she'd make after church.

Despite his best attempts to ignore them, Casper's words gnawed at Cole for another hour before he grabbed his coat and headed over to Lighthouse Memory Care. Fine. He'd check it off the list and, besides, sitting around wasn't his M.O. It certainly wasn't going to heal the wounds of the past, but maybe the visit would distract him from the fact that he still had to survive a wedding with Megan and make his grandfather's house marketable.

The care center sat on Fifth Avenue, the exterior a dull gray that blended in with the colorless sky. Tired and forgotten.

The door buzzed open and Cole entered the care facility. The sharp smell of disinfectant permeated the air and a flush of heat stifled the corridor. The building was set up with a central entrance at the front and the reception and nurse's station acted as a hub where three hallways converged, like spokes on a half-wheel.

An older woman stood at the reception desk, her expectant gaze on him.

This was a mistake. Cole turned to catch the door before it latched.

"May I help you?"

He paused. Took a breath. "I'm here to look in on Edgar Barrett." The door clanked closed behind him.

"Are you family?"

The dryness in his mouth made it hard to speak. "Yes, ma'am."

She lifted a brow at him.

"I'm his—I'm his grandson."

"Well, okay." The woman shuffled through a file drawer and withdrew a manila folder. "Here it is. I'll need to see photo identification."

Cole handed her his license and she began clicking away on her keyboard.

"Hmm," she said, looking up at him.

"Is there a problem?"

"There's a note here in the system. One moment. I'll need to have his case manager speak with you." She disappeared into an office behind her and then re-emerged. "Miss Chase is available now, Mr. Barrett. Come on back."

This couldn't be good.

The office was painted bright white with pale green accents, and the woman behind the desk looked younger than Cole. Her dark hair was pulled back in a ponytail and she wore a purple blouse with snowmen all over it. Something light-hearted.

"Mr. Barrett, I'm glad you stopped by. I didn't have a phone number on record for you." She extended her hand. "I'm Camilla Chase, your grandfather's case manager. We're short-handed on the administrative side, so I'm trying to assist with some of the financials and billing, too."

He shook her hand, and despite every instinct telling him to back away and find safer ground, he took the seat she offered.

She picked up the file. "The February billing went out yesterday. Your grandfather has some benefits through the end of January that insurance will afford him due to his injury. The church paid for an additional thirty days, but after that, he'll have to be transferred to a VA facility in Duluth unless there's funding to pay directly for his care."

"Insurance doesn't cover it?"

"He doesn't have extended coverage for memory care. It simply isn't covered by regular policies. And after his hip fracture, I really think this is the best place for him."

"I don't know anything about a hip fracture."

"In December he had a fall. He's been doing rehab here, which is why he currently has coverage. We have a physical therapist on staff and it's considered acute care."

"Okay. Thanks."

"Can I add your information to our system?"

Cole gave her his contact information and she began typing.

"This is your first time seeing him in a while?"

"Yes, ma'am."

"How long has it been?"

"About fifteen years."

"I see." She blinked. "Do you have experience with Alzheimer's?"

"No." He darted another look at the door.

She stopped typing, turned to him. Her voice softened. "Dealing with Alzheimer's can be difficult for both the patient and family. Their reality in the moment is their reality, and nothing you can say will cause them to think the way you or I would."

Cole nodded, and he planted himself, refusing to bolt. But man, the door called.

"We ask visitors not to argue, correct, or try to reason with patients. You can distract them, redirect, and even reminisce. Patients sometimes live in a past time of their life and that's what we see most often with your grandfather." She handed him a care guide brochure. "Mr. Barrett, your grandfather has only had two lucid moments in the past four months."

"What does that mean?"

"It means you shouldn't expect him to know who you are. When he was lucid, he understood what was going on with his diagnosis. He understood he would continue to get worse, but the rest of the time, he hasn't been in the moment of the present-day world."

Cole nodded, stuffed the brochure into his back pocket. Maybe this would be better for another day. A day when he hadn't exhausted himself clearing snow from parking lots and shoveling driveways.

She stood and led him down the wide corridor. "He's in what we call our rec room. Patients like to gather and socialize. We do have an outdoor area for summertime, but our doors are kept locked and you must be buzzed in or out. Alzheimer's patients have a predisposition to wandering off due to their confusion. Our outdoor area has an eight-foot fence and is securely gated. It's monitored with staff and cameras."

She gestured to an open doorway. A balding man sat in a chair at a table, facing two other patients and a caregiver, talking. One of the residents, another man, stared out the window. The other, a woman, worked on a puzzle with the staff member. Cole stared at the man speaking, whose thin wisps of hair jutted out in all directions. The years hadn't been kind to Grandpa.

All Cole caught was the mention of Vietnam and a medevac.

The raging monster in his teenage memories sat frail, small, and utterly lost to reality. Broken beyond repair.

The sight gripped Cole's throat, closing off his airway. The man who'd been his childhood hero until he succumbed to alcoholism and the devastation of grief.

"He often talks about his service like the memories are fresh." Camilla's quiet words stilled him.

Cole nodded to acknowledge her, and the movement caught Grandpa's eye. The man squinted. "Jimmy?" His jaw dropped open, his eyes wide. Frail, aged. "What are you doing here?"

James, Cole's father. He turned to get guidance from Camilla, but she'd disappeared down the hall. He started to step back out of the room.

Grandpa gestured toward Cole. "This is my son, Jimmy. They live in Minneapolis, but he always brings his son, Cole, to spend summers with Rosalind and me."

Cole swallowed. *Don't argue. Don't try to reason.* He stepped forward. "Thought I'd say hello and see how you are doing."

"Did you bring Cole with you?" He beamed, leaning back in his chair. "That boy. He's going to be a professional hockey player someday." He turned toward the other residents and they lifted their attention to him. "And the last time we went fishing, that boy caught the biggest walleye I've ever seen."

The other man nodded. "There's some big ones."

What? Cole tried to not let his grandfather's words needle into him and pierce his heart.

"I need to go now." Cole backed away. Air. He needed air.

"When will you come back?" his grandfather asked. As if he might actually care.

"I'm not sure." Cole didn't know what else to say. Everything began closing in on him as he made his way back past the central hub and bolted toward the exit door, giving a nod to the clerk when she buzzed him out.

For the first time, twenty degrees didn't feel cold enough to soothe the fire in his heart.

He stood there, drinking in the frigid air. He needed to get out of this town.

"Hi, Cole." Nathan Decker approached from the parking lot. Under his winter coat, he wore dress slacks and the knot of a tie snugged against the base of his neck like he'd come from church. He looked from Cole to the care center. "I'm glad you made it over here. How did it go?"

Cole opened his mouth. Closed it. Paused. "I don't know how to answer that." He hated the thickness in his voice.

"It's difficult to see the changes with Alzheimer's." Nathan placed a gloved hand on Cole's shoulder. "I like to volunteer here. I've known Edgar for quite a few years. He really had become a changed man. Sobered up. Spoke with regret about his past choices."

Cole looked away. "He thought I was my father."

Nathan pressed his lips together, nodded. "This is a good place for him to be. At this care center, no one is forgotten, even when they've forgotten who they are. The staff treats each one of them like family."

Cole nodded. "That's a mercy, I guess." A mercy time hadn't given him. He looked at Nathan. "I need your help to find a place for Megan to live. And it can't cost more than her current rent. And it has to allow pets."

"That's going to be tough." Nathan pulled out his phone and began making notes.

"I've been told you're the best."

"So, that's how you're going to play this one?" Nathan smiled. "I'm no miracle worker, but I'm pretty good with real estate." He paused, considered. "So, a two-bedroom apartment, reasonable rent, allows pets."

"And maybe some room for storage."

Nathan raised a brow.

"She has some wedding stuff she stores in the first floor of my grandfather's garage."

"Okay, with storage."

"And a nice yard area for kids to play in."

Nathan stopped thumb-typing. "Are you trying to make it impossible for me to find a place? Because the initial request was fairly challenging right out of the gate."

"No, it just needs to be the right place for her to want to move into it."

A place she could call home. Because everyone else seemed to have forgotten his brutal family history—who the real bad guy was. If Cole kicked out Megan and her son, leaving them homeless in the winter, one thing was certain. Instead of his grandfather, he'd be the one forever remembered as the villain of Deep Haven.

Megan could do it all. Plan, decorate, and execute two weddings at the same time.

What she could not do was reach the ceiling hook for the lights.

She stood at the top of the ladder, glowing twinkle lights wrapped around her torso like Rambo, and wondering exactly how dangerous the "Not a Step" rung on the ten-foot ladder really was.

If there were awards given out for speed decorating, Megan was going to win, hands down. She'd arrived at Deep Haven Community Church early and began setting up tables and chairs before the sun came up. Anything to minimize contact with Cole and secure the Black Spruce down payment.

She'd filled all her spare time the day before by volunteering on a Meals on Wheels route after church, dropping off snacks for the hockey team, getting both brides through a rehearsal, and picking up Mrs. Olson's prescription.

Indispensable. That's exactly what Mrs. Olson had said. The word still swelled in Megan's chest.

Megan startled when the doors to the fellowship hall flew open. She grappled to wrap her fingers around the top edges of the ladder, bobbling.

"Whoa, Mae!" Cole set down the box he carried and jogged toward her. He climbed up the ladder to rescue her, locking his arms around her. "Gotcha."

"What are you doing here?" She took slow steps backward down the ladder, trapped between his strong arms.

"I was helping Seb Brewster unload some food boxes. Got to talk hockey with the mayor for a bit and thought it would be good to check in with the boss before I run some errands."

She turned when her feet reached solid ground.

Oh boy. He wore a dark blue Henley that had the unfortunate effect of taking his eyes from dangerous to absolutely devastating. It molded around the muscles of his chest and arms, and she was pretty sure a man couldn't possibly smell any better. Something woodsy like pine. Earthy and altogether appealing. Completely despicable.

And he called her Mae. His childhood nickname for her.

Again, oh boy.

"I couldn't reach the ceiling hook to hang these." She gestured to her luminous wrap.

"Please don't do that again." He put a hand on her arm. It had the full effect of an electric shock tingling through her entire body. "Can I help?"

She cleared her throat, stepped away from his concerned gaze. "For the record, I was doing well until you came in." Sort of. She'd stayed busy because when she slowed down, the nagging voice in her head asked her what in the world she was going to do if Cole really did kick her out.

"There's a reason it says 'Not a Step.'"

"Okay, Ranger. Then, yes, I need your help."

A smile hitched the side of his face. "All you had to do was ask."

He scaled the ladder and hooked the string over the ceiling mount. "Where do they go from here?"

"I was thinking about putting them across the tables and over the place where the band will be playing."

"What if we zigzag them across the entire room? Do you have more strands?"

She looked at the coils in his hands. "I do."

"Let's try it. It looks like there are hooks along the wall for hanging banners. You could use those."

She climbed the step behind him to take the coil and walked it toward the wall to another ladder where the lower hooks were within her reach.

They continued to work back and forth around the room until the entire place was aglow in a warm wash of light. Why hadn't she thought of doing this before?

Megan stepped back to survey the space.

Cole still stood on the ladder, his face triumphant. "It looks—"

"Wow—that's magical!" Claire stood in the doorway holding an empty vase. "You two make a good team."

Not a team. *Not* a team. Because teams stuck together. Worked together. Were in it for the long haul. And she couldn't lean into the possibility. Because he was leaving just like he always did. And the sooner he did it the better. The last thing she wanted was Josh getting hurt.

Cole descended the ladder and folded it, then hauled it out into the hallway before returning.

Megan studied the room. The circular tables were draped in white cloths. At the center of each, she'd placed a miniature lantern with silver-covered branches and pine cones. Under the lights, the room became ethereal.

She turned back to Claire. "You don't have the flowers, do you?"

"No, not this early. I had to pick up this vase left in the storeroom and couldn't help but sneak a peek." She lifted the vase. "I'll see you guys later. Good job!"

Cole dropped an unlit strand of lights into the box. "It does look really good, Mae."

She swallowed. He needed to quit calling her that. It felt too personal. Too familiar. And it made her want to lean into too many good memories.

She stepped away, putting distance between them. "I think we're set." She flipped off the twinkle lights and led the way to the foyer.

Cole picked up his coat. "I need to run. What time do I need to be here tonight?"

Megan looked at her watch—quarter to nine. "Be here at four?"

"Yes, ma'am." He turned to leave, paused, and turned back. "No more ladders?"

She held up three fingers, Girl Scout style. "No more ladders." *Today.*

Megan spent the rest of her morning finishing the decorations at the Art Colony by herself, followed by a mad dash through the grocery store and too much attention given to what she'd wear to the weddings.

It irked her that somehow tonight's weddings felt different. She changed her dress for the third time, slipping into a blue one. For some reason, what she wore mattered. Which didn't make any sense because she had no one to impress.

Nope. No one. Definitely not Army Ranger Cole Barrett. Because that would be a terrible idea.

Maybe worse had been her decision to accept his help. Or to consider the fact that it would be very possible to find a job in

Minneapolis working for one of the big event companies. Yep, she was getting waaaay ahead of herself.

Besides, life in Minneapolis would mean a big school for Josh. Losing his friends. Having to sit in after-school programs while she worked to build someone else's company.

Saying goodbye to her dreams. Nope. She wouldn't leave Deep Haven. Not for anything—or anyone.

Oh, for Pete's sake. Cole had been here for less than seventy-two hours and she already had Prince Charming stamped on his head, completely forgetting who he was and why he was here.

She stared out at the white landscape. The relative warmth of the day had melted some of the snow. Neighbors walked down the sidewalk, stopping to visit in clusters along the street.

Josh shrieked with laughter from the living room floor where he played some form of improvised charades with the babysitter—a senior from the church youth group, Kayleigh Nelson.

No. Deep Haven was their home and she wouldn't let Cole derail that life. And if that meant working with him tonight, then so be it. She'd be one small step closer to buying the Black Spruce.

Claire had delivered the flowers for the second time in as many days, and Alexa had spent the morning messaging Megan with updates on the bridal party's progress from Duluth. The roads were clear and they'd made a quick trip up the highway.

So, that was it. This might be an epic failure. An end to her career.

Or, they just might pull this off.

"I'm heading over to the Art Colony." She grabbed her planning binder and purse. "There's leftover pizza in the refrigerator and you might even find a pan of brownies." She winked at Josh.

"Brownies? Yes!" Josh threw his hands in the air.

"I should be home by nine."

"Okay, thanks, Ms. Carter." Kayleigh smiled.

"Bye," Josh answered before jumping up and pantomiming something that resembled a monkey playing a ukulele.

The sidewalks were clear the entire way to the Art Colony. The bride, Jessica Mullins, was already halfway dressed when Megan arrived, her bridesmaids giggling like school girls and her mother gently pulling up the zipper.

"Eager?"

"That obvious?" Jessica giggled. "I've been waiting nine months for this day. I'm so ready."

"My other wedding is at the church, but I have an assistant helping with that one. I'm going to do a walk-through and make sure everything is set."

"Okay, thank you."

Megan had finished her final check when her phone buzzed with a text from Cole that everything looked good there.

Okay, then. Two eager brides. Check. Two well-dressed grooms. Check. All bridal party members where they were supposed to be. Check.

And she didn't have to face Cole until the end of the evening. They could do this. Right?

Thirty minutes later, Megan stood at the back of the venue watching Jessica and Garrett exchange vows. Maybe it was the stress of the weekend. The juggling of the day. Having to spend so much time with Cole. *Mae.* But somehow this time, the promises said at the altar stung. Reeled her back to the day she'd picked out her own dress and thumbed through books of floral arrangements.

Until, of course, Trevor broke off their engagement.

You're the one who planned out our whole future together without ever asking me. You roped me into this—let's be honest.

Her stomached tightened. Like the moment she'd realized what a fool she'd been. Naive. Blind.

There's a simple solution to this problem. Just make an appointment.

But she couldn't hide from God. No matter what, she couldn't hide.

She stepped out of the former sanctuary to check on the reception hall. The multi-use building held a variety of creative classes during the week, but was also still a popular location for weddings and special events.

Her tall boots clicked across the tile, and she stopped to smooth the bow on her wrap dress. Nope. She didn't need a man in her life and she was definitely not wearing the dress to impress.

She had nothing to fear from this night. Or Cole Barrett.

CHAPTER 5

The last thing Cole needed was a failed op.

Unfortunately, the success of Operation Aisle Run hinged on Cole wrangling the three-year-old flower girl down the aisle with her basket of rose petals. In truth, he'd met his match.

He tugged at the knot of his tie and squatted down to face the enemy.

"Stand here." Cole pointed to the spot he'd marked with tape. She twirled around in her fluffy white dress. He handed her the basket of flower petals. "Okay, princess. You're up." He aimed her through the open doors and stood next to her.

She looked up at him with big, green eyes. Her feet didn't move. *Come on, kid.*

This was so far out of his element. Cole had avoided weddings like a fish taco sitting all day in the summer sun. Maybe he was a little embarrassed at how he had let the memory of his parents down. Marrying a girl "just because" and throwing away the model they'd demonstrated.

He patted her head. "All you do is walk toward your mom.

SUSAN MAY WARREN & RACHEL D. RUSSELL

See her sitting up there waiting for you? Drop those petals from your basket, just like you practiced, okay?"

She nodded and grabbed his hand.

He knelt down, sliding his hand from hers. Clearly, she didn't understand the rules of engagement. "I don't go with you."

She froze, and her face turned splotchy and scrunched up as she drew in a deep breath.

His mission was headed south in a hurry. The musicians repeated the interlude to cover the delay.

"You like cake, right?"

She nodded.

"As soon as you finish your job here, you're going to get a big slice of cake. But everyone needs you to do this one job, okay?"

She narrowed her eyes and held up a finger at him. "I get a big piece."

"Sure." He pointed toward the open door and this time, she tromped down the aisle, chucking handfuls of petals in the air and letting them rain down on her like confetti.

Whatever worked. Mission accomplished.

Once she'd landed in the hands of her mother and the bride had been escorted down the aisle, he closed the sanctuary doors and went to the fellowship hall for a walk-through. The catering staff unloaded carts of food and prepared the buffet line at the far end of the room. Savory smells of prime rib and roasted vegetables permeated the room.

He'd hardly eaten all day between helping Megan decorate the church and his marathon trip to Duluth with Casper so he could return the rental car. He'd also scored a suit and some winter apparel. When the U.S. Marshals Service called, he'd be ready for his interview.

He plugged in the twinkle lights and lit the candles inside the table lanterns. White and pink roses centered each table in tall glass vases. He had to admit Megan was good at what she did.

At least they'd managed some sort of truce. When she'd teetered on the ladder, it had sent an alarm firing through every nerve in his body. Caused her nickname to slip from his lips and pressed him to offer to help after assuring she was safe.

If he could survive this night, he'd be one step closer to leaving town.

One of the light strands flickered and went out. He took off his suit coat, grabbed a chair, and started the slow process of checking each bulb until he found the loose one and snugged it back into place. The entire strand lit.

Returning to the foyer, he waited outside the sanctuary during the ceremony. There was no need to further torture himself. In a few minutes, the sanctuary doors opened and the bride and groom came through. He turned away for their private post-ceremony kiss.

No need to rake up old, broken memories.

The wedding party and guests filtered into the reception hall, taking their seats at the designated tables while the bride and groom stood in the receiving line. Cole was standing at the entrance to the hall, on the lookout for trouble when Marianne Berg, mother-of-the-bride, exited and placed her palm against the far wall, her skin ashen.

"Ma'am? Are you okay?"

"This can't be happening." The bride's mother looked up at him, tears and makeup streaming down her face.

Oh no.

"What's wrong?" His voice came out too hard, almost demanding. Probably he needed to remember this wasn't one of his teammates, and this wasn't really one of his ops.

She let out a heaving sob. "He's going to ruin the entire day. Who invited him? And how did we end up being placed at the same table?"

"Who?"

"Alexa's father!" She began searching through her purse. "Please, you've got to do something. I can't deal with him." Pulling out a well-worn tissue, she blew her nose. Looked back up at him. "And, really? He brought his wife?"

And now, heaven help him, she released a full-on, all-out wail. What the—? He just stood there.

A man in the center of the room talking with several guests caught his attention.

Right, Alexa's father. A long-haired brunette hung on his arm. He seemed unencumbered by any disruption their presence was causing.

Nice. They had a terrorist in their midst. "Come in here." He tugged Marianne into an empty Sunday school classroom and handed her a box of tissues from the side table. "Please, sit." He pulled out a chair for her.

She sank into the chair, pulling out a half dozen tissues. "After all the snow and delays. How is it that he shows up to ruin it? And now he wants to flaunt his happy life seated at the table, next to me?"

"I'm so sorry. Let me see what I can do."

"Can you make him leave? Kick them out?"

Cole was starting to think a little brawl might be just the thing he needed. "I'll be right back."

She nodded, and he headed into the hallway, pulling up Megan's callback number. As much as he'd like to go mano a mano with this guy, he couldn't get himself into trouble over an unwanted wedding guest. He knew when to call for reinforcements.

"We have a problem."

"What's wrong?" Her voice was low and he could hear music playing in the background.

"I don't know the whole story—Ms. Berg said Alexa's father and his wife showed up, and she's hysterical. I don't know what to do with her—the tables are all full and she said she's seated next to them."

"Oh no. He'd told Alexa he would be coming alone, but I must have used my standard seating chart when I gave it to the caterer. Usually the bride's parents are at the same table. It's my fault. I'll be right there."

She must have run the half block to the church, because a few minutes later, she burst through the door with flushed cheeks and a few strands of hair hanging loose from her twist. She tugged off her coat, revealing a bright blue dress that hugged her curves, flared at her hips, and ended just at her knees. A nice change from her puffy jacket and jeans look.

"She's in here." Cole opened the door so Megan could slip into the classroom. Ms. Berg looked up at her and started sobbing again. He went still as Megan dropped to her knees and embraced the distraught woman. Held her like she was a dear friend, clearly possessing the right touch to save the day.

Cole seized the opportunity to vacate. "I'll go...uh...check on things."

Megan tugged several more tissues from the box. "Here, let's get you put back together." She nodded to Cole and he stepped out of the room.

Cole cruised through the reception hall, where the bride asked for her mother, worry furrowing her brow.

"She's with Megan."

Alexa's eyes fell on her father speaking with guests across the room. "What was he thinking? He brought Karlie. Is my mom okay?" Jason stood next to her, dutifully holding her hand, and his family stood behind them, taking in the scene.

"Can I help with anything?" Jason's father asked. His eyes were on Alexa's father. Clearly he'd been better briefed than Cole.

"I'm sure everything will be fine. I'll go see what the holdup is." Cole headed back to the classroom. The door was open a

SUSAN MAY WARREN & RACHEL D. RUSSELL

few inches and he could hear the soothing tones of Megan's voice.

"Thank you, Megan. You've been the most amazing coordinator."

"Again, I apologize for my part in this mix-up."

Ms. Berg gave Megan another hug before smoothing out her gown and tucking a loose lock of hair behind her ear. She gave Cole a nod before leaving the room.

He turned to Megan. "Wow. What did you do?"

"I'll tell you later. Right now, we need to run and fix the place settings."

"Right." He led her into the reception hall. Ms. Berg must have clung to Megan's words because she artfully moved about the reception hall mingling with guests while avoiding a confrontation with the skill of a special operator. Megan spoke in quiet tones with several guests who nodded. She deftly swapped the place cards, giving Ms. Berg a spot several tables away, facing the opposite direction of her ex.

And here he'd been ready to dump the guy on the curb—a tactic that, while very satisfying, would have probably resulted in any number of additional problems for all parties involved. Including Megan.

"Do you need to head back to the Mullins wedding?"

"Probably. Soon." She looked him up and down. "You're a little mussed. Was Ms. Berg just a little too much for you?" She grinned as she reached up to his tie. "Nice duds. Where'd you find the uniform?"

Her rose fragrance enveloped him and she deftly worked at his tie, finishing by smoothing the fabric down his chest. His throat went dry. A woman hadn't touched him in years, and the feeling of her palms against his chest heated his entire body.

"You're all set now." She pulled her hands away, tucked them behind her back.

He swallowed. She looked radiant beneath the lights, and he

couldn't take his eyes off her. He cleared his throat. "I know how much you liked that minivan, but I took it back to Duluth. Picked up a few things before getting a ride back. You know, a suit, anorak. A couple sled dogs. Though, I did manage to get Grandpa's Jeep running."

"Stop. It isn't that bad."

"Says the girl who's lived here her whole life."

"You grew up in Minneapolis. And here."

"I've been gone a long time."

"Yeah." She looked up at him with her golden eyes. "I should, uh, you know, go." She tilted her head toward the exit.

"Yeah. Okay."

"I'll be back later."

He sure hoped so.

By the time she returned, her steps had slowed. She sent the bride and groom off with an arch of sparklers, directed the caterers to save the cake topper, and started to take down the twinkly lights. He came over to help. "Thanks, Cole. I couldn't have done this without you."

"You know, I'm starting to think you could have. Why don't you let me stay, chase away these last few guests, and finish cleanup? You've done enough for everyone today."

Jason's father approached them and held out his hand to shake Cole's. "Thank you, both, for making this all come together despite the crazy weather." He leaned in closer. "And unwanted guests."

He shook Megan's hand and then tugged an envelope from his coat pocket. "Miss Carter, this is for you. For going above and beyond and making this day so special. I don't know how you rescheduled the entire wedding, from flowers to musicians, but you did it. Outstanding work."

Megan took the envelope. "Thank you, sir. You all have a wonderful evening."

He nodded and escorted the rest of his family out the doors.

"So, what did you say to her?" Cole said as he returned with a ladder, setting it up to help her take down the lights.

"Who?" She set the envelope down and stood on a chair in bare stocking feet, holding one end of the lights.

"Ms. Berg. How'd you get her to calm down? I probably shouldn't tell you the solution I was thinking of."

She raised a brow at him and shook her head, a hint of a smile on her lips. He unstrung the lights, and she rolled them up like a climber. "I don't know," she said. "I just let her know I understood her pain, I guess. You know, a bad relationship. Mistakes you can't take back."

"You mean your ex-husband?" He moved the ladder and unhooked another string of lights.

She wound them up too and disconnected the strings from each other, putting them in a box. "We were never...never married." She wouldn't look at him and frowned. "Trevor McAllister. Swept me off my feet during my freshman year of college. Maybe I was so in love with the idea of being loved, I missed all the warnings. You know, like the fact that he always had a reason to not take me home to meet his parents." She wrung her hands together. "Still, I wanted so much to please him. I believed the promises he made. Actually, he says he never made me any promises." She lifted a shoulder. "I guess his plans for law school didn't include a small-town girl and they definitely didn't include a child."

He shook his head at her words. The implication. He worked quietly, unhooking lights, one after another. Glanced at her. She still wouldn't look at him.

Oh, Megan.

"So, anyway, when I found out I was pregnant with Josh, he was angry. He thought I'd done it on purpose. I wasn't even nineteen and he thought I should..." She stood up. Swallowed, forced a smile as he gave her the handful of lights.

His gut tightened because he knew what she was going to say.

Wanted to groan when she did.

"He thought I should get an abortion, which, of course, wasn't an option. Said I'd ruined everything."

Aw. And he couldn't help himself. He reached out and covered her shaking hand with his. All the years between them evaporated. "I'm sorry."

She stilled. Then nodded and pulled away. Rolled up the lights. "That's about it. He broke things off. I dropped out of school and moved back here to raise my son. I'd always hoped for redemption—hoped he'd come for us. Even prayed for it, maybe so I could find a way to redeem my own mistakes." She gave him a wry smile. "Trevor's sent cards for Josh here and there. Never been reliable or consistent. I stopped expecting much of him years ago."

Dropping the next coil into the box, Megan kicked it over to the final row of lights. "He's shown up a few times over the years, but mostly, he'd get Josh's hopes up, then something always caused him to cancel. I just avoid him now. Less heartache for Josh." She shrugged. "What about you, Ranger? How come there's no ring on your left hand?"

And now it was his turn not to look at her. He moved the ladder and retrieved the last of the lights. He'd played it off with everyone else. But somehow, in telling Megan, he could still feel the sting. "Divorced, two years ago." He paused, considered his words. "I met Rebecca at the off-post bar where she worked. We got to know each other a bit and, I don't know...started dating." That's what he'd called it. In hindsight, they were two desperately lonely people looking for something—someone—to hold on to. "I guess I wanted a home. A family." He let out a sharp laugh. "While I was on deployment, I got a letter saying she'd become a Christian and had fallen for a guy at church."

He hadn't realized that Megan had come over to the ladder.

And when he turned, she reached for the lights. The expression on her face undid him.

"Oh, Cole," she said softly.

Her words had the effect of a roadside bomb, taking apart his defenses.

He swallowed and climbed down the ladder. "She begged me to go to counseling with her—that she knew how wrong it was." He shook his head at the sting. "That was pretty rich, you know?"

She just held the tangled mess of lights. "Did you? Go to counseling?"

"Absolutely not. The trust was gone." He stared across the vacant room and scrubbed a hand through his hair. "It was a stupid, short courtship and we didn't really know each other at all." He shrugged. "Obviously."

"And here we are." She let out a sad, sharp laugh. "Sending couples off into the world together."

"With twinkle lights and roses."

She stood there for a moment, as if stymied, and he took the lights and wound them up. Walked over to the box.

"You know, I still believe in it," she said softly, a wistful longing in her eyes.

He nodded. "I know. I'd expect nothing less from you, Mae." He pointed to the envelope left on the table. "Don't forget your envelope."

"Oh, yeah." She retrieved the envelope and slid it open to peek inside. Her eyes grew big and her mouth dropped open. "What?" She pulled it out and turned the check around so he could see it.

One thousand dollars.

She slid a note out. "It says, 'From the Thomas family, Thank you for your amazing work. You went above and beyond. Best wishes.'"

"That's fantastic."

Except, she put her hand over her face and—oh no. She was…crying?

"Mae, what's wrong?" He took a step toward her.

She swiped a tear away. "I'm fine. I just can't believe he did that. It's one step closer to buying the Black Spruce. This is a huge boost. I want this so much for me and Josh."

"You deserve it." How he wanted to touch her. To pull her into his arms.

To feel that closeness again, like he had this morning on the ladder. Her, safe in his arms.

Man, this wedding business was going to his head.

"Thanks." She stepped away from him. "Ready to get out of here? I can clean up the rest tomorrow."

He nodded, his heart thudding dangerously. "Let me drop you off. I'm heading to Casper's for one last night. Tomorrow is moving day. It's time to settle in at my grandfather's house so I can start making repairs."

He stripped off his tie on the way out the door. The sooner he was out of this monkey suit and back on task, the better.

Not even the sunshine of the morning could lighten the darkness that clung bone-deep in Megan's body.

She'd replayed the evening with Cole a thousand times staring at the ceiling in her apartment, tossing the night away, trying to push every last thought of him out of her mind. Oh, she was such a fool.

A jealous fool. Because she couldn't deny the sting that hit her when she noticed the eyes of several bridesmaids following Cole around. The whispers and giggles. Yes. The giant green-eyed monster assaulted her when one of the beauties dared to approach him. Engage him in conversation. She was young and cute, her body lean and muscular. Her bridesmaid dress fit in all the right places and the sweetheart neckline showed off her flattering curves.

But how could they *not* notice him? He was stunning any way she looked at him, despite her efforts to not look at him at all. There was something entirely delectable in the way Cole's undershirt snuck out just a tad below his dress shirt when he'd removed his tie.

She hadn't meant to let him in—to show how far wrong her life choices had taken her. He'd caught her in a weak moment, telling him how she'd talked Ms. Berg back from the ledge. And he'd looked at her, gutted. Yeah, well, she'd disappointed herself too. Fallen for Trevor's caramel-sweet promises. Sold out all her values and morals.

The shame was still enough to choke her.

And Cole had reached out to her. The same electricity she'd felt when she straightened his tie she felt when he had wrapped her hand in his. How she'd missed the warmth of his hand when she pulled hers away, much like she'd missed him when he disappeared from her life.

But it was for their own good.

A doorbell ring snapped Megan out of her dark places. She hustled down the stairs and opened the exterior door to Raina.

"I've lost my houseguest and you've gained a neighbor." She nodded toward the Victorian, and Megan peeked out the door just in time to see Cole disappear through his front door. He wore jeans with an untucked, blue flannel shirt under his leather jacket and his green rucksack slung over his shoulder.

Perfect. Now the enemy was camped at the gate.

"Can I come in?"

"Please," Megan said. She led the way back up to the apartment, and Raina stepped inside, slid out of her coat, and followed Megan to the living room. Except for the bathroom and two bedrooms, Megan's apartment was an open concept.

Her only couch sat in front of the large picture window that faced the Barrett house.

"So I have to know. How, exactly, did Cole end up staying with you guys?" She sat down on the couch and gestured for Raina to join her.

"Casper brought him home." She lifted a shoulder. "His house doesn't have running water so I'm assuming that's first on his agenda today." She gave Megan a look. "When you described him, I was picturing more of an ogre. Flattened nose, pointed ears. Gray skin and maybe horns. Definitely a snarl." She leaned over for another peek at the culprit, now carrying a box inside. "He's actually rather cute."

"I don't think cute is the right word for him. It's a little like calling Casper docile. That scar says dangerous."

Raina laughed, her amber eyes sparkling. "How about rugged? Handsome? Focused?"

"He's focused, all right." Megan would let the rugged and handsome part slide. Even if the reminder of him dressed up in a suit had made her heart betray her with a flip-flop. "He's got his mind set on becoming a Deputy U.S. Marshal. And there's no reason they won't take him. He's been a Ranger, for goodness sake. The man lives and breathes service to his country." She wrinkled her nose. "I'm the one person standing in the way."

"You couldn't have known what would happen when you rented this place."

"The sooner I can make the money I need, the better." Megan got up and pulled the window blind. "As much as I can't let him force me out, I can't hold him back from his own dreams."

"You still care." Raina's eyes held Megan's.

The declaration stirred the emotions Megan had tamped down. She could hear the disappointment threading through Cole's words from his story last night. Married and divorced. Sitting in the dust of a foreign land and discovering his wife's betrayal. Well, that had ripped a hole through her heart.

SUSAN MAY WARREN & RACHEL D. RUSSELL

She cleared her throat. "Against my better judgment, I suppose." She returned to the sofa, and Puck climbed into Megan's lap and flopped. She stroked his pale fur and he blinked against the sunlight, purring with complete contentment.

At least one of them was at peace.

Megan hadn't meant to let the shame of her past relationship slip out, but when Cole had reached out to her, the temptation to lean into that strength and familiarity nearly overwhelmed her.

She had to be stronger than this. She couldn't give her heart to another man who was moving on. Whose plans didn't include her and her son.

"Why?" Raina said. "What do you mean, against your better judgment?"

Megan lifted a shoulder. "I found out he's been married before." And by the rancor in his voice, he wasn't a man who would be looking for another relationship. Ever.

"Does it matter to you that he was married before?"

And there went those flames of jealousy again. Yes. Maybe. Probably not. "It doesn't matter either way. We're just childhood friends who lost touch." The words felt like a lie as they left her lips.

"I have the feeling there's more to it than that."

"Look at me, Raina." She gestured to herself. "Who would want me? Single mom, small-town girl. I can't compete with…" *Exquisite women like the ones at the wedding.* Unencumbered. Carefree. Their bodies unmarked by the scars of motherhood.

Raina leaned back in her seat. "The right man will love you, no matter what."

She looked over at her friend who was expecting her second child. If anyone could believe that, it was Raina.

Yeah, well, Casper was different.

"No. I had my chance. This is my life. Besides, Cole deserves,

I don't know. More, maybe. More than this small town. More than…me." Like one of those cute bridesmaids.

"More than you? Why?"

"I'm just…I'm just not enough."

"Are we talking about relationships still? Or you, in life? Either way, if it's shame you're dragging around, you've got to let that go." Raina reached out and gave Megan's hand a squeeze before releasing it. "I know that's hard, but it's the only way you can embrace today."

Megan shook her head. "I don't know. Both. It's what I know, who I am." She let her fingers slide through Puck's fur. "When Lillian was born, I could see the strain it put on my parents' marriage. Her heart defect meant a lot of bills, appointments, worry. I worked so hard to put everything I had into being helpful. Removing burdens from them."

"And it felt like that was your place in the family?"

"Maybe. I guess I thought if I sacrificed for her, I'd still feel important to them. I'd still be…special."

Raina repositioned herself, her hand gently rubbing across her swelling abdomen. "Did it work?"

"No." Megan's voice dropped to barely a whisper, the disappointment clogging her throat. She blinked the moisture that filled her eyes.

"Megan?" Raina swallowed. "What happened?"

Megan let out a long breath. "When I was in third grade, I had a supporting role in the school play." She scratched Puck's chin when he tilted his head up to look at her. "I know it sounds silly—I was the bakery owner and I had four lines. Just four. But they were *my* lines and I wanted so much for my parents to see me. Anyway, for one reason or another, my parents had missed every performance, and it came down to the final night. My mom had to stay home with Lillian because she'd developed a high fever. At breakfast my dad had promised me he'd be there

—that nothing would keep him away." She fell silent, picked at a ball of lint on the afghan.

"He didn't come." Raina's quiet words filled the silence.

"Nope. He never showed." Megan swallowed, wiped her eyes. "I waited outside afterward for an hour. He didn't even come to pick me up. When the director had closed up the theater, she found me sitting on the ground, bawling my eyes out. I just didn't understand why I wasn't important enough to them. She packed me into her van and took me home."

Raina nodded. "I'm so sorry."

"It was the first of many broken promises. My tenth birthday party that never happened. The no-show at honor band awards." She lifted a shoulder. "Saying it out loud, it all sounds so selfish, but I so longed to be seen. To be important, and I wasn't. I'm not. I wanted them to choose me. I thought if I did more—if I could be all the things they needed—I would be enough."

"None of us are ever enough, Megs. We can't meet the needs of everyone—we can't even meet our own needs. Let's be honest. We wouldn't need our Savior if we could." Raina reached out and scratched Puck's chin. "But that doesn't mean you aren't valuable, that you don't matter. You do matter, simply because you are you. And unfortunately, people do break promises, make mistakes, but that doesn't mean they don't love you or that God doesn't love you."

Megan looked down at the floor, tried to find the words. "I know God loves me up here"—she tapped her finger against her temple—"but I don't feel it in my heart." She swiped away the moisture in her eyes. The admission stung.

"Megan." Raina's voice dropped, low and soft. "I used to carry that same burden. Thought God's love was for everyone except me. That God didn't see me. It's a lie."

"I want to feel..." Megan paused, thinking of the way her clients looked at each other. There was something precious and elusive in the way they held hands. The secret looks they exchanged across the room.

"Treasured," Raina finished for her.

The word struck the most tender place in Megan's soul. "Yes." *Treasured.*

"You don't believe it's possible."

"Maybe it's too improbable. I don't let myself think about it."

"You matter, Megan. You don't have to do or say or be anything more than you are."

She leaned away, the conversation lodging a rock in her throat. "Right now, what I need to do is figure out how to make enough money to finalize the Black Spruce purchase. Once I can do that, then Cole can follow through on his plans." Puck stood up, arching his back in a quivering stretch before jumping to the floor.

"How do you propose to do that?"

"I don't know. I'm already booked up for weddings, but I won't make enough for it."

But she'd find a way to make it work. In this one area of her life, she had to be enough.

CHAPTER 6

*J*ust when Cole thought he might be free of tragedy, a new day brought temperatures that hit unusual highs.

Which meant thawing.

Which meant water in the basement.

Cole's feet sank into the eight inches of water lapping in the darkness of the basement stairs. The dark water wicked up the walls and soiled his trousers. His to-do list had just gotten much longer. Between broken appliances, light fixtures, molding, and tile, he already had enough to keep him working around the clock.

He clicked on his Maglite. Add to that list all new drywall and plaster for the basement.

Ugh. The supplies were already straining his small financial reserves.

The place where the electrical panel used to be was stripped bare. Grandpa had rewired.

Perfect. Maybe now he could get electrocuted too. He followed the wall around, looking for a new panel.

Nothing. If the panel wasn't in the basement, where would he have put it? The new garage?

Admittedly, he was in a humdinger of a mood. Maybe because his conversation with Megan kept drilling at him all night.

And not just the one about his ex—but what Megan had gone through. He'd like to get his hands around her ex's neck.

For the first time in years, he wished he'd never left Deep Haven.

And that put him in an even darker mood because he was about to do it again.

Cole climbed back up the stairs and looked out across the yard. Yeah, the box had to be in the garage. It made sense Grandpa would have had to rewire when he built it.

He had no idea where to even start looking for a spare key, which meant finding Megan.

She hadn't been home all day—not since she'd knocked while he was pouring his first cup of coffee. He'd opened the door and discovered a plate of fresh scones on the porch. No Megan, though he'd heard the rumble of her car engine as she'd headed down the street.

Yeah. Those flaky scone layers with vanilla glaze had been a perfect pairing with his brew, but they'd added a little bit of torment to his day. Because he couldn't get used to those kinds of surprises.

He looked at his watch. If he had to make a guess, they'd be finishing up after-school practice at the rink pretty soon and he'd bet money he'd find her there.

He hopped in his Jeep for the short drive to the rink. It seemed everyone else was enjoying the warm spell. He got a few looks and waves on his way down Third Avenue. Everyone probably recognized his grandpa's Jeep.

His phone started buzzing as he parked at the ice rink.

SUSAN MAY WARREN & RACHEL D. RUSSELL

Nathan Decker's name scrolled across the caller ID. Maybe he'd finally get some good news.

"Hello?"

"Hey, Cole, it's Nathan."

"Yes, sir, did you find a place for Megan?"

There was a pause on the other end of the line. "No. Nothing yet on an apartment or any other housing options. The market's pretty tight for that right now."

Cole pressed his hands to his temples. Great.

"I wanted to touch base with you, though, to see if we can find some flexibility—does it absolutely have to allow pets?"

"Yes, sir. Josh has a cat."

"Okay." Nathan let out a sigh. "I'll keep searching. Is the house ready for listing photos?"

"No. Not at all. A pipe broke in the basement. I'll be doing repairs after I pump the water out of the basement."

"Oh. Wow. Sorry to hear that."

"Thanks."

"But I should keep looking? For an apartment?"

And for the first time, he paused, his throat tightening. But, "Absolutely. Of course."

"All right. Keep me posted."

What was he thinking? Truth was, he'd liked working with Megan at the wedding. Her tactful approach balanced his directness. They'd always made a good team when they were kids. And if the wedding had proven anything, they could still be a strong team.

No, no, what was he *thinking*? Cole tugged his knit cap over his ears before walking to the rink. The outdoor rink hadn't changed much, except there were a few more stands on the long side and at the far end, a one-story building sat back off the ice a little. Snow had been cleared from the exterior arena walls and piled into large berms on the back side, opposite the parking lot.

The teams were running a scrimmage game. He studied the players for Josh, finding him on the offensive, his team driving toward the goal. The puck slid across the ice behind the goal, and Josh hung back, waiting on the near side of the goal instead of chasing it. Smart. A teammate brought it around from the other side and the goalie deflected it. And there Josh was, ready to snap it in before the goalie could regain his footing. Nice goal.

Cole whistled. "Good job, Josh!"

Josh looked up as he skated past, a smile lighting his face.

Cole took in a breath, the cold air stinging his nostrils.

And just like that, he was Josh, his skates sliding against the slick ice. *You've got this, Cole. Pull the puck back, let those defenders freeze on it, then bring it through to your backhand. Keep it tight.*

His dad, always on the sidelines. Always cheering for him. How many times had he skated past his dad, just like that? The memory fisted in his chest.

"He's a good kid." A large, dark-haired man approached. Even without the Evergreen Lodge Outfitter embroidery on his jacket, Cole would have recognized the telltale blue eyes of the Christiansen boys.

"You've got to be Darek." Cole extended a hand to him. "Cole Barrett. Not sure if you remember me."

The man smiled, nodded, and shook the offered hand. "Yes. I sure do."

"Man, you look just like your dad," Cole mused.

"Thankfully, I still have more hair than him." Darek laughed. "Casper said you were in town, Cole. Good to see you again." He nodded toward the ice. "It's nice to see Josh connecting with you."

"He seems to do all right out there on the ice."

"Yes, he does. There's a tournament coming up they're all hoping to play in. He's been a star wing for the team."

"Nice. Where will they be playing?"

93

"Minneapolis. Well, the tournament is in St. Paul at the Xcel Energy Center. The hotel is in Minneapolis."

"Got it." He nodded. "They should have found somewhere warmer. Somewhere without snow." He laughed. "A nice indoor rink, somewhere in the South." He gestured toward the mounds of snow piled at the end of the parking lot. "I'm getting a little tired of having to plow snow constantly."

"Casper says he'd hire you for the city crew if he were the guy in charge."

"I definitely picked the wrong time of year to try to sell a house." Cole leaned around Darek to get a better look at the stands. "Have you seen Megan?"

"Yeah. She's talking with my wife, Ivy, in the warming house." He pointed to the newer, small building along the side of the rink.

"The attorney, right?"

Darek laughed. "That's the one. But don't let her intimidate you. She's got a big heart." He slid his hands into his pockets and smiled. "Some days, I don't know how I did it before she came into our lives." He shook his head. "It's crazy the curveballs life throws at you." Darek leaned against the light pole and turned his attention back to the ice. "As I recall, you used to play."

"I did." Cole paused, rubbed his hand against his chest as if he could push the memories of his father back inside where they were safe. Less painful. "You have a son who plays?" Only a parent would be standing out in the cold, watching practice. Except him. Josh took another shot on goal, this one deflected by the goalie. Cole lifted his collar around his neck against the breeze.

"Yeah. And this year, he's a junior coach for the peewees. He's thirteen." Darek nodded to a tall boy skating on the outside of the play. He looked like he'd be built just like his dad when he filled out.

"What brings you to peewee practice?"

"I need to get the keys to the garage from Megan so I can turn off the power from the fuse box. The basement is currently an indoor swimming pool."

"That's always fun. Last time I had that happen was in one of our cabins. What a mess."

"Yeah. That's about it. A complete disaster."

"What are your plans after the repairs are done? You're still selling?"

"Yeah. Just buttoning up my grandpa's affairs."

Josh skated by again, shot him a grin.

Darek turned from Josh back to Cole. "Have you thought about staying?"

"Staying? No. Definitely not." That didn't make any sense. "Besides, I don't know what I'd do here. I'm waiting for a call to get on with the U.S. Marshals."

"We don't have any of those around here, but the sheriff's department has a slot that just opened. Casper said you were a Ranger. I bet that came with some skills the county would find helpful." Darek considered Cole. "He said you mentioned the issues we have with our emergency resources—or lack thereof. We could use a strong leader. Someone with a vision."

"I'm focused on getting the house repaired. Nathan Decker will be listing it for sale." Cole toed the snow at the edge of the rink wall. "My grandpa didn't keep up on any of the maintenance."

"Ouch. That's no fun. I tell you, the maintenance at the resort is a full-time job. Every season I work with my dad, there's more and more."

"I'll stick with one residence to repair, thank you." He watched the other team try a shot on goal, stopped by the defenders. He loved the scrape of the skates across the ice and the snap of the puck. "You don't know where I can get some large industrial fans, do you?"

"We actually have a few in the storage shed out at the lodge. I can bring them by this afternoon."

"Perfect." He turned back to the rink to watch as Josh again took the puck down the ice, heading for the goal. "C'mon, Josh!"

The kid slapped it into the net, just past the outstretched glove of the goalie.

"Yes!" Cole pumped his fist.

Next to him, Darek laughed. Cole glanced at him. The man was shaking his head.

"What?"

"Nothing. Just...are you sure you're not staying?"

He was going to see her spying on him, Megan just knew it.

But what did he expect? Somehow, the man had the power to enter a space and command all attention to himself. At least, her attention. Just by standing there. Looking good in his hiking boots and jeans, a heavy navy jacket, the collar snugged up around his neck and a blue beanie on his head. And from her vantage point in the warming house, she could see Josh skate past him and give him a little wave.

Oh boy.

He looked so serious standing at the edge of the ice. What was he talking to Darek about?

"Um, hello?" Ivy nudged her.

"What?"

"You didn't hear anything I just said, did you?"

"I, uh..."

"Yeah." Ivy leaned forward and looked out the window. "I see where you're looking. Is that him with Darek?"

Megan swallowed, turned back to the game. "Who?"

"Nice try, Megs. Nice try. You've watched more of their

conversation than the scrimmage. So, that's Cole Barrett, Army Ranger and all-around hottie?" Her green eyes sparkled.

Megan's flush warmed her face. "Stop that. And, I have not. I've been listening to you and watching the game."

Ivy folded her arms and gave her a look. "Repeat one thing I said to you over the last two minutes."

Megan wrinkled her nose. "Okay. Fine. I have no idea what you just said."

"I can see why you're preoccupied." Ivy shot her a sly smile.

"Stop. There's nothing happening." Nope. Not at all.

"How did the crazy wedding schedule go on Monday? Did he pan out as your new assistant?"

Megan took another look at him at the end of the stands. He was still deep in conversation with Darek. "He did great, actually. He really came through for me—in fact, because of him, I made an extra thousand dollars." The team gathered on the center of the ice and she zipped up her coat. "He was a bit of a superhero."

"That's fantastic!" Ivy turned to her daughter, Joy, who sat at the back of the room. "Time to start packing up your books." She faced Megan again. "Has he changed much? Since you were kids?"

"Yes and no."

"Taller, darker, more handsome?" Ivy waggled her brows.

"Stop."

"I saw him cheering for Josh a little bit ago. And did you see Josh's face?"

She had. The smile had both lifted her heart and torn it a little. "Yeah. Josh seems to be getting a little attached to him." Too fast.

"So, would you ever consider it?" Ivy gave a nod toward Cole. "Could you fall in love again?"

"The last thing I need is to fall for him. He's made it clear he's selling the house and getting out of town. Really, we're just in the way. And I don't want Josh too involved either. I won't risk him getting hurt."

"You're in the business of happy endings."

"This is the best ending I'm going to get. And that's okay. I'm all right with it."

Ivy glanced at Joy and lowered her voice. "What about Josh?"

"I don't know how to protect him. How to keep him from getting hurt. I keep reminding him that Cole isn't staying and he says he knows, but then, it seems like he doesn't. I know how hard it is to impress Josh. He's been hurt so many times." She wrung her hands together. "But I can tell—I can see it on his face. He already looks up to Cole like he's a hero."

"He kind of is."

Joy tugged a bag of apple slices out of the tote bag. "I'm going to go outside."

Ivy nodded to Joy. "Okay, Dad's still out there." Joy exited the warming house and Ivy placed a hand on Megan's knee. "You want to protect him from hurt. I get that." She paused. "But you also don't want to raise him up to be a man afraid to love because he's afraid it will hurt too much."

Right. Because then she'd have exactly what was in front of her. Cole. A man on the move. On a mission.

Although admittedly, a part of her would like to know about this woman who had stepped out on him. Her heart had certainly broken a little for Cole, wanting to find his ex and tell her exactly how she'd messed up.

Maybe. But then he might have never come home.

Oops. Not home. Back to Deep Haven.

"So," Megan said, "it's better for Josh to get a broken heart now? To learn he can survive it?"

"Who says it has to end with a broken heart? What if it could be something special? What if it's God's plan?"

Megan swallowed. She'd botched God's plan in college.

Ivy picked up her buzzing phone to read a text. "Awesome!

They just did the final counting for the fundraising efforts. The team's raised enough money to go to Minneapolis for the tournament."

"That's great news! Josh has had his heart set on it."

Outside, Coach Williams blew the whistle and the team began clearing the ice.

"Tiger's really enjoying being a junior coach."

"By the way, Josh raved about their snowmobile ride." She still wasn't thrilled with that little adventure, but he'd been just fine. Tiger knew the trails well.

"They had a great time. Tiger adores being a big brother to Joy, but he likes time with the boys too."

The players piled off the ice.

"We'd better make room for the boys." Ivy pulled her hat on over her red hair before she handed Megan her own.

"Thanks." Megan held the door for the team and then followed Ivy out, the snow crunching beneath them as they walked along the length of the rink toward the parking lot.

"Hey, I almost forgot!" Ivy grabbed Megan's arm. "Grace's husband, Max, used to play with the Blue Ox, and one of their friends—a current player—has had a bit of a wedding plan catastrophe. They're hoping you might be able to help."

"What happened?"

"There was a mix-up with their wedding venue when the company changed scheduling systems and they ended up double-booking them. They're in a pinch to relocate because their families have already bought their plane tickets to Duluth. Because it was their coordinator's own lodge, she's now dealing with all the fallout, so they're needing to completely shift gears. They need a coordinator, a venue, a caterer—everything. The only thing they do have is the date."

"When it is?"

"The second Saturday in February."

Megan pulled her phone from her pocket and scrolled

through her phone calendar. "Bummer. There's no way. I already have a wedding that day. Hannah Swanson and Erik Klein—they're my older couple."

"Older couple?"

"Yes, marrying their high school sweetheart after all these decades. High school! And they're both retired. Can you imagine?"

"That is amazing." Ivy clasped her hands together. "But, if you could do it, Cameron said they'll make sure you get listed with the North Woods Premier Wedding Planners."

"What?"

"I know! Can you imagine, Megan? That would be a coup! They want an über-private, upscale venue for about sixty guests. Are you sure you can't figure it out?"

Having to say no made her feel a little sick. She'd dreamed of being listed with Premier Wedding Planners, but only the most sought out and elite ever made it.

Darek and Cole came around the end of the rink toward them.

"Hi," Cole said. "Sorry to bother you. I need to get the garage key to access the fuse box."

"Hi," Megan answered. "Sure. Everything okay?"

Before he could answer, Josh came running up, his cheeks flushed. "Hey, Cole, did you see my snap shot?" He rubbed a towel across his face and shoved it into his gear bag.

"I did, Blades. That was pretty awesome." Cole held up his hand and Josh slapped it with a high five.

Blades?

"I taught him that," Tiger said, joining the group.

"I believe it." Darek held out a fist bump to Tiger. "You've always had the knack to get it in just the right spot." He turned to Ivy. "Ready to go?"

"Almost," Ivy said to Darek and turned back to Megan. "So,

you're sure you can't do that wedding? I'll need to let Cameron know."

Aw, she hated turning down an opportunity. "I'm really sorry. I can't make both weddings work that day."

"What wedding?" Cole asked. In his jeans, work boots, and jacket, he looked like a local. Except none of the other locals made her heart do that annoying skip thing.

"One of the Blue Ox players has to switch up his wedding plans last minute and they were hoping Megan could do it. Their star center, Cameron Crawford, and his fiancée, Mariah Lee. Everyone else is booked. But it could land Megan on the Premier Wedding Planners list."

"Cameron Crawford?" His eyes held admiration and surprise. He turned to her. "Why can't you take it?"

"I'm already booked that day too."

"What if I help again?"

She stared at him. "Are you my new assistant?"

He smiled, something slow and devastating. "Yes, ma'am. You need the money, right?"

She lowered her voice. "I can't pay you."

"I did thoroughly enjoy the fresh scones you left this morning. And you have to admit, I did rock the Berg-Thomas wedding."

Ivy leaned in, clearly listening. "You did say he rocked it. Actually, you said he was a superhe—"

"Stop." Megan held up her hand to Ivy and gave her the don't-say-another-word look.

A sly grin curved the corners of Cole's lips as he turned to Ivy. "She'll do it."

"Hey! You can't just show up here and make commitments for me."

"It's Cameron Crawford. Are you kidding me? Mae, you seem to struggle with what to say yes to and what to say no to. I'm here to help. This is a definite yes."

She turned to him, exasperation threading her words. "Where would we even hold this wedding? A private, indoor venue, big enough for over sixty people? There's nothing like that available."

Darek leaned against the rink fence. "When Ivy mentioned it this morning, I checked with Jensen Atwood. Guests could stay at Evergreen and you could hold the ceremony at Jensen's Pine Acres Resort. Claire and Jensen aren't living there right now."

"That's a great idea," Ivy said. "That would be beautiful." She turned to Megan. "It has enormous floor-to-ceiling windows that look out onto Evergreen Lake. And the guest list isn't massive. They want it to be a private, intimate setting. Pine Acres would be perfect."

"And it's already available?"

"Yes. And Claire said she can do the flowers," Ivy added.

"Is there anything left for a coordinator to do? Or do I just need to show up, point them down the aisle, and collect the check?"

"There's plenty more to do. I mean, this is a celebrity wedding. You've heard about how celebrities always have those eccentric ideas. But you'll do it?" Ivy raised a brow.

"I really don't know—"

"Yes. We'll do it," Cole answered.

"Wait." Megan held out a hand. "You can't say I'll do it."

He turned to her, and now his voice softened. "You can do this, Megan." And if the way he used those blue eyes against her wasn't bad enough, he added, "*We* can do this."

"Excellent." Ivy crossed her arms like she'd rested a case she knew was a win.

Megan may have just doomed her business, agreeing to a wedding without even having an adequate venue set up. What if Pine Acres wouldn't work for what they wanted?

"You said you need access to the fuse box?" Megan turned back to Cole.

"Yes, ma'am. My basement is flooded."

"That's terrible!" She started pulling her garage key from the ring and turned to Ivy. "Can we get going? Apparently, I have a new wedding to work on."

"Sure." Ivy looked to Darek as Tiger slung his gear bag over his shoulder. "Are you guys ready?"

"I need to run down and make sure Coach Williams doesn't need any help getting things put away, then I'll meet you at the car and we can drop Megan and Josh off," Darek said.

"You didn't drive?" Cole asked Megan.

"No, we rode with Ivy. I had to drop my car off for an oil change."

"You can ride with me."

"You're sure it isn't any trouble?"

Cole stared at her. "Is it any trouble to drive back to my own house with two extra passengers?" He smiled. Something friendly and kind and maybe even a little sweet. "No, ma'am. No trouble."

Trouble. He was the trouble. Because, just like when they were kids, his smile had the power to make her knees go a little soft. Cloud her judgment. But it was far worse now because she was a grown woman who knew better.

She climbed into his Jeep while Josh threw his gear in back, then climbed in behind Cole.

It felt way too much like a family headed home from a game. And it had to stop.

When they arrived home, she handed Josh the keys. "I'll be in soon."

Josh bailed from the car and headed inside with his gear.

Cole raised a brow. "Is this where you yell at me for accepting the job on your behalf so you can pay for that bed and breakfast you've got your heart set on?"

"I'm not going to yell at you." She took a deep breath, bolstered herself. "Every summer, I always looked forward to you coming. And then, when you moved here—under the worst of circumstances, I know—but that year, your friendship..." She swallowed. "You saved me from so many things that year. It was so hard at home with Lillian, but I had your company to look forward to. And then...you left." She blinked back stupid tears, cleared her throat. "It took me a long time to get over your leaving. I sent you letters and you'd promised you'd write. Promised you'd come back. And you didn't. I don't want to count on you and then go through that again."

He stared at her, quiet, his expression a little stripped. Maybe that was way too much. Maybe she'd read into this and—

"I'm sorry, Megan," he said quietly. "I couldn't face you. Didn't know what to write. I was embarrassed and confused." He turned away, his hands on the steering wheel, looking at his grandfather's house. "And I didn't understand all the ramifications of going into foster care. How fast and how far they'd move me. And maybe I couldn't quite shake the feeling that I was to blame." He got out of the Jeep.

Megan slid from her seat. "How could you possibly be to blame?" She followed him into the lower level of the garage and pointed to the far wall where the utility panel was just barely visible behind storage. He began moving the boxes that blocked it.

He lifted a box and carried it to the other side of the open bay, set it on the floor. "The day my parents died, I should have been with them. Instead, I stayed in bed. Tired from being out with friends the night before." His friends had begged him to join them for the last football game of the season. "I didn't even say goodbye when they left for church. My mom—" He shook his head, lifted another box, and Megan took it from his hands. "My mom called up to me that they'd be home later. And I—" He swallowed. "I rolled over and went back to sleep."

He put his head down and kept moving boxes.

Megan set the box down and grabbed another one. "That doesn't make it your fault, Cole." She put down her box and placed a hand on his arm. "You were a child. What could you have done?"

"I could have been with them." He looked away, kept working. Box after box. "Who knows? Maybe I could have seen the oncoming car. Or pulled them out before the fire—" He ran his hands through his hair, closed his eyes for a moment before continuing. "I even ignored the knocks on the door at first. They persisted, so I threw on a T-shirt, went downstairs, irritated. Two police officers, their faces grim. And I knew. I knew something was terribly wrong."

His words scooped her out, left her hollow, aching. She swiped the tears from the corners of her eyes, covered her mouth with her hand to stop the cries of her heart.

"And then, when I arrived here, I knew Grandpa would make it okay, somehow." He shook his head. "I longed for something familiar. The man who'd take me fishing and tell me about honor and duty. Sacrifice." He shook his head. "I needed him more than ever, but something had changed."

"Was he already drinking?"

"I think so. But it wasn't obvious at first. You know, a slow fade. I know he'd turned to drinking after Vietnam. It was the reason my dad never drank. But Grandpa hadn't touched alcohol in decades. Not in my lifetime, up to that point." He shrugged a shoulder. "Maybe he started again after Grandma died." He tossed a bag of potting soil across the garage. "The more he drank, the worse it got."

"He hit you." Megan closed her eyes, the words nearly strangling her.

Cole nodded. "The first time, I wouldn't admit it to myself. A shove, into the hutch cabinet." He picked up a shovel from the mass of tools lined against the wall behind the boxes they'd cleared. Tossed it onto the pile of debris. "An accident, right?

The second time, when his palm smacked me across the face, I convinced myself I must have deserved it. I mean, why would the man I looked up to hurt me?" He picked up a rake. "But, the third time, when he punched me—"

Cole hurled the rake across the garage. It landed with a crash, knocking over several boxes from the stack and sending debris flying. "That's when I knew the man I loved was gone. I was all alone." He turned, the look in his eyes brutally raw. "Except for you." His words sliced through her. "I didn't have my grandpa the year my parents died, but I had you."

Oh, Cole. She nodded, unable to speak. And she was going to full-on ugly cry if she didn't get out of there fast.

He reached the panel, flipped the breakers. "I can't stay here, Megan."

She stilled.

"But while I'm here, you can count on me. I promise, you can count on me."

She pressed her lips together. Swallowed. Knowing he was leaving already rubbed a raw spot in her heart. "I understand. We'll do this wedding so you can move on. Win-win, right?" She hoped her voice didn't betray the loss she was already starting to feel. The void his departure would leave. At least now she understood what he was running from. Why Deep Haven could never be his home. Even if it did tear out a piece of her soul.

"Right. Win-win."

But his voice didn't sound like a win. And in her heart, she couldn't help but fear that she and Josh were about to lose more than they could bear.

CHAPTER 7

*S*even days of industrial fans humming in the pumped-out basement should feel like progress, but after eight trips to the hardware store, five hours with the plumber, and two hours with an electrician, Cole's repair list had only grown longer.

On top of that, he wasn't sure exactly what he'd committed himself to with this wedding, but it apparently required less Ranger and more grunt because the to-do list Megan texted him included everything from the florist to the photographer. And where in the world was he supposed to locate an ice cream truck in February? In northern Minnesota?

Celebrities.

He lugged a bucket of drywall joint compound, a scraper, and tape toward the house, Megan's words from days before kicking around in the back of his mind. Maybe even his heart. Her confession in the car had soaked into him. Raw and honest. And she'd managed to pull from him his own confession. *I didn't have my grandpa the year my parents died, but I had you.*

Of course, that had always been part of her magic. She could make him see—and admit—the truth.

Or most of it. *I can't stay here, Megan.*

Yes, those words had been bugging him too. But the house had to be sold. He had a job practically lined up. He had plans. Still, he hadn't been able to scrape away the sad shadows he'd seen in her eyes.

"Good afternoon." Seb Brewster came up the walk, his black hair curling out under his knit hat and a smile on his face. "Looks like you've got some work ahead of you. Need a hand?"

Cole nodded. "Sure. You can grab that other bucket of joint compound sitting in the Jeep."

Seb hefted the bucket from the back seat and followed Cole inside.

"You can set that over there." Cole gestured toward the growing collection of construction materials in the living room. "How can I help you today, Mayor?"

"I heard you have some ideas regarding emergency management. Organizing things so we don't get gridlocked when the heavy storms hit—or even activating assistance when someone needs it in the greater Cook County area."

"I don't think my ideas are anything unique or earth-shattering. Can I get you a cup of coffee?" He headed into the kitchen.

"Sure. Black is fine. I don't mean to keep you from your work, though."

"It's okay. The discussion won't take long." Cole poured a cup of coffee and handed it to Seb before pouring his own. "In a nutshell, your crisis management and response is terrible. But you know that, don't you?"

"I do."

"As far as I can tell, you don't have any kind of plan—just wishful thinking that volunteers will show up with the necessary skills. You've been lucky to have people like Casper Christiansen jump in, but one person getting things done isn't an actual plan. Neither's a well-intended bucket-brigade when you could have an actual fire hose."

Seb laughed. "Your analogy is spot-on. We've limped by on that for all of history." He took a sip. "Seriously, our problem is we have people willing to help, but it's hard to get them where they need to be *when* they need to be there. We don't have the organizational structure to best utilize our resources, and truly, we are a little short on resources and skill sets."

"Someone better fix that before people die."

"I hear you, I do. Our teams are volunteer and many of them live remotely across the county." Seb took another sip of coffee. "We need something better."

"Right. It's called a Crisis Response Team, and you're in dire need of one."

Seb stared into his mug. "We had a deck collapse this past fall during a birthday party event. More than thirty people went into the lake, and even on a good day, it's cold." His voice thickened. "There were children and adults in the water fighting the cold and the waves. It was chaos."

Cole closed his eyes against the thought of Megan or Josh being caught in the frigid water.

Seb swallowed. "We didn't have a cohesive team to organize the rescue, and in the panic, people were unaccounted for. And since more than half the volunteer rescuers were involved in the initial incident, we had to rescue the rescuers."

"Your volunteers went into the water?"

"Yeah. Many were part of the party. If we'd had a team like you mentioned, we would have been able to manage the crisis without the panic that ensued." Seb shook his head. "It was terrible—and that's just one example. If someone gets lost in a remote area or we have a community emergency, we don't have the means to mobilize fast enough."

"You're right. And that *is* what a team would do for you."

Seb nodded. "I also heard you were a Ranger."

"Is there anything in this town that remains private?"

Seb smiled. "Not much."

"Yes, I was a Ranger." Cole took a drink.

"And in a leadership position?"

"Where's this going?" Cole knew exactly what Seb was fishing for and he wasn't biting.

Seb seemed to know it, because he paused, took a breath, and then met Cole's eyes, pulling no punches. "Deep Haven could use someone with your skills."

"I haven't seen any insurgents walking around town."

Seb set down his mug of coffee. "We know you did a lot more than that. In fact, I did a little research. I think you have exactly the skills we need."

"You did *what?*" Cole set down his coffee too. "No. Don't look at me. I'm not sticking around."

"Of course I'm looking at you. Why not? We have a deputy sheriff position open. You could step in and coordinate our resources—create this team."

"I can't."

"Cole, we need a proven leader under pressure. You're fast-thinking, organized, decisive. You know how to run training, know how to deal with equipment needs." Seb rinsed out his cup from the now-working faucet.

"I'm not staying here."

Seb turned from the sink. "Maybe God's brought you back here for a reason."

"God wouldn't do that." Cole was usually better at keeping those things private. Protecting himself.

"I used to think that too. In fact, I never wanted to come back here." He set the mug upside down on a towel near the sink amidst other drying cups. "Too many bad memories."

Oh. Cole sized up Seb. "Why'd you come back?"

"God redeemed my mistakes—but only because I realized I had to allow Him to do it. Stop blaming everyone else for my mistakes." Seb wiped his hands on a nearby towel. "You just don't know what God's up to sometimes."

God and I aren't that close anymore. Cole couldn't say the words out loud. Instead, he stared out the window at the snowy landscape and gave a noncommittal shrug.

Seb took his silence as an invitation to continue. "My mom left town when I was in high school and my dad's preferred coping mechanism was drinking himself into oblivion and passing out with his face over the toilet bowl. If he even made it home. It took me some time to realize there's a lot more here than the darkness of those years." He leaned against the doorframe, his arms folded. "Let me tell you, I may be mayor now, but I made a lot of mistakes in my youth. All kinds of stupid things that hurt others and myself."

"And you still came back?"

"I did, but man, I was bitter. Used what had happened as excuses for selfish decisions. I blamed God—railed against him. It was a miserable way to live."

Seb's words, like live rounds churning the dirt around his feet, sent Cole for cover. "I appreciate you stopping by, but I should get back to work."

Seb straightened, nodding. "Here's the deal. The deputy position closes in a couple weeks. It'd be great if whoever filled it could do collateral duty as the Crisis Response Team coordinator. Create a plan for this city, this county." He stood in the doorway and met Cole's gaze. "I think that's you. I think that's why God brought you home."

Seb was wrong. God didn't have any kind of happy ending for someone like Cole. If he cared, He would have shown it a long time ago. Besides, Deep Haven wasn't his home.

"I've got an interview coming soon with the U.S. Marshals Service. I have plans with one of my Ranger buddies." Plans reinforced by David's call early in the morning to discuss his current timeline. Although, the thought of a bachelor pad and microwave meals had grown less appealing, even with David's company.

"Yeah. Josh mentioned that."

This guy knew how to press all the right buttons. And with them came the memory of Josh, snuggled up with Puck, asking five hundred questions about life as a Ranger while Cole tried to plan a wedding with Megan at their tiny dining room table. Talking about his plans to go fishing and camping, hoping he could tag along with the Christiansens.

Except, Cole could take him, couldn't he? And that was exactly the kind of thinking that would decimate his future.

"He thinks a lot of you." Seb smiled, warm and genuine.

"He's a good kid." Cole washed out his cup and set it on the towel.

"He has a giving heart like his mom." Seb grabbed his jacket. "I should get going, but seriously, give our little town and county some thought. Sometimes we can serve best in the last place we think we'd choose."

When Cole closed the door behind Seb, the emptiness of the house thundered around him.

Thanks a whole lot, Seb.

Because he liked how Josh and Megan's voices filled the void. He looked forward to spending time with them. Enjoyed the company. Found comfort in days that didn't revolve around orders and operations but in hockey and house work.

Sheesh, he was turning into a homebody.

Truth was, being with Megan did dangerous things to his heart and mind. Made him offer to do crazy things, like help her make dinner after he'd walked her through his wedding plan. Or ask about sledding down Honeymoon Bluff. Or think about how much fun it would be to watch the Fourth of July fireworks over the water with her and Josh.

But that would be summer and by then, he'd be gone. Wearing a new uniform. Eating restaurant takeout with David.

Alone.

Because staying seemed not only improbable, but impossible. It would mean facing the darkness Deep Haven held in his heart. Living—where? In this house? And what about Grandpa's care?

No.

This wasn't home. He didn't belong here. Not with all the dark memories to haunt him.

The light knock on the door was almost so faint he didn't hear it. He opened it to Megan, who held out a plate to him. In her other hand, she carried an oversized basket. All kinds of temptation, right there in his doorway. He pressed away Seb's words.

"Hi." She wore jeans and a T-shirt under her green flannel, her hair tucked up in her pom-pom hat.

"Are those brownies?" He stepped aside and motioned for her to come in.

"They are, and they're still hot." She toed off her boots and followed him into the kitchen. "And your basket. You won one of the raffle baskets."

"The what?"

"You bought raffle tickets for the peewee fundraiser. You won the 'home spa' basket." She held up a green bottle of lotion with cucumbers on it and a fuzzy, pink eye mask, waving them in front of him.

"I guess this means I didn't win the autographed jersey."

"Nope. Sorry. Edith Draper won that."

"That seems like a waste. I mean, it's probably been forty years since she's attended a live game."

"You're wrong there. She still attends several Blue Ox games each season. You know those crazy fans yelling for a fight?"

"No, she isn't."

"I've heard rumors..." Megan smiled, and he couldn't tell if she was serious or not.

He stared at the brownies. He'd probably gained five pounds simply inhaling their rich decadence. "You don't have to keep paying me with food. Especially the super-sweet variety. I have a PT test to pass, you know."

"I had to bake a batch for the team and had leftovers. I didn't think I needed to eat five myself." She set the plate down on the counter and grabbed one of the brownies. She let out a little moan as she took a bite. "They're good. It's a new recipe." She gave him a smile. "I promise, I'm not trying to sabotage your fitness test."

Oh, her smile. Every time she smiled at him, it lured him into her warmth. Made him want to drink it in, take his fill. Her eyes were bright, and the rays of sunlight that came through the kitchen window highlighted the flecks of gold and the deep amber.

"Did I see Seb here earlier?"

He surrendered and took a bite of brownie. "Yes."

"What did he want? You didn't dent someone's car with a snowplow, did you?"

"Funny." He noticed she still licked her fingers like when she was nine. "He was just checking on things." No need to tell her that Seb had dangled a job opportunity in front of him. Or that he'd, even briefly, considered it.

She tugged off her knit cap and let her long waves tumble around her shoulders. He should make her go. Send her away with her plate of double-chocolate brownies and the enticing companionship that came with them.

Because he had a future and a plan and...other important reasons not to hang around. He just couldn't quite remember them right now.

Megan had exactly ten minutes to make Pine Acres Resort look presentable before her call with Cameron Crawford's high-society fiancée, Mariah Lee. It might be a picturesque winter wonderland if it wasn't in the middle of a remodel—a small fact that no one had bothered to share with her. No wonder it was available.

She'd already spent a good chunk of her Thursday between calling vendors, internet searches for supplies, and a stop by the church to talk to Pastor Dan.

Claire entered the house behind her. "I feel wholly under-dressed now."

"Don't. You look fantastic and far more comfortable than me. I just—I don't know, I wanted to impress Mariah. Look like I'm already a wedding coordinator to the stars." Megan knew the high-heeled boots were as impractical as her long skirt and silk blouse, facts verified by the gust of wind that met her when she'd exited her Subaru outside the resort. The wind had raked in over the whitened expanse of Evergreen Lake and shivered a spray of snow off the pine trees around the cabin. Still, the wedding pictures would be glorious.

If they avoided the stacks of paint, flooring and supplies piled in the hallway. Or the current absence of a working kitchen. "I didn't realize it was currently under remodel."

"Oh, no!" Claire laughed. "This must be a shock."

"Yes. It is." Megan looked around at the scaffolding, plastic sheeting over the floors and finished white-quartz center island, obviously protecting it from the light gray paint on the walls. "It looks like there's a lot left to do."

"The contractor has assured us it'll be done within the next two weeks. It looks much worse than it is. Go ahead and look around." Claire headed back for the front door. "I forgot to grab my notes from the car."

Megan unwound her scarf and set it by the door before sliding out of her long coat.

Wow.

As much as Ivy had raved about it, her description hadn't quite done the place justice. With the soaring windows that overlooked the lake, and the massive great room big enough for a half dozen tables plus a dance floor, it was more magnificent than Megan would have dreamed. Exquisite. Yet the hand-crafted trim and scrollwork up the stairs gave it rustic charm. If one ignored the paint and plaster buckets. Those made it a little too rustic.

She began moving the smaller supplies to the hallway. And if she shot with her back to the windows, maybe Mariah wouldn't notice.

Megan toed off her boots and paused to stare out across the frozen lake. Serene. But as the quiet soaked into her, her thoughts ran a replay on her last visit with Cole.

It had probably been a mistake to take those brownies to him the day before, but his confession in the car had been niggling around in her mind. *I had you.* And especially, *But while I'm here, you can count on me.*

She was still trying to reconcile the man he'd become with the boy she'd known. At least more of it made sense now.

Ivy was right, though. Taller, darker, and, yeah…incredibly handsome. He'd been working on the house while she ate her brownie and how could she not notice the way his T-shirt snugged tight around his biceps? The way his jeans hung on his hips, the promise of a taut six-pack underneath?

She'd give the Army one thing. They knew how to keep a man in shape. Now, she pressed her fingers to her lips, as if she could hide from herself the smile the memory brought.

That was it—no more brownies. No more cookies. Definitely no more time alone together because her stupid, romantic heart would get ideas, and those ideas could only result in absolute and total devastation. Not to mention doing something ridiculous like letting him see that she cared.

Cold air blew through the doorway with Claire as she returned, toting a notebook and floral catalog. She glanced up at

Megan standing at the window. "What do you think? Will it work—minus the building supplies, of course?"

"Will it work? This place is stunning. They'd be crazy not to hold it here."

Claire smiled. "Thanks. I thought the great room would be perfect for the ceremony, with the lake as the backdrop."

"Yes. I can imagine it. Spectacular." Megan pulled her phone from her bag and looked at the time. "Should we show her? I'm really excited about this location, and she should be ready for us."

"Yeah, let's do that. See what she thinks." Claire pulled out a pen.

Megan punched in Mariah's number. They'd already had a few long calls to discuss the wedding and Mariah had a very clear vision.

"Hey—how's it going?" Mariah appeared on the screen, her long, pale blonde waves cascading around her face and her ring light reflecting off her bright blue eyes. The woman was photo shoot ready.

"Good. I'm here at Pine Acres with Claire Atwood. Are you ready to do a walk-through with us?"

"Sure. I'm excited to see it." Mariah adjusted her phone in her hand and Megan could see a sleek, modern kitchen in the background. White cabinets and black stone countertops. Yeah. Megan's entire apartment would fit inside that kitchen.

Megan took care to angle her phone so that only the lake and windows showed. If Mariah's own home said anything, it said luxury. "I need to warn you, first. There's some remodel work going on. It's a bit of a mess right now."

"Oh?" Concern tinged Mariah's voice. "Is that going to be a problem? I mean, will it be done in time?"

"Yes." Megan looked at Claire who gave a reassuring nod. "Absolutely."

Megan stepped out of the way so the camera picked up the

SUSAN MAY WARREN & RACHEL D. RUSSELL

windows, the expanse of snow, the frozen waters of Evergreen Lake. A private, remote location. Exactly what Cameron and Mariah asked for.

"What do you think?"

There was a long pause on the other end and Megan turned her phone to make sure Mariah was still there.

"It's gorgeous. But what about the remodeling project?"

Megan turned her phone to show the unfinished kitchen. "It's a little hard to imagine right now, but it will be gorgeous. We'll put a massive floral arrangement on the center island, around hors d'oeuvres, for the cocktail hour, and then we can easily serve from the kitchen."

She turned her phone back.

A furrow had creased Mariah's brow and it wasn't fading. "I've got to be honest with you. After the last fiasco, I'm kind of gun-shy about getting tangled up in a venue that could fall through."

"It won't, I assure you." Even if Megan had to paint and install the cabinets herself. She was pretty sure she could figure out how to use a screw gun and not lose her fingers.

Mariah chewed her lip. "I'm really worried about this, Megan."

"I won't let you down. It will be magnificent." She stepped over three buckets of paint and a toolbox. Time for the sell. "Imagine the chairs will be set up here." Megan walked away from the windows across the half-finished floor. The couches were draped in plastic drop clothes. "Those couches by the fireplace will be removed." She turned back toward the center of the room. "We can put the aisle runner here. And—look at this." She turned the camera toward the high ceilings with open beams and the broad fireplace along the back wall. At least one thing was untouched by the remodel.

"It is beautiful. I can see the potential."

"Privacy won't be an issue and your guests can stay at the

Evergreen Resort across the lake." Megan had carefully inventoried every one of the bridal party's needs and wants. All two hundred and sixteen of them. And Pine Acres—a fully remodeled Pine Acres—exactly matched their dream location. "We're about six miles out of town."

"What about the photographer?"

"Cole—my, uh, assistant—has secured and scheduled the photographer you requested."

"And the fire and ice roses?"

Megan handed the phone to Claire.

"I confirmed with my supplier I can get those. Did you see the photos of the sample arrangements I sent you?" Claire said.

"I did. I sent you a reply back, but now that I've seen the room, I think we'll want to go with four of the large displays."

Claire wrote a few notes. "Okay, perfect." She handed the phone back to Megan.

"Megan, I can't believe all you've been able to pull together on such short notice. Thank you for doing this."

The knot in Megan's gut released. "My goal is always to give the bride and groom their dream wedding, regardless of how much time we have to plan."

Claire's phone buzzed and she pulled it from her pocket to read a message.

"Oh no." She groaned. "I'm so sorry, ladies—I have to run. Apparently Ruby has a fever and is vomiting all over the babysitter, and Jensen's still on EMT duty." She shook her head. "Parenthood." She tugged her coat back on. "Would you lock the door on your way out?"

"Sure, I can do that," Megan said.

Claire leaned into the phone picture. "Thanks. Mariah, I'll catch up with you later to finalize your flower order."

"Absolutely. I hope your daughter feels better soon."

Claire left, and Megan started down her preparations checklist with Mariah. By the time Megan finished the tour of the upstairs dressing areas and detailed discussions, the sun hung low, the last rays of light disappearing from the western sky in deep purple and magenta, casting a kaleidoscope across the snowy landscape.

She locked the door on her way out. The house had been cool, but it was nothing like the icy gust that hit her when she headed to her Subaru. She'd have to pick up dinner before getting Josh from practice. She turned her heat on high and backed out of the parking spot.

They'd need to plow the road better for the wedding guests. The private road hadn't been cleared regularly—only what Jensen had done with his tractor. The pine trees edging the drive hung heavy with snow, icy crystals sparkling in the twilight. She steered the car down the winding road and glanced at the clock. Hopefully practice ran long tonight.

She began her mental list of everything left to take care of. Cole had taken control of the plan, but it was still her name on the business. Her responsibility. Her future.

A dark blur blasted out of the trees.

Deer!

She slammed her brakes, locking her seatbelt, and her gaze immediately searching for a second deer—they always came in twos. Yep—right in front of her, the first deer having escaped.

Her car slid on the ice, out of control, heading for the beast.

She screamed. Closed her eyes. Ducked.

Please let her not kill it.

Please let it not destroy her car, pulverize her windshield.

Bam! The car slammed into something, jerking to a halt. She opened her eyes when the tilt of the car brought up images of plunging down the embankment toward the frozen lake. Her notes were scattered across the floorboards along with the contents of her purse.

No sign of Bambi.

But she'd plowed into another tall berm of snow. In the

moonlight, she could see a thin swirl of steam rising into the night from her hood. She threw the gearshift into reverse, nudged the gas. It didn't budge. She turned down the heater fan and listened to the rumble of the engine. Didn't sound too bad.

She pulled out her cell phone. Just a little bit of juice left in the battery.

If she called Cole, he'd come. But then of course there he'd be, back in her life, all muscular and rescue-y and frankly, her heart couldn't take it.

Besides, she'd managed on her own for a long time. She didn't need to be rescued.

What she needed to do was put on her big-girl pants and hike back to Pine Acres for a shovel like she'd have done any other time this had happened. In fact, like she'd done any number of times in her life. Just not in heels. She snugged her coat collar up around her neck, gauging the distance she'd driven. If only she hadn't dressed up for today's appointment. Her high-heeled boots and skirt were less than ideal for trekking cross country.

She got out, tucked her chin, and headed back down the dark road. Several times she thought she heard the long howls of wolves, but when she paused, she only heard the wind shifting the heavy-laden branches.

By the time she reached Pine Acres, her feet had numbed to the pain and dark shadows chased her the final steps. The cold bit at her and, despite locking it herself, she tried the front door anyway with the dim hope she might not have latched it.

There had to be a window unlocked, right? She tried the first window. Locked. Then the next. Again, locked.

Unfortunately, Pine Acres Resort had been skillfully secured. But the house sat on a rise above the lake, creating a daylight basement that opened on the lake side of the house. Megan hiked through the deep snow—maybe someone had left the door unlocked.

She'd lost feeling in her feet a half hour ago. Even if she found a shovel, it was too cold to hike back to the car.

The wind off the lake tore tears from her eyes when she ventured toward the lower level, feeling her way down the slope in the inky darkness. Her eyes strained to focus on the steps to the lower level, lit by a small outdoor light over the second story.

Just as she reached the door, her foot slid on a patch of ice, pitching her body backward. She scrambled in her slick-soled boots, unable to find any purchase, then landed flat out on her back, staring at the clear, cold night sky.

Oh, joy.

She caught her breath, rubbing her right elbow with her other hand. It smarted where it had hit the snow and ice-covered deck. Okay, come to think of it, most of her body hurt. She tried to roll to her side, but her right foot was stuck. Pushing herself upright from the ground, she squinted into the darkness. Her boot had wedged through damaged slats in the decking.

She tugged. It wouldn't come free.

"Are you kidding me?"

The harder she pulled, the more the wood slats dug into her ankle.

She yanked out her phone and tried to revive the dark screen. Resisted the urge to chuck it into the snow when it refused to light up.

And then she thought of the fisherman who'd had to amputate his own arm to survive.

Umm... No. Not that desperate. Yet.

She unzipped the boot, trying to release her foot from it. Better to go barefoot than be stuck in the snow. She couldn't get it past her ankle bone. The wooden slat had locked her in. She pulled harder, the wood digging into the thin leather over her swelling ankle.

Oh, God. Please.

She kicked at the boards with her other foot until the bones began to ache and the icy chill had found her core. Her whole body began to shiver. Not even her thick Minnesota hockey-mom coat could keep her warm forever. Her fingers and toes burned. The temperature had been dropping since the sun went down and the wind whipped the air around her.

"Help!" Her voice soaked into the night. Thin. The universe of stars looking down on her. Reminding her how very small and alone she was. How maybe nothing really mattered at all. Maybe *she* didn't really matter at all.

And even the very hairs of your head are all numbered. So don't be afraid; you are worth more than many sparrows.

The verse Pastor Dan had read during last Sunday's service.

Her body shook as the cold burrowed in and she hunched sideways against the steps, trying to conserve heat. Josh would be wondering what happened to her. That troubled her more than anything. More than the cold that burned her fingers, despite her gloves.

No. This couldn't be happening. She kicked at the boards again and again, twisting her ankle back and forth to break free until the throbbing became too much.

Her entire body screamed with the cold.

"God! Please!" She didn't care who else heard her. But her voice died in the frozen grip of the night, falling back to her. Again, not enough. Not even for God.

CHAPTER 8

"*H*ey Cole, it's Darek. Is Megan there with you?"

Cole tried not to panic at the tone in Darek Christiansen's voice through the cell phone. "No, I haven't seen her. Why?" He set down his hammer, tossed nails into the box on his living room floor.

"It's just that she didn't show up to pick up Josh from practice. That's not like her."

Not like her at all, and that added a fist to his chest. "I haven't seen her this afternoon, but she's probably over at the church." He hoped for it more than believed it. Nothing would keep Megan from being there for Josh.

"Everyone else has left the rink. I told Coach I can take Josh home with us, but we're getting worried about her. Ivy tried to call her cell phone several times and it goes straight to voice-mail. I'll call around to a few more people. Maybe Claire knows something."

Cole was already picking up his keys. "If you find her, let me know." He was out the door even before Darek hung up. Sliding into the Jeep, he drove around the corner to the church. Pastor

Dan was at the entrance, just locking up. Cole rolled down his window.

"Have you seen Megan?"

Outside, the twilight had surrendered the sky to night.

Dan turned from the door. "Earlier today. She left several hours ago."

"If you see her or hear from her, please tell her to call me."

"Will do."

Cole's phone rang as soon as he got back onto the street. Darek again. He clicked it to speaker phone. "Did you find her?"

"I just heard back from Claire. She said she had to leave Megan at Pine Acres because her daughter got sick."

Pine Acres. The venue for the Crawford wedding. "Can you give me directions?"

"Sure."

Cole pulled off the road and jotted down the directions to Pine Acres Resort. It didn't make any sense that Megan would miss picking up Josh and not call.

"We're taking Josh home with us for dinner," Darek said. "Let us know if you find her at Pine Acres."

Ten minutes later, Cole put his Jeep in low gear on the partially plowed road. Megan was no stranger to driving on these back roads. She'd made it clear that Minnesota flowed in her veins.

He came around a curve and his headlights lit up a vehicle jammed into a snowdrift on the side of the road. Megan's Subaru, off the road and canted sideways into the ditch. At least he'd found her.

Maybe she'd had another PB and J mishap. He let out a breath as he stopped his Jeep next to her car.

He grabbed his flashlight from the console, jogged to the vehicle, and opened the door.

Empty. His heart sank. Scattered paperwork was strewn across the floor mats.

Why would she leave the car? Whatever would have made her go out into the freezing darkness?

"Megan!" His voice echoed in the night. "Megan!"

His light bounced around in the darkness as he searched for footprints.

A small-heeled shoe print, headed back the way she'd come. Toward Pine Acres. Good—at least she wasn't outside because by the feel of it, the temperature had dropped back into the single digits.

He drove down the road, watching for any redirection of the footprints, but they went all the way to the main estate house. But when he drove in, the house stood dark, lifeless.

And the little hairs on the back of Cole's neck stood on end.

No Megan.

Please, God. Please keep her safe.

He didn't know if it qualified as a prayer, but the words lifted from his heart. She was somewhere out in the cold, frigid blackness.

He left the vehicle, scrambling through the snow to the front door, his gut tight. "Megan!" He knocked and rattled the front door. "Megan, are you here?" Only silence met him, cut by the faint cry of wolves in the distance.

His flashlight scraped across more footprints that traveled around the side of the house, toward the lake, and he followed them, stepping into the deep snow

He cupped his hands around his mouth. "Megan!"

"Help!" He heard her faint call and rounded the house.

The snow fought him, but he forged through it, finally sliding down the hill in his scramble to get to her.

The sight nearly unraveled him. She was lying on her back in the snow, her foot wedged through the deck planks. And she shook, the cold deep in her core.

"Mae." He crouched over the top of her. He wasn't one to

panic, but the sight of her collapsed, clearly hypothermic, unraveled the last hold he had on his calm.

She gave him a half smile. "H-Hey, Ranger. I c-can't tell you how good it is to s-see you." Her teeth chattered, tears splashing down. "It's so c-cold."

"Shhh, Mae, it's okay." He tried to free her boot. It wouldn't budge so he began working her boot off. "How did you do this?"

"I d-don't know. I was trying to f-find an unlocked door or w-window and I slipped. Couldn't get my f-foot back out. D-dumb way to d-die."

"You aren't going to die." He stripped off his coat and wrapped it around her before trying to free her foot a second time. The board held fast. "Your ankle's swollen and it's not coming out of that boot. I think if I lift you, we can pry you free."

"Okay. W-Whatever you need to do. It b-beats amputating my leg."

"We're not amputating your leg."

"I was trying to be f-funny."

He slipped off a glove, pressed his hand against the bare skin of her face. "It's not funny, Megan. You're freezing cold." He tugged his glove back on. And got behind her, wrapped his arms around her, and pulled her up, into his arms, moving her body forward.

She cried out, and he bit back a groan but managed to reach down and free her heel. Then he scooped her up to carry her. Now to get them inside, because he didn't have time to drive them back to town. Not the way her body heat was dropping.

"How long have you been out here?"

"I d-don't know. An hour?" She curled her gloved fingers into his coat. "The house is locked. I already tried. I'm l-late to get J-Josh."

"He's with Darek. We need to get you inside." He debated carrying her back up to the front, but probably couldn't nego-

SUSAN MAY WARREN & RACHEL D. RUSSELL

tiate the big drifts. "I have to put you down for a moment." He set her on the stoop, then used the butt of the flashlight to break a small pane in the glass by the door handle. He knocked the loose glass away and unlocked the latch.

The lower level was outfitted for winter and summer fun, with a large entryway filled with ski equipment, fishing gear, and lifejackets.

And further inside, a big stone fireplace and a small kitchenette.

He settled her onto a leather sofa, tugged off her snow-covered outer layers, and then knelt before her. "This will probably hurt."

"It's numb," she said, but tightened her jaw.

He doubted it was numb enough to stop pain from spiking up her leg as he eased off the boot. And he was right, judging by the way she closed her eyes and made a tiny, pained whimper.

"I'm sorry—"

"It's fine," she said, leaning back as he finished pulling off the boot. He tossed it aside. and took a look at her ankle. Maybe not broken, but definitely badly sprained, given the swelling and the purple and red bruising along the bone. "Let's get some snow on this, then I'll make us a fire."

But in the meantime, he had to stop her shaking. He found a small linen closet in the hallway and pulled out a thick wool blanket, brought it back and wrapped her up in it. Her body still shook.

He needed a fire, ASAP. Grabbing an empty stuff sack from the entryway, he stepped outside and filled it with snow. Then he returned and wrapped it around her ankle, moving her leg high on the sofa to elevate it.

Her eyes were closed.

"Hang in there, Mae."

He could thank his Minnesota roots for one thing—he knew how to build a good fire, fast. Once he had a blaze going, heat filling the room, he dug around in the kitchenette and found some peppermint tea. He set an electrical kettle to boil while he took cardboard and plugged the broken window and cleaned up the entryway.

When she continued to shiver, he toed off his boots and slid onto the couch beside her, pulling her into his arms maybe as much for his own relief as to warm her. He held her against himself and pressed her cold hands between his own until they warmed.

No doubt she could feel his heartbeat, the elevated rate revealing exactly what she was doing to him. He nearly let his fingers weave into her silky locks, the smell of her hair twining through him.

"My body is on fire," she said. She lifted her head, her eyes glassy in the firelight.

Mmmhmm. But he knew what she meant. "Yeah. Thawing is going to hurt." He lifted her hands and inspected her fingertips. "You're lucky not to have frostbite. You aren't exactly dressed for an outdoor hike."

"It's the stupidest thing. I dressed up to impress Mariah." She grimaced when she tried to move her ankle.

"How did you end up in the ditch?"

"I swerved to miss a deer." She shook her head. "The deer fared better than me."

"Funny how that works." At least dressing up in winter still included wool socks, gloves, a heavy coat over her dress, and boots. "You do look really nice." Nice. What kind of compliment was that? He cleared his throat.

"I look like Jack Frost."

"Definitely not. Jack doesn't wear a skirt."

"Hilarious." She shifted against him, the heat between them filling the space.

"So, why did you feel you needed to impress Mariah?"

"She's going to marry Cameron Crawford. That's the closest

thing to a celebrity client I've ever had. Their recommendation —or not—could make or break my business."

"You're impressive, all on your own, Mae." He met her eyes, caught in the glow of the firelight.

She stared back at him for a long moment before she tried to sit up. "I can't do this." She tugged the blanket around her shoulders.

"Can't do what?"

"I can't…" She looked away. "I can't *breathe* around you, okay? And you can't do that—you can't…I don't know—call me Mae. And be dependable and just…you know, rescue me!" She closed her eyes, shaking her head.

Rescue her? But, "Yeah? Why not?" He pushed the hair from her face and snagged her hands into his again. "What if I like rescuing you?"

She just swallowed, then looked at him, her eyes reddened. Oh no, she wasn't going to cry, was she?

"Because then I might like it too," she said quietly. "And then I'll be in big trouble."

Silence slipped between them, his heartbeat banging in his chest.

She looked away from him. "Maybe I'm already in big trouble."

He frowned.

"I could have died out there if you hadn't found me. I was lying out there in the cold, my foot stuck in those stupid planks, and I couldn't believe that was how God would end things. I've never felt so alone in my life."

He reached for her, pulling her against himself. She surrendered. "Mae. You aren't alone."

But she sighed, then pushed away from him. "That's the problem, Cole."

He shook his head because he didn't see that as a problem at all.

"I started begging God to please, please help me." And now her eyes were filling. "And He sent you. I'm not sure what to do with that."

He could think of several things to do with that, regardless of whether or not it was luck or God who'd brought him here. Because with everything inside him, he wanted to rescue her. To pull her against himself and hold her, and frankly, it was starting to drive him more than a little crazy.

Was it getting hotter in here?

"It's just like the time you saved me from drowning in the lake."

"I don't think things were quite that dire, but I'm not sure what you were thinking trying to swim all the way across the inlet."

"I wanted to impress you. Show you I could keep up with you just like the Christiansen boys."

"You never had to prove anything to me." No, because she didn't have to try to impress him that summer. That was the summer after he'd come to live in Deep Haven. He'd realized his childhood friend didn't look like "one of the guys" anymore. Nope. And she did crazy things to his twelve-year-old brain. Kind of like his adult brain, now. Only this was far worse.

"Yeah. Kids do silly things. But then you rescued me, and... and then, after the summer was over, you left." She looked up at him. "But that's the thing. You've always been there to step in and help. I really wasn't surprised you became a Ranger."

He swallowed. "You know my dad was in the National Guard."

"Yeah. I remember you talking about it."

"They'd have family weekends sometimes. Like, all-day outdoor picnics and activities. I loved tagging along behind him." His throat thickened. "One weekend, they let us go on this huge obstacle course—well, it was huge to me. I was only seven at the time. He and I were teammates and I remember him boosting me over the last obstacle. A towering wall." *Oh, Dad.* He could still see his dad's arms thrown over his head in victory. "We won. I snagged the flag at the top and, I don't know—that feeling of being part of something bigger than myself? It stuck with me. I wanted so much to be like him."

"You are, Cole. You're exactly like him. You make a difference. A huge difference. I just wish—" She stopped herself. Didn't finish her sentence.

"Wish what?"

"I just wish you didn't then leave."

He frowned. "Are you talking about the fact I left Deep Haven?"

She was rubbing her hands, as if trying to ease away any lingering cold, and he took them in his grip again.

She looked down at the floor.

"You know I didn't have a choice, right? I told you—"

"No, I don't." She pulled her hands away from him. "I just heard rumors about social services showing up at school—you didn't really say anything about it, other than you promised to write. Promised to come back. And then you were gone. Not a single response to any of the letters I sent...then they started coming back as returned mail. I thought I'd never see you again." Her voice softened and she looked up at him. "And then you rescued me again, from the ditch."

Yes, admittedly, he saw a pattern.

She sat up and met his eyes. "Cole? What happened before you left?"

One would expect after all these years he'd be ready for that conversation, especially after everything she already knew. He sat up, put his feet on the floor, and stared into the fire.

She leaned against him and wove her hand into his.

"One night, my grandpa woke me up around two in the morning. He was in a rage, reeking of alcohol. Angry. Miserable and looking for someplace to put all that. He pulled me out of bed and started yelling at me, dragging me across the floor. I begged him to let me go." He closed his eyes. Remembered flailing to get loose from his grandfather's grip. "Somewhere during our scuffle, we knocked a chair over. He picked it up like he was going to hit me with it. I just kept thinking—"

He paused, scrubbed a hand over his eyes.

Her hand in his squeezed.

It was enough.

"I kept thinking if he caught me...I wouldn't survive. He was so mad. I was really scared and I ran. I ran out the front door and I just kept running. Barefoot, in my pajamas."

"Where did you go?"

He could still feel the cold pavement under his feet, the chill in the fall air. "Lucky for me, Eli Hueston, the old sheriff, was on his way home. He spotted me and stopped his car." He swallowed. "He took one look at me, shucked off his coat and wrapped it around me, and hauled me to the police station." He paused. Let the memory settle. "He gave me some clean clothes from his locker."

She raised a brow. "He was four times bigger than you."

"I didn't say they fit. But when I changed, he saw the bruises and he said I wasn't going back home." He turned to her, saw her blinking back tears. "The next day, he took me by the house to get some things and change before dropping me off at school. I think he had words with Grandpa, though. Then the social worker came and I told you I was leaving. She sent me to Duluth. Into foster care."

Megan was quiet. Then, "I knew it was bad. I didn't know it was that bad. I should have figured it out—found a way to help you."

He looked at her. "You can't blame yourself. Not at all. I didn't want people to know. I bounced around a few foster homes, and then when I graduated, I joined the Army. It sort of became home for me."

"And you left Deep Haven long behind."

He nodded.

"What did you do as a Ranger?"

He let out a long breath. "Sometimes quick raids on a compound. Seizing and securing airfields. I don't know." He ran his hand through his hair. "All kinds of stuff."

"And you liked it?"

"For a long time, yeah. It felt like I had a purpose for the first time in my life. And I was good at it." The logs in the fire shifted, popped.

"So, why'd you leave? What changed?"

He paused, considered the best way to filter the ugly story. "We were on the ground working with a foreign army to combat terrorist cells and were handed a high-risk mission involving an ISIS leader. Normally, we'd train with everyone on the mission. Memorize our exact plan. Have all our contingencies. It wasn't done, despite David and me speaking up." He shook his head. "It seemed someone in Washington wanted to have a token achievement to put into the press. The odds were against us from the beginning."

The memory of the sunrise ambush still made the hairs on his neck stand on end. "We didn't have the proper air support for the mission and the enemy was waiting for us. Lost communications with one of our vehicles and got separated. Turned back. Got pinned down. David nearly died during the firefight and if it hadn't been for a medic who defied orders...it isn't likely he'd have survived." He shook his head. "She probably tanked her career that day, but David survived because of it." He looked back into the fire. "Unfortunately, not everyone was so lucky." The weight of it still crushed him. "We lost two good men that day."

"I'm sorry." Her fingers curled around his even tighter.

"I decided it was better to get out than get myself in trouble." He played with a silky lock of hair that fell against his fingertips.

"I got into a few scuffles that could have landed me in some disciplinary action. We were back in-country. David was healing and he felt the same way—it was time to get out." Maybe leaving is what he did best.

"And now you want to be a Deputy U.S. Marshal."

"Yes, ma'am. That's what David's doing now. He's been putting in a good word for me, hoping to get an interview lined up. A new career. A way we can stick together."

"Where you can leave Deep Haven behind, permanently."

He frowned, but nodded. "He's in DC and they have Deputy Marshal openings there." He blew out a long breath. "David—he's family to me."

She tried to get up, then winced and fell back.

"What are you doing?" He caught her, pulling her into his arms.

"I think I'm warm enough. And I need to get back to Josh."

"I think you're still cold. You should stay here."

She looked up at him, her breathing hard. Her eyes had the power to make him completely lose his mind, especially when added to the confusion, even tenderness, in her gaze.

"Is that what your scar is from? When David got hurt?" Her fingers skimmed the jagged mark.

"No." He cringed. "Nothing heroic or courageous."

"Really?" She scrunched up her nose. "I hardly believe that—but you don't have to talk about it."

She was still looking at him like he was Captain America and, as much as he liked it, he couldn't mislead her. "No, really." He let out an embarrassed laugh. "It wasn't."

She tilted her head, gave him a sidelong glance.

"Fine. I was playing an impromptu game of football in the barracks with the guys. Slipped. Sliced it open on the metal desk." He still remembered the looks on his squad's faces when the blood began staining everything. He knew he'd need stitches and there was no way they weren't going to get in trouble for it.

SUSAN MAY WARREN & RACHEL D. RUSSELL

She gasped, her hand over her mouth. "Seriously?"

"Yes, ma'am."

"So, no more football in the barracks?"

"We were smart about a lot of things. I can't say that was one of them—but we did make sure we didn't have metal objects in the end zone from then on."

She shook her head and laughed. The sound of it threaded through him, settling in his chest and bolstering a different kind of courage.

"Since we're reminiscing, are we ever going to talk about the first time I kissed you?"

"You never kissed me." She quirked a brow at him, the firelight dancing across her face.

He gave her a smile. "Not yet, but if we're going to be able to talk about it…"

Her eyes widened, and his gaze roamed her face.

Then she smiled, and he couldn't stop himself. He pulled her close, leaning down so his lips brushed across hers.

"Mmm." The sound from her came out soft and sweet. Then she just about stopped his heart when she curled her arms around his neck and pulled him down to her, returning his kiss with a hunger he hadn't expected.

She tasted like mint and winter and the thrill of flying down Honeymoon Bluff. She was fun and familiarity and yet, suddenly surprising.

He deepened their kiss, exploring the uncharted trails of their relationship. He didn't know how he ended up with her cradled under him, but footsteps thundering down the stairs broke them apart. He still held her in his arms, however, when the basement door burst open.

Megan froze, her eyes wide as Jensen Atwood stood in the doorway, his hands on his hips, a dubious smile on his face. "I'm glad to see you're both okay."

Okay was one word for it.

Another might be breathless, caught in a place he'd never imagined.

~

Nothing had changed.

Megan had spent the past two days trying to shake off the kiss Jensen had interrupted, uncertain if she was grateful for the intrusion or disappointed. Not that she should have been kissing Cole Barrett, former Army Ranger and soon-to-be Deputy U.S. Marshal. But she'd been confined to her sofa, her ankle on the mend, which gave her exactly the right vantage point to watch him from her apartment window, in and out all day, working on the house.

And slowly, she'd realized—while kissing him had rocked her entire world, it had clearly meant nothing to him.

Megan stood and looked out the window. He was still marching full speed ahead on his house repairs, and it wouldn't be long before the For Sale sign would go in the yard. And Cole would be gone. Of course he would be.

He'd told her that from the first.

But she couldn't get past the fact that her hero was leaving town. Leaving her. Again.

"This is really bad, Ivy," Megan said, watching him carry in Sheetrock.

"Your cookies?" Ivy asked from her barstool perch in the kitchen.

"Him." The oven timer buzzed and Megan limped to the kitchen to pull the cookie sheet out. She set it on the cooling rack and looked at her happily married friend with a sigh. "I'm falling for him."

"And?"

"And I *can't* fall for him."

"And the way you not fall for him is by baking cookies?" Ivy's question was charged with all kinds of accusations.

"Yes. Chocolate chip cookies. And I'm not sure I'm going to share them with you." She began to lift the cookies off the sheet.

"Why is it every time I turn around lately, you're baking something?" Ivy reached for a gooey cookie, catching it in her hand before it fell apart. "Let's see, there were the scones. The coffee cake. Brownies you claimed were for the team. The lasagna—with garlic bread. You're going to fatten that guy up."

"Stop. I'm not making him fat." No, not at all. Because she distinctly remembered him lifting her from the snow and her being pressed against his solid form. And being held in his arms when he chased away the cold with the warmth of his body. He hadn't an ounce of fat on him. "Besides, why do you assume it's for him?" She began to scoop more cookie dough onto the sheet.

Ivy took a bite of her cookie. "These are really good."

"Of course they are. They're Mona's Footstep of Heaven Bookstore recipe she published in the *Deep Haven Cookbook*."

Ivy took another bite. "So, you're clearly denying any attempts to fatten up Cole Barrett and hypnotize him into staying through your baking magic."

Megan held her spatula in the air like a jouster. "I don't owe you an explanation."

"So you aren't carting those downstairs to him when you walk me out?"

"You're right about one thing." Megan narrowed her eyes. "It's time for you to go."

Ivy laughed. "Fine. But I'm totally on to you. I think you're cooking up more than baked goods and if your goal is not falling in love, I think you're going about this totally wrong."

Megan shook her head. "It's worse than that."

Ivy quirked a brow, waited.

"We may have, well, our lips may have possibly collided."

138

"What? Like your face fell and his lips caught yours?"

"I kissed him, okay? Actually, he kissed me." She used the spatula to point toward the window facing his house. "He started it."

"When did this happen and why am I only now hearing about it?" Ivy set down her cookie, put her elbows on the kitchen peninsula and her chin in her hands.

"At Pine Acres. The night I nearly froze."

"What?" Ivy gasped, comprehension filling her eyes. She sat up. "Wait a minute—is *that* what you were doing when Jensen found you?"

"What? Why? What makes you ask that?" Megan reached for a cookie.

"Because when Jensen called to tell Darek he'd found you, he told us you seemed to be 'better than fine' and you had refused medical care. Were you, or were you not, kissing Cole?"

Heat flushed Megan's cheeks. "Don't go all prosecutor on me."

"Are you denying it?"

"Can I plead the Fifth?"

Ivy narrowed her eyes, answered slowly. "Noooooo."

Megan squirmed. "Do I qualify as a hostile witness?"

"Definitely not." Ivy crossed her arms. "Were you, or were you not, kissing Cole Barrett?"

"Okay. Yes." Megan made a face. "And we probably looked like a couple of teenagers breaking into a vacant house to make out."

Ivy's eyes were huge saucers. "Wait, this wasn't just a kiss."

"It was, though. I mean, look at him—" Megan pointed out the window toward the Barrett house again with her spatula. This time, a chunk of dough plopped onto the counter. "He's been working overtime like he can't get it repaired fast enough. Like he's on the *run*."

"Or maybe he just wants to not have to be working on the house all the time."

"So he can *leave*." She scooped the dough off the counter with her fingers and ate it. "Don't forget, he's the same dashing stranger who rescued me and tried to evict me all in one day."

"He didn't know either one was you, so I think he should be pardoned on those counts. What if he's working so hard because he wants time for other things—like kissing you?"

"Stop. We were just—we were just caught up in the moment. You know, stress kissing. Let's not forget I almost died that night."

"Stress kissing isn't a thing and you still haven't told me the rest about that night. How you *almost died*."

"Yes, I did. I drove off the road. Hiked back. Fell."

"Yes, I know all that part. I meant the part about when he found you and *what, exactly, happened before this kiss?*"

Megan stared at the plate of cookies, letting the memories soak into her. He'd carried her into the house. Taken care of her. Kept her warm. She'd felt safe.

And when he'd talked about his past, being a foster kid and a Ranger, she longed to be that safe place for him too. Home, where the warrior could find rest.

She put the next batch of cookies in the oven, then turned to Ivy. "When he found me, I nearly started bawling. I mean, I really thought I'd die of hypothermia before anyone came along. I was praying, and then he showed up—got me unstuck and carried me into the house." She plated the fresh tray of cookies. "That's about it. We talked, you know, and then, he kissed me."

"You're leaving so many details out." Ivy raised a brow at her.

Yeah. Like the hard planes of his body he tucked her against. Strong arms, holding her close. The laughter that danced in his eyes when he asked about their first kiss. And, hello, she'd have remembered kissing him when they were kids. But that kiss at

Pine Acres. It was all grown up, and very much worth waiting for.

"Are you blushing?"

She looked up to meet Ivy's gaze. "Wouldn't you? Yes, it was a great kiss, but...stupid. Oh, so stupid. He's clearly leaving, and I'm making the old familiar mistake of giving out my heart without thought."

Ivy shrugged and reached for another cookie. "I bought my husband at a bachelor auction. There wasn't much thinking involved in that."

Megan smiled. "Yeah, but it all worked out for you—I have Josh to think about."

"Darek had Tiger. He was a single dad. You're a single mom."

"That's different."

"How in the world is that different?"

"You always knew you wanted to stay here. You knew Darek had roots here." Megan shook her head. "I don't want to risk my heart or Josh's on someone who isn't sticking around. I can't see Josh get hurt like that."

"It wasn't always easy. For a time, Darek really missed the fire lines." She pushed the plate of cookies away after snagging one more. "What if Cole turns out to be the best thing that ever happens to you and Josh?"

"You're such a romantic, Ivy."

"I'm just saying, keep an open mind."

"Look at all the evidence, right? If I look at all the evidence, it points to one conclusion. He'll be leaving as soon as he can."

"I say there's still reasonable doubt."

"What do you call it? A preponderance of evidence. From the Sheetrock to his history, Cole leaves. And he will again, just like when we were kids."

"Megs, I still say you're wrong, but that reminds me—I'm so glad Josh can spend the night tonight."

The timer dinged on her last batch of cookies and Megan

pulled them out of the oven. "I'll bet he is already on the back of a snowmobile." She grimaced.

"Yeah. They were heading out to the lodge with Darek. They were all smiles, and my in-laws love to have kids around."

"Josh was so excited to be able to go again, but I've gotta be honest. It scares me a little to think of him riding around out there." She scooped the cookies off the pan. "But I know it'll be a fun night for him."

"And Tiger too. He loves getting to share his outdoor playground."

"He doesn't mind that he's got four years on Josh?"

"No, not at all. He loves playing the 'big brother' role. Joy's not into what he considers the really fun stuff." Ivy looked at her watch. "Speaking of, I told them I'd pick up pizza and take it out there. I should get going."

"Let me fix you a plate of cookies to go." She piled cookies onto two plates and trailed Ivy to the door.

"I don't know that you should be using stairs."

"The doctor said I need to get it moving and today's been a good day. I'll go easy. I promise."

"If you fall, I *will* say 'I told you so.'" Ivy winked.

"Of course you will. I'd expect nothing less." She followed Ivy downstairs, one step at a time.

"Trekking that road to Cole's heart," Ivy said, gesturing to the second plate.

"Leave me alone. I'm just doing some recon," Megan said and shuffled to the Barrett house with the other plate of cookies, shaking her head when Ivy gave her a knowing wave and smile.

She knocked on the door.

"Come in!"

She stepped across the threshold into a light, bright living room. The peeling paint was gone, new light fixtures hung from the ceiling, and the old armchair had been replaced with a pale blue, barrel armchair. Cole stood in a flannel shirt and jeans, holding paint samples to the light.

"Wow, you've gotten a lot done."

"Should you be out walking around? Take a look at these paint chips." He gestured toward the coffee table where more paint samples covered the surface. Mostly browns, but some grays and blues too. "You can help me pick a color scheme for the kitchen."

"I can't sit still. Let's see them." Why not help him move out faster, taking her heart with him? But she was a glutton for punishment, handing him cookies, pitifully wanting to be in his life. "I brought you a few cookies. They're still hot." She even *sounded* desperate, but how else could she catch a glimpse of what he'd been working so hard on all day?

"Thanks." He took a cookie from the plate. "Mmmm... I thought we agreed you weren't going to sabotage my PT test."

"I'm not. These are a local favorite. What do you think?"

"Delicious, as always." He grinned at her, and she felt it all the way to her bones. "How's the ankle doing?"

"Better."

Her eyes fell on a detailed repair list stuck to the door of the refrigerator. Basement drywall. Plumbing. Interior paint. Lighting. Front porch. A ruler-straight line cut through many of them, and any small piece of hope she'd latched onto sunk.

His phone began ringing on the table. He glanced at the number, not answering, and continued to eat his cookie.

"Should I get that for you?"

"No. Let it go to voicemail. It's Seb."

"The mayor? What's he calling about?"

"He wants me to be part of a new Crisis Response Team."

"You're starting a team?" How had she not heard about this?

"He's pushing for me to. Keeps telling me I should put in for the vacant deputy position that's closing soon."

"Really?" Huh. Like he might stay. She wasn't sure how far she wanted to step out on that ice.

"I'm ready to take a break. Should we go grab a pizza?" He paused, smiled. "Or, we could order in."

And, oh, there was danger in those blue eyes. She should go. Grab her plate of cookies and run. Or at least, hobble.

He took a step closer, and the musky scent of aftershave and the heat of work practically reached out to taunt her.

Oh, dear. "Yeah, we could order in," she heard herself answer.

Yep. She'd completely lost her mind.

He leaned in, placed his hands on her waist, and his glance lowered from her eyes to her lips.

Her phone rang in her back pocket.

"You don't have to get that."

"It could be a client." She dug it from her pocket.

"Don't—"

"It's Ivy, and Josh is at her house for the night. He probably forgot his toothbrush again."

He relaxed against the wall, leaving his hands on her waist, and she clicked the button and winked at him. "Don't worry, Ivy, I'll save you some cookies."

"I'm sorry, Megan—I just got a call."

Her breath hiccuped and Megan's smile vanished. "What is it?" She stepped away from Cole, into the living room, her heart pounding in her chest.

"Josh and Tiger..." She took a breath. "They've been in a snowmobile accident in the woods beyond Evergreen Lodge. They're both being taken to the hospital."

She didn't know how Cole had moved up next to her again, hadn't even realized he'd touched her shoulder, but when she looked up at him, he just nodded. "Tell her we're on our way."

CHAPTER 9

*H*ospitals still had the nauseating effect of snapping Cole back to the day his parents died. By the time the officers had escorted him to the trauma center, both of them had passed. His father first, followed minutes later by his mother.

He walked down the corridor, beeps and buzzes coming from the rooms they passed on their way to find Josh's exam room.

Poor Megan. When he'd overheard Ivy on the phone, he almost felt like his world had imploded too. He'd followed her almost by instinct when she'd walked away, her face blanched.

Their short drive across town took an eternity. She'd prayed aloud the entire drive to the hospital, panic threading her voice.

Lord, please keep Josh safe. Let him be okay.

And then, the part of the prayer that had pierced him through and through, like a bullet.

Please don't make him pay for my mistakes.

Oh, Mae. He'd reached over and slid his hand around hers. Squeezed.

They approached the urgent care reception desk, Megan's

limp hardly slowing her down. "We're looking for Josh—Joshua Carter."

The woman looked up. "Friends or family?"

"Family," Cole answered.

"I'm his mother." Megan fished her driver's license out of her purse and gave it to the woman. Her hands shook. The nurse nodded and began typing, reading her screen. "Looks like they're just loading up at Evergreen Lodge to transport."

"They aren't here yet?" Cole gripped the edge of the reception desk. "We thought they were already on their way."

"No."

"How can they not be here already?" Megan looked up at him. "Does that mean it's bad?"

He pulled her into an embrace. "I'm sure he's fine."

"Do you have his insurance information? I can start the registration process."

Megan nodded, dug out a card, and handed it to the emergency room receptionist.

"I'll be right back with this."

"Okay." Every time her voice wavered, it tightened the fist around his heart.

When she finished with the receptionist, he led her to the waiting room.

He couldn't sit. Just began to pace at the window. Waiting for someone else to get things done wasn't his MO. He was used to being the guy in charge. Planning and executing the attack.

The helplessness ate at him. He finally slid into the seat next to Megan, wrapped an arm around her, and let her lean into him.

"This is my fault," she whispered.

What—? "Megan. How could you even think that?"

She shook her head, looked away.

"Ms. Carter?" A woman in scrubs stood in the doorway.

Megan jumped to her feet. "Yes."

"Your son has arrived. We'll let you back in a little bit."

"How is he?"

"I don't have any information right now, other than that he's stable and alert."

Megan nodded, her eyes red. She slid back down onto the seat.

He'd nearly worn a rut into the linoleum floor by the time an ER nurse came through the interior set of double doors. "You're his mother?" she asked Megan.

"Yes."

"You can come back now. He's asking for you."

"Is he okay?" They followed the nurse down the hallway.

"Preliminary findings are a sprained wrist. They've already taken an X-ray and are waiting on the final confirmation. That's one lucky kid."

The nurse stopped outside a room and pulled back the curtain. "I'll give you a few minutes."

Megan nodded. "Thanks."

Josh sat on the bed looking like he'd just been expelled from school. The bed engulfed him. He spoke before Megan could. "I'm sorry, Mom."

"I was so worried about you." She wrapped her arms around him.

"Really, I'm okay, Mom."

For his part, Cole barely held himself back from doing the same thing. Stupid kid, scaring them all that way.

Josh looked up at him. "Hi."

"Hey," he managed, irritated by his irrational anger. Josh didn't do anything wrong. And still, Cole wanted to wring his skinny neck. "Looks like you fared pretty well."

"Yeah. You'll have a fancy sling to show off at church tomorrow," Megan said, sounding far more lighthearted than she looked.

She blamed herself—for what? Wanting a night off? Letting her son go have fun with a friend?

"Are you coming to church too?" Josh was looking at Cole.

Megan looked at him.

"Me? I—uh—"

"Sorry to interrupt." Ivy stood in the doorway. "Jensen was looking for you, Cole."

Ivy looked pale.

"How's Tiger?" Megan asked.

She swallowed and blinked back tears. "He's good—he got a couple tiny scratches from brambles, that's all." Ivy set her eyes on Josh. "We're relieved you're okay."

Josh looked down. "Thank you."

"I'll be back." Cole reached out, squeezed Megan's shoulder.

Megan nodded and Cole stepped out, leaving Ivy with her. The small waiting room had a crowd. Jensen, Darek, Tiger, and Seb. Two sheriff's deputies dressed in SAR gear. Tiger had a couple fresh scratches on his cheek that had been cleaned up and a little bruising around his eye.

"He's got a bad sprain but is otherwise in pretty good shape, all things considered." Cole gave his report to everyone in the room.

"That's great news," Darek said. He wrapped his arm around Tiger, who looked devastated. "Tiger bailed out of the exam room nearly as fast as they could flush his cuts."

"I told them I didn't need the ambulance." Tiger's voice cracked. "I don't know how it happened. We must have gotten off the regular track. It was still fresh snow and I thought I knew where we were, but then we hit a culvert and—" Tiger clasped his hands together and stared at the ground.

Cole touched his shoulder. "Hey, it's not your fault and he's okay. In fact, I think you should probably go in there with your mom and see for yourself."

Tiger nodded and slid from the seat, making his way to Josh's room.

Cole turned to Jensen, who'd been the EMT on duty. He hadn't seen him since they'd left Pine Acres after the whole kissing scene Jensen had walked in on. "Thanks for taking care of him. They must have both been pretty scared."

Jensen nodded. "Of course. Yeah, once we got to them and did a preliminary examination, we were relieved they were stable and didn't have visible injuries." He paused. "You saw, though, how just getting to them—it took a lot of time." He paused, as if chewing on a thought. "Seb mentioned a Crisis Response Team and he dropped your name in with it."

Super. "I just told him the town needs a better plan."

"You're right, we do. This was only a snapshot of what could happen. We could have reached Josh a lot faster if it didn't take so long to mobilize." Jensen shook his head. "And we need better equipment. We pulled him out with another sled and toboggan. But if he'd had a head injury or internal injuries, we would've had no way to airlift him out of there."

"All true," Seb added.

"If Tiger hadn't called with the general area where they were, we could have been searching for them for hours—well after dark and temperatures dropping. Exposure over that many hours..." Darek didn't finish.

He didn't have to. Even without critical injuries, the two boys couldn't have survived that long in temperatures below freezing.

Cole's phone buzzed. Nathan. He'd already called twice and left voicemails asking for a callback.

"Sorry, I need to grab this."

Cole stepped away and lifted the phone to his ear.

"Hello?"

"I think I've got a buyer for your house."

It took a moment for Cole to catch up. A buyer?

For his house. Right. "That's great news."

A pause. "It doesn't sound like great news. It sounds like I just told you that your cancer tests just came back positive. What's going on?"

Cole paused. "Sorry. I'm at the hospital. Megan's son, Josh, got into a snowmobile accident."

"Is he okay?"

"Yeah. Likely just a sprained wrist. But it could have been worse." And he didn't know why, but all the worse things kept jangling around in his head.

They did need a better emergency response team in Deep Haven.

"Thanks for the update, Nathan."

"I'll keep you posted," Nathan said and hung up.

Megan came down the hall. "They'll be releasing him soon. The X-rays came back clear."

He didn't know why, but he reached out and pulled her close.

By the time Josh was released and Cole helped Megan get him home, up the stairs, and into bed, it was near midnight. Cole tucked the blanket around Josh and followed Megan out of the bedroom, turning off the bedroom light and pulling the door closed.

She sank onto the couch, pulled the afghan blanket around herself.

"He's so lucky." She swiped a tear away. "When Tiger told me they'd hit a culvert and Josh went flying... He's lucky he had his helmet on. Lucky he didn't hit a tree. And lucky, too, it's only a sprain." She laughed, nothing of humor in it. "I keep saying lucky, which is kind of funny since I don't believe in luck. God watched out for him today."

And she finally fell apart. The brave facade she'd put on unraveled and suddenly she was sobbing. "I don't know what I'd do if I lost him."

"You didn't. You won't." He wrapped his arms around her and she curled into him, holding on to his T-shirt and letting out little huffs of breath.

"It feels like it's my fault. I know he asked to go—but I wanted to have the time too."

Time...with him. She didn't say it. Didn't have to. Because that was exactly what he'd wanted too. And when he'd found out Josh was safe and let the relief pour out of him—well, shoot, his own eyes were burning.

He cleared his throat, and she picked then to lean away. He wiped the tears from her cheeks. "Do they think he will be healed in time for the tournament?"

"I hope so. I think we'll know more over the next few days. For now, he has to keep the brace on." She wrinkled her nose. "We never got our pizza."

"No. That's okay. I forgot I was hungry."

"Me too." She looked at him, a solemnness in her eyes. "Thank you for being there tonight. For being here."

"Of course."

He let his fingers glide through the silky lock of hair that had fallen over his hand.

She smiled. "Do you remember the time we rode on the Evergreen Lodge Fourth of July float?"

"As I recall, it was more of an Evergreen truck and flatbed trailer." He'd been so proud to be included. An outsider, invited into the fold.

"Of course. That constitutes a bona fide float in this town. With hay bales and balloons. Candy to throw," she added. "And we got so burned."

The memory reached in, wrapping its tender grip around his heart.

"Not only sunburned, but I remember having our fill of watermelon, and someone—" He gave her a squeeze. "*Someone* trying to rig the water fight."

She shrugged half-heartedly. "I didn't see anywhere in the rules that we couldn't ask to join the fire crew's team. They could have said no."

She looked up at him, her eyes luminous, the furrow gone. Instead, she bore a softness and smile that could stop him in his tracks. Wow. She could take his breath away.

"That's the kind of life I want to give Josh."

"The sunburn?" He gave her a smile, pressing away the niggling memory of David's last call with him. *Get that house sold fast, man. We've got plans.*

"No, Ranger." She gave him a light jab in the ribs. "Community. You know, a hometown. That feeling of family."

The words had the full effect of reaching straight into his soul, destroying all his protective barriers. Because he couldn't think of anywhere else he'd rather be than right here, with her in his arms, especially as she leaned against him again, her breaths growing heavy, and Josh, asleep in his room. With, yeah, that feeling of family.

The smell of chocolate chip cookies still permeated the air. This little apartment was so much more a home than he'd had in years. Reluctance held him there for another twenty minutes, until propriety required him to slide out from under her and ease her back against the cushions. He tugged the afghan up and wrapped it around her before pressing a kiss to the top of her head.

He locked the door on his way out, pulling it closed as quietly as he could.

Darkness filled his own house. Not even the new light fixtures seemed to brighten the room enough. He shivered, turned the heat up, and sat down on the couch.

He looked at his phone. He had text messages from Darek, Jensen, Casper, and Seb. In the two weeks since his arrival, Megan had helped weave people into his life. Because not a single message was asking about what he could do for them in regard to the team. No. These were personal. Either expressing gratitude that he'd been there for Megan or following up to see how Josh and Megan were doing since they'd left the hospital. Because, somehow, he'd become part of their world. Someone who belonged. Like a hometown boy.

And now, with Nathan's call, he was going to leave it all behind.

∿

Clearly, church was the last place Megan was supposed to be today. First of all, she wasn't paying attention. Second of all, even though she sat in her usual third row pew and Pastor Dan was speaking, she'd heard barely a word of what he was saying. She'd only caught snippets. Like, *When we are weak, He is strong.* But the reality was her brain wasn't on the sermon. It was scrolling through the list of friends she could contact.

Because after last night, the only thing that mattered was to find a new place to live. And sitting in the pew wasn't going to help her. As terrifying as the experience had been with Josh, she'd leaned on Cole. Relied on him to hold her together. To be there for her. With direction and comfort. Spilling her heart. A solid rock she could cling to.

Yikes.

She needed to extricate herself from his life. He'd gotten way too far into her heart. That kiss at Pine Acres had tangled up her brains and she needed to remember Deep Haven was her home. And he. Was. Leaving. The last thing she needed to do was prolong the agony. She needed to get out of his life as soon as possible.

At least she had these two hours of safety. Time to regroup. Because she'd been setting herself and Josh up for absolute, catastrophic heartbreak. It was time to put a cease and desist on everything related to her current landlord and business assistant.

A jab in her ribs jerked her upright. "Stand," Josh demanded.

Megan realized everyone around her was standing, several members offering up prayer requests as the service neared its end.

A frail voice spoke from the second pew. Edith Draper, asking for praise and thanksgiving. Her driveway had been cleared for her during the snowstorm.

Ivy nudged her. "Wasn't it Cole who did that?"

"Shh. Don't talk about him." Of *course* it had been Cole. Ranger. Hero. Snow shoveler extraordinaire. And, she couldn't forget, wedding coordinator.

He was the last person she should be thinking about. Especially during church. Especially the way she remembered him from last night, the steel of his chest beneath his snug T-shirt. The beat of his heart in her ear. His concern for Josh. The way she fell asleep against him. He felt like...home.

Oh boy.

Now everyone was bowing their heads in prayer. Guilt crawled into the pew beside her and wedged itself into the tiny space between her and Josh.

She'd had no business leaning on Cole all night, letting him be her emotional rock.

The congregation sat.

Ivy leaned toward Megan and whispered in her ear. "Did you know Cole was coming?"

"He's *here*?"

"Sitting down in the back." Ivy nodded toward the back of the sanctuary.

Megan tried not to look. Tried not to let her casual hair flip and glance over her shoulder look exactly obvious.

Lovely. And there he was, clean-shaven and wearing a dark green button-up under his leather jacket. Seated on the edge of the back pew like he was ready for a helicopter to drop in and extract him before things got too dangerous. Yeah, she might need one of those extractions herself.

Maybe he hadn't seen her. She could duck out the side door.

"Is it hot in here?" She tugged at the collar of her blouse.

"No." Ivy looked at her with narrowed eyes. "It's February. What's wrong with you?"

"I don't want him to see me." She slid down against the pew, putting Ivy into a blocking position between her and Cole. "Why did he have to pick *today* to have his come-to-Jesus moment?"

"Are you serious? Isn't that a good thing?"

Darek leaned forward from the other side of Ivy and gave Megan the same look he might give Tiger for goofing around during the service.

The music began for the final song and Megan flipped through her hymnal.

"'My hope is built on nothing less—'" She lowered her voice more and leaned closer to Ivy. "Because. I mean, I want him in church, just not in *this* church and *this* service. I need some distance." Because she couldn't think straight when he was in the same room. "As soon as everyone gets up to leave, I'm going to grab Josh and go out the side door."

"'But wholly lean on Jesus' name.'" Ivy shook her head and put her lips to Megan's ear. "Don't you think you're overreacting? The last time I saw you with him, he was helping you."

"'All other ground is sinking sand.'" Megan let out a long breath and whispered, "No. Not at all. Nothing has changed for him. He's still leaving, I'm still staying." She closed her eyes, lowered her voice even more. "I can't risk Josh's heart too."

Darek leveled a look at her and lifted his hymnal, his strong baritone rising over their whispers. "'In ev'ry high and stormy gale—'"

"Is this about that kiss?" Ivy's eyes grew round, the light of

155

realization spreading across her face. "There's been more than one, hasn't there?"

"No!"

Ivy put her fingers over her mouth and gasped. "I thought he was looking at you like he might break into a million pieces last night at the hospital."

Megan closed her eyes. "Stop. He was not and there hasn't been. But that's exactly why I need to get out of here."

Josh bent forward to look at her. "What are you talking about?"

"Shh," she said to Josh. "Nothing."

"'When all around my soul gives way—'" She turned back to Ivy. "Maybe he won't even know I'm here."

She let that bolster her voice, singing out the final chorus and finding peace in the blending of voices around her.

"'On Christ, the solid Rock, I stand, all other ground is sinking sand. All other ground is sinking sand.'"

See? It was a sure sign. Jesus was her rock. Her only rock.

The song ended and Pastor Dan moved back to the podium. "Before you all dismiss, I do want to recognize we have Josh Carter and Tiger Christiansen with us today. Both of them are doing well after their snowmobile accident. I know the families appreciated all your prayers last night. Can you boys please stand so we can pray for you before we go?"

Megan slid back against the pew, her cover blown. She wanted to squirm in her seat as much as Josh, who'd taken to playing with the Velcro on his wrist brace.

A soft murmur buzzed through the congregation. Megan looked around. All eyes turned toward their pew. Pastor Dan held up a hand to quiet the packed sanctuary. "We'll continue to pray for Josh's sprain to heal quickly." He winked at Josh. "We don't want that to keep you from the tournament games."

Pastor Dan closed the service with a prayer, and Megan turned to Josh.

"Hey—let's head out of here quickly, okay?"

"I'm not ready to leave. I want to see my friends." Josh looked up at her from under his long dark lashes.

Megan squeezed Ivy's hand. "If Darek asks about the chit-chat, tell him it was prayer support. Best-friend counseling." She smiled and shrugged. "He has sisters. He'll understand." Megan turned to grab Josh's hand. He was gone. "Where did—"

Ivy nodded toward the back of the sanctuary. "You'd better hurry. Cole has a fan."

Megan followed Ivy's line of sight to where Josh was weaving his way through the conversations on a clear mission in Cole's direction. "Oh, no! Now what am I going to do?"

Josh reached Cole, threw his arms around him, and Cole leaned in, wrapped Josh in a hug that made the boy look positively tiny.

Ivy placed a hand on her arm and gave her a consolatory look. "Looks like there's no escape. I gotta run—I need to grab Joy from children's church."

Megan nodded and watched Ivy retreat.

Great. Left alone. She ducked out into the hallway, still slowed by her sore ankle. At some point, Josh would finish his little man-chat with Cole and he'd look for her. And she'd give him the mom eye. The one he knew meant *You'd better get your britches over here right now or there's going to be trouble.*

"Megan! I was hoping to run into you today." Evelyn Hunsaker placed a hand on Megan's arm, as if holding her in place, her sturdy form an anchor.

"Oh?"

"Yes. I was going through the Sunday school curriculum for spring. I need to line up teachers for the nine- and ten-year-old class."

Megan knew exactly where this was going. Because everyone knew she couldn't say no. At least it gave her a place to hide out and wait for Cole to leave. Eventually Josh would get bored and search for her.

Evelyn droned on and Megan tried to nod politely at the appropriate junctures and pauses. Sure, she could make time to teach. Yes, she'd love to get copies of the materials in advance. Design crafts? Um...

"I'd love to," Megan heard herself say.

"Excellent!" Evelyn released her grip on Megan, as though now that she'd secured exactly what she wanted, the conversation was over. And Megan had added far too much to her packed calendar. She watched Evelyn's round figure retreat, already trying to figure out how to say no, after the fact.

"Good morning." Cole's warm tenor jolted Megan.

She turned. And if she thought he looked good in the pew from afar, she'd forgotten the way the man smelled. Clean and freshly showered, and up close, his blue eyes swept her voice from her throat. "Oh," she croaked. "Hi."

"How are you?" He studied her, his brow raised and head tilted.

"Good. Doing good." She licked her lips. "And, Josh. Josh is doing good."

"Good."

"Yep. Everything's good." She looked past him, hoping to see some great reason to excuse herself from the conversation and save her mushy brain.

"Yeah. Okay. I'll see you at home." His forehead scrunched up and he pursed his lips together.

"Home?"

"Yeah—we're supposed to hammer out a few details for the wedding of the century, remember?" He rubbed his chin.

Oh. "I'm not sure I can do that today." She'd buried that calendar item somewhere between falling asleep in his arms and waking up to reality. "I don't think I have time." She needed to put some serious distance between the two of them.

Because she could not, would *not* fall asleep in his magnificent arms again.

He gave her a look. "We don't have that much time left. Today's as good a day as any, right?"

Despite the screaming in her brain, she relented. "Okay. Fine. I have to run a couple errands with Josh first."

"Sounds good. Just come by the house when you get back."

"Okay." She could keep it all business.

He walked away, out the church door. Just like he'd do in a few weeks. Right out of her life. She probably needed to write that down somewhere for her mouth to remember next time it started babbling agreements.

"Hey, Megan—before you go, I need to talk to you." Ingrid Christiansen broke away from a conversation with Pastor Dan and tucked a lock of blonde hair behind her ear. She reached out and placed a hand on Megan's arm. "How are you all doing this morning?"

"Much better, thank you."

"I can't tell you how many times the boys gave me heart palpitations in their youth." She gave a wry smile. "And some of them even in adulthood." She winked.

"Yeah, it's hard not to want to put him under lock and key. Not let him leave the apartment."

"Speaking of the apartment, Ivy mentioned you're looking for a place."

Megan let out a long breath and wrung her hands together. "Yeah, we are. Cole needs to sell his grandfather's place."

"Noelle and Eli Hueston are out of town for a few months while they travel. I've been dropping in since their original house sitter ended up having to head to Kansas due to a family emergency, but they really prefer someone on-site."

"So they need someone to *live* there?"

"Exactly. Someone to shovel the snow, keep the pipes from freezing, water the plants, just keep an eye on things."

"That sounds perfect—as long as they'd allow us to bring our cat."

Ivy joined the conversation with Joy.

"Yes, I made sure of that when Ivy mentioned you as a possibility."

"Then, I'm in." A home. For *free*, even. Maybe God did still see her.

"You're going to do it?" Ivy asked.

"Absolutely—why wouldn't I?"

Ingrid nodded. "I'll get the key to you later this week and then we can do a walk-through. I'll show you where everything is."

"Thank you for thinking of us." She had somewhere to go. The resolution to her problem should feel good. Instead, it left her with an ache in her chest.

Ivy pinched her lips together. "Are you sure you want to do that? You really want to move out?"

"I have to. He's selling the house." Megan shoved her hands into her coat pockets.

"You could stay there. See what happens. He doesn't actually have a buyer yet." Ivy quirked a brow at her.

Stay? So that she could keep bringing him brownies, or worse, so he could come over and spend time with Josh? Maybe snuggle on the sofa with her?

And, more.

Yeah, no. "I can't stay. He's leaving and the sooner I accept that, the better."

Her gaze rested on Josh who was standing with Darek, Tiger, and Cole, laughing. Like father and son.

Her heart thudded hard. "Better for all of us."

CHAPTER 10

*M*egan didn't strike Cole as the kind of girl to play hard to get. And yet, that's exactly the vibe he'd gotten from her the entire church service. He hadn't missed the way she ducked behind Ivy. Nor the way she jetted straight out the side door as soon as the service ended, hobbling as fast as her wrapped ankle allowed.

If it hadn't been for the robust lady who'd cornered her in the hallway, all evidence pointed to her intentions for a prompt departure, aka, getaway.

As if his head wasn't already spinning from Dan's sermon—a sermon that somehow felt like it was written on the fly, just for him.

The words were still burning two hours later while he waited for Megan to stop by. *God does not waste our suffering.*

He stared at the church bulletin he'd set on the kitchen counter. Psalm 80. *Come and save us... Restore us.*

Cole wasn't sure which part of the sermon had rubbed him the most. Maybe it was the acknowledgment that sometimes people didn't know a specific reason for suffering. They were simply supposed to trust that God is good and allowed suffering for His purpose.

Why? Why was that the answer? How was it that God's people still held confidence in their future deliverance?

Before he could dissect it, Megan knocked at the door.

"Hi," he said as he held the door open.

"Hi. Sorry I'm late. I had to drop Josh off at a friend's house." She didn't look at him, walked past him and carefully selected the chair across the room instead of joining him on the couch.

Huh.

Not thirteen hours earlier, she'd held on to him. Let him be part of her world.

She wore jeans and a striped, green T-shirt that did crazy things to her eyes and made the soft pink of her lips nearly irresistible. He remembered exactly how she'd tasted when he kissed her. And the curve of her body when she'd finally relaxed against him.

She fired off a barrage of questions about the work he'd already done for the Crawford wedding until she'd satisfied herself that he was, in fact, very good at putting together complicated plans. He'd even pulled out the work he'd done for the Swanson-Klein wedding.

Then she got up to leave, as if the briefing was over.

Uh-uh. No way. He blocked her exit. "Are we going to talk about why you're avoiding me?"

Again, she wouldn't look at him. "I'm not avoiding you."

"Oh, please. You won't even look at me."

"I'm not… I'm—" She lifted her gaze, something sparking in it. "Fine. Okay. I think we need to step back." She swallowed. "I think we've gotten a little carried away, and it needs to stop."

Oh.

"Cole." Her voice softened and she sighed. "Let's not kid ourselves that you're sticking around. You made that clear. You're leaving, I'm staying. Just like always."

Her soft tones had the power to dig into his soul, leave him aching. Because, for the first time, he wanted to believe he could belong here. Stay. As if life could bring him full circle.

Wanted to believe that Pastor Dan was somehow right—that the wounds of his life could lead to deliverance.

But before he could get any of that out—and not sure he should—Cole's phone vibrated on the table. Nathan's name flashed in the caller ID.

"You'd better answer that," Megan said, and started to push past him out the door. He got desperate and put up his arm to block her.

"Really?" She put her hands on her hips.

"Just wait!" He picked the phone up, pressed the button. "Hello?" He didn't actually mean to snarl.

Nathan didn't seem to notice. "I'm on my way with a buyer."

Megan was staring at him, annoyance in those pretty eyes.

"Now's not a good time."

She looked up at him, her eyebrows drawn together in question.

"Well, it has to be because they fly out of Duluth later tonight and they're extremely interested and we're right around the corner." Nathan paused. "Cole. They have cash."

It still felt like a punch, deep inside.

So much for his wounds leading him to deliverance. See, he'd been lying to himself again. Cole let out a long breath. "Fine. See you soon." He hung up, looked at Megan. "I'm sorry, Nathan's coming by with a buyer."

She nodded, smiled, but it didn't touch her eyes. "That's... great. Really great. See? Can I go now?"

And if he wasn't mistaken, those were tears in her eyes.

He didn't know how he'd turned into a jerk, but he shook his head. "Not like this. Megan. It's just a showing." He caught her hand and squeezed.

"I get it. I know you need to sell this place." She forced a smile. "I'm happy for you. Really."

He swallowed. Nodded. She was right, wasn't she? He needed to sell the place. It's what he'd said all along. He had plans, a future outside of Deep Haven. Away from the past. A future with a purpose, which didn't seem very important at the moment.

Restore us.

So why was he having such a hard time letting her walk out the door?

Maybe because...he could do it, couldn't he? He could actually walk away from the house and drive right out of town. And that truth suddenly set his gut to roiling.

Before he could measure the words to say, the doorbell rang.

"I should leave," Megan said, letting go of his hand.

"No, stay. In fact, I can help give the tour. You—you don't move."

She quirked a brow at him and he opened the door.

"Welcome." He held out his arm toward the living room. "Come on in. I thought it'd be good if I helped Nathan show you around."

Cole saw the question in Nathan's eyes, but he ignored it. Because no, Cole didn't have a clue what he was doing.

The couple, in their mid-fifties he guessed, looked like they were right at home in the wintry north woods. The woman was dressed like she'd come in from cross-country skiing and her husband from chopping wood. She wore pale pink snow pants, and when she shrugged out of her matching jacket, a high-collar white performance shirt was underneath. Her husband stood beside her in his red-and-black flannel, his dark wash jeans stacked on his hiking boots.

"Thank you for showing the house on such short notice," she said. "It looked perfect when Nathan sent us the preview listing. I'm Karen Ashforth and this is my husband, Ray."

"Nice to meet you, ma'am, sir." Cole shook their hands. "Cole

Barrett."

Ray turned and began perusing the room. "Is this the only common living space? Or is there a family room too?"

"This room was originally the parlor," Nathan said. "There is also a sitting room. I believe it is currently in use as an office." He looked to Cole for confirmation.

"Yes, sir. That's correct."

"I see." Karen looked around, her eyes bright with appreciation. "They don't make houses like this anymore, do they? With these extra touches." She ran her hand along the chair rail molding. "It has good bones."

Megan looked like she was trying to make herself as invisible as possible on the corner of the couch.

Nathan moved forward into the room. "Cole's done an excellent job bringing the house up-to-date. You can see in here where the light fixtures really create a modern Victorian style." Nathan flipped the switch for the living room and dining room fixtures.

The drum light over the dining room table had a dark pewter finish with an intricate cutout design and a crystal drop at the center. Fancy enough for the Victorian without being gaudy. Cole had been pretty pleased with the find.

Ray pointed to the living room lights. Simple wall sconces that matched the pewter cutout of the drum fixture.

"Wow. Those are lovely." The woman looked at her husband, who nodded in agreement.

"Yes. Those actually look a lot like the ones on your wish list." The man squeezed his wife's arm.

"Yeah, it was my first time installing new fixtures, but I think I did okay. They seem to be working. Haven't burned the house down yet." Cole gave a laugh that came out weird and unfamiliar, and Megan frowned at him.

He looked away from her.

Karen's brow creased. "Oh?"

"That's funny, Cole." Nathan shot him a warning look.

Nathan led the clients and Cole into the kitchen. "You have new stainless steel appliances—a stove and dishwasher."

"Had to do something after the plumbing burst," Cole said.

Nathan gave him another look, but Cole couldn't seem to stop talking.

"The trick here is the floor's not level, so this pantry door doesn't open during winter unless you shimmy it upward." He showed them the trick for closing it.

Nathan gave a hollow laugh. "Adds character, doesn't it? And you can see the kitchen has well-appointed upgrades the chef of the house will appreciate." Nathan opened the oven door. "If you haven't cooked with a convection oven, you'll love it."

As Karen looked inside, Nathan glanced at Cole and gestured with his head. Leave? Why? He was doing a great job.

"Let's move on to the bedrooms." Nathan started up the stairs, then paused and turned back to Cole. "Maybe you should wait down here for us."

"No, I'm glad to help," Cole said and followed the group upstairs. "Do you have a cat? The pest management company felt a cat might help keep the rodents away. I did thoroughly clean the mice droppings upstairs."

The woman drew in a breath, something of horror in her expression.

"Is that a problem here?" Ray asked. "Do you have a lot of rodents?"

Cole opened his mouth to tell them that, in truth, he had found only one—a large mouse, long dead—in the basement in one of Grandpa's traps.

But Nathan cut in. "You know, we all have to be proactive to prevent unwanted houseguests." He ran his hand across his throat in the universal sign to stop, frantically shaking his head at Cole.

What? Fine. Cole held his tongue as they ventured through

the bedrooms. Karen looked in the corners, as if scrutinizing the carpet for any sign of rodent droppings. He wanted to tell her that it wasn't in the bedroom, but in the hallway, near the vent—

"Let's go back downstairs," Nathan said.

They followed him down to the first floor.

"It's got a lot of lovely potential," Karen said, exchanging a look with her husband.

"I know the windows are a little thin," Cole said, "but if you put plastic over them in the winter, it holds the heat nicely. And the boiler only cut out once since I've been here, but it was a pretty big storm so—"

Now Megan was looking at him again, her eyes wide. She gave a little shake of her head.

He frowned.

"Um, I think we need to discuss it before we'd consider making an offer," Ray said.

"I'm—I'm not sure this is the right place for us," Karen responded.

Nathan looked deflated. He turned to Cole on the way out. "Next time, maybe don't be here."

What? But Nathan left before he could follow up. Whatever happened to full disclosure?

Megan rose from the couch with her stack of notes in hand. "Is everything okay?"

"I think that went well."

"Seriously? Cole. You sabotaged that entire showing!" She put a hand on her hip. "I could hear the whole thing—even when you were upstairs. Those poor people were horrified."

"I...no I didn't. I was just being honest. They need to know what they're getting into."

And then she smiled, something sweet, and now he was completely confused. "What?"

"Nothing," she said, but her eyes were shining.

Huh. But she wasn't leaving.

And that gave him all the encouragement he needed. "I think we're done planning the wedding for the day." He pulled the notes from her hands and tossed them onto the chair.

He stepped closer. Close enough to smell her sweet floral fragrance.

"Um…Cole?" She stood there, looking up at him like maybe, just maybe, she didn't really want to leave. The amber-gold of her eyes caught the glow of the afternoon sun.

He captured a stray golden lock, let the silky length slide through his fingers.

"What are you doing?"

"Maybe something I should have done before."

Because everything in him wanted this moment to be his life. A home. A family.

Megan. Josh.

A life that he could sink roots into and never leave.

"I should go." Her protest was half-hearted.

"I think you should stay."

"Why?"

He leaned toward her, let his lips brush hers. Testing. And when she let out a soft sound, it lit the fire in his core. He wrapped her face in his hands, drew her closer.

She pressed her hand against his chest, like she might push him away. Paused. Then curled her fingers into the fabric of his shirt, gripped it, and molded her body against his.

Oh, Mae.

She drew back. "Cole, what are you doing?" Her words, husky, soft against his cheek, could unravel him entirely.

"I'm deviating from the mission." He leaned back, searched her eyes for permission, caught his breath. Because in them he could see the same longing. Desire. Hope.

He slid his arms around her and she returned his kiss with the same eager hunger, wrapping her arms around his neck. She tasted like chocolate, sweet and rich and tempting, and all he could do was surrender because nothing, not one thing, had ever felt so perfectly right in his entire life.

She finally moved away and met his eyes, smiled. "One thing's for sure. You should never become a real estate agent."

$\sim$

He wasn't leaving.

Megan wanted to believe it in her heart, even before Cole had kissed her three days ago.

She inhaled the rich smells of Java Cup, sank her teeth into a fresh maple Long John, and stared at the game board, the red and black squares blurring out of focus.

Those kisses hadn't felt like goodbye. No, they felt like flying out over the water of Evergreen Lake on the rope swing. Like the Fourth of July fireworks over Lake Superior. Like white water rafting on the St. Louis. She'd been mesmerized by the strength and tenderness of his touch. Exhilarated.

Nope—he wasn't leaving. He just didn't know it yet. So, how exactly was she going to make everything work out?

"Are you waiting for spring showers?" Raina leaned forward, hands on her chin. "Or are you going to take your turn today?" She picked up her coffee cup and took a long sip.

"Maybe." Megan blinked. Focused on the game board. She'd almost told Cole about moving out—would have if she didn't feel she needed to talk to Josh first.

Except, if he wasn't leaving, then she didn't have to move to the Huestons', right? But...she'd promised. They were counting on her. And how in the world would Cole stay?

She moved her piece. He'd need a job to make that work.

Raina promptly countered. "King me." She gave Megan a smug smile of triumph.

A few patrons gathered in the doorway, zipping their jackets and snugging on their gloves before pushing open the door, their heads tucked against the cold. The breeze that swirled through the closing door caused Megan to shiver.

"Fine." She picked up a black disk from the table and fit it onto the checker and then began fiddling with the two she had left, clacking them together.

Raina reached across the table and poked a finger in Megan's arm. "You aren't paying attention. I thought you invited me for coffee so we could chat." She waggled a brow.

"I'm sorry. I know." But what could she say? Because she could still feel Cole's lips on hers and smell that woodsy scent that made her lose her mind. The last thing she needed to be doing was fancying any kind of future with the man, right? No matter how much his kisses curled her toes. Cole couldn't stick around, and in reality, he was the guy who moved on. Didn't look back. Especially with his Ranger buddy waiting for him.

Oh. He was so confusing.

She took a sip of her drink, a sweet caramel and chocolate blend they'd named after her because she'd helped the Java Cup's owner with a wedding fiasco.

"Spill. What in the world has you so bunched up that you can't even manage a game of checkers?"

Megan looked around, checked the doorway for ears. "Okay. Here's the deal. I'm supposed to be moving temporarily into the Huestons' so I can watch their house for them while they're out of town for a few months." Megan took another drink. "And that was supposed to be a good thing. But, now, I'm not so sure." She bit her lip and stared out the window at the waves crashing against the frosty shore.

"So this is about Cole." Raina tore a chunk of her chocolate glazed Bismark off and popped it into her mouth.

"Maybe."

"Come on. You were staring at him in church last Sunday."

"I wasn't staring at him." Megan moved her piece. Heat

flooded her face and she tossed another look over her shoulder. She'd kissed him back. Like, all-in. The excitement still swirled in her gut.

"Yes, you were." Raina leaned in and jumped Megan's pieces. Twice. She scooped the pieces off the game board. "And you think if you move out, he'll see that as a reason to sell the house and leave. An open exit door."

"Yeah. Because he doesn't have a job here right now. His grandfather needs the money. It's probably the right thing for me to do." Megan rubbed the back of her neck.

Raina looked at her with an unbroken gaze.

Megan squirmed. "What are you doing? Why are you looking at me like that?" She repositioned in her chair.

"What happened?" Raina leaned back and crossed her arms.

"Nothing happened." Nothing she was ready to share. Because Cole was stealing her heart. Again.

Why couldn't she do something halfway? Why did her heart run away with plans?

"Right. Something happened." Raina opened her hand full of pieces. "Because checkers may not be your best game, but you have lost three times already. Three. That's got to be a new record and by the looks of this game, you aren't faring too well. And I'd expect to hear you jabbering nonstop about the weddings you've got lined up—like, you know, maybe *Cameron Crawford?*"

"Fine. Probably. Yes. I don't know. I really like Cole. I don't want to like him." She covered her face in her hands. Under no circumstances was she going to tell Raina right there in the middle of the Java Cup about the kiss. "I'm too old for this."

"You're not making any sense. Why can't you like him?" Raina took another bite of donut. "He's nice. And—um, hello— good looking." She sat back in her chair. "He's been very helpful to Casper. What are you too old for?"

"The uncertainty." Megan peeked out between her fingers

before dropping her hands. She let out a long breath. "I'm afraid he'll leave again."

"This is the boy who came every summer when you were kids."

Megan jumped Raina's pieces twice, finally gaining ground. She would not lose four times in a row. "Yep. He's the one."

Summer. She could almost hear the pebbles hitting her bedroom window and the gust of cool morning air when she would push it open. She'd lean out and smile. He'd call up to her. *Let's go.* And she'd race down the stairs, hollering to her parents on her way out the door to meet him.

Raina slid her game piece into an edge spot. "It seems like maybe you've loved him longer than you've admitted."

Oh.

"Loved him? We were just kids." Megan tried to laugh but it came out a sharp snort. She could still taste Cole's kiss on her lips. The warmth of his breath against her neck. And the bold determination with which he took her in his arms. She had to stop thinking about it.

"Yes, but you loved him." Raina smiled like she'd just found the secret recipe for Edith Draper's no-bake chocolate oatmeal cookies.

"No. Quit saying that. King me." Megan was on the verge of finally winning. She was due a victory.

"Why are you denying it?" Raina's eyes narrowed in accusation and she moved her checker.

"Shhh—not so loud." Megan sat back and let Raina's words soak into her. Let the childhood fondness meld into the current quickening of her heart every time he came near. "Fine. Maybe, a little, but now?" She moved her game piece. "I don't know. He's selling the house and moving away. Or, maybe not. I mean, he's been so helpful around town. You saw how he jumped in and helped Casper clear snow from some of the parking lots and roads. He's helped me with these weddings that got doubled-up due to the crazy weather. Our time together has been, um, nice."

All the conflict and confusion whirled in her brain like a stormy tide. "And Josh? Josh is kind of wild about him and that terrifies me. But he's leaving—he has to, right? And the Marshals Service would be idiots not to hire him. His friend is *waiting* for him. And I have the Huestons' place to move into temporarily. But if I leave the apartment, he'll leave town—do what he wants to do. Probably needs to do, right? Should I leave? Should I stay?" She gripped the edge of the table. "What should I do?"

Raina smoothed the fabric of her tunic over her abdomen, looked across the game board at Megan, and stared at the Long John sitting on the plate. "I'm still hungry."

"Really?" Megan laughed. "I understand you're eating for two, but I'm serious. I don't know what to do." She handed Raina the rest of her Long John.

"Have you talked to him about it?" Raina ripped off a bite and ate it.

"I'm afraid to. Maybe I'm not ready to know. What if I can't fix it?"

Raina reached a hand out to her, interlaced their fingers together, and squeezed. "You don't have to fix it."

Except sitting, waiting wasn't in her nature. She thought of Cole, his friend David. His visit to see his grandfather. Moving out was the right choice. Besides, she'd already made the commitment. They needed someone on-site and she'd agreed to it.

She swallowed, the decision pressing down on her.

Raina plucked one of her double-stacked checkers from the board and jumped her piece across Megan's last two, scooping them from the board. "You lost. Again!"

Megan slumped in her chair. Yep. That's exactly what she was afraid of.

CHAPTER 11

C ole blamed Megan for why he was sitting in the dark of his grandfather's room. He hadn't planned to spend his Thursday morning in memory care, listening to the soft snores and grunts of a sleeping man lost to the ravages of Alzheimer's.

Megan had been MIA since their rendezvous Sunday afternoon, and Cole wasn't sure if the space was a good thing or not. But one thing he did know—kissing her had completely muddled his brain and plans.

If there was any possibility of a future in Deep Haven, he needed to talk to his grandpa. Because somehow, the very man who drove him out of town was the same one who held the answer now.

Cole needed to make a decision.

Heavy curtains closed out the morning light. The care center had done their best to make the institutional setting seem more like home. Landscapes by local artists hung on the walls, depicting area landmarks—Split Rock Lighthouse, Palisade Head Cliffs, Eagle Mountain—as though hoping to anchor the patients somehow to reality.

The man hadn't stirred, but Cole couldn't help but start sorting out the problem. He leaned forward in his chair, looking at the old man.

"I know you were hurting when my dad died. I know you'd lost Grandma, and really, I can't imagine the pain of losing your own child." Cole swallowed, thinking of Josh. Not his own son and yet, so much the child he always envisioned having. And the night they rushed to urgent care—every minute they waited passed in agony. "But I never understood why you couldn't protect me from your own pain."

He scrubbed his hands through his hair and stared at one of the paintings. It looked like the annual Fisherman's Picnic. Booths lined Main Street, a big blue Fish Burger sign in the middle. He remembered going with Grandpa to get a fish burger from the Lions Club and watch the logrolling competition.

A dark-haired nurse entered the room in smiley-face scrubs, her rubber-soled shoes silent as she padded to the bedside table to remove the breakfast tray.

"Good morning." She paused, looked at the sleeping man, and turned back to him. "Are you Cole?"

"Yes, ma'am."

"It must be hard to see him this way. Yesterday he had a pretty good day. He talked about you. By that, I mean he told me all about his six-year-old grandson and one of your fishing trips. I hope that brings you some comfort—those good memories sustain him. He's been doing really well here."

Cole nodded. He faintly remembered those fishing trips.

She left as quietly as she came, and Cole continued to sit in the shadows until his grandpa stirred, opened his eyes.

Panic filled them. "I'm late." He sat up, his thin hair stood on end and his pale blue pajamas were half buttoned, twisted on his tiny body. He pushed to his feet.

"Hey! What are you doing?" Cole stood, not sure if the unsteady legs would keep his grandpa upright.

His grandfather focused on him, squinted, maybe seeing him for the first time. "Are you the new supervisor?" Then his voice turned to a low growl. "I know who you are. You're the one Jack sent to get me fired." He stepped toward Cole, his spotted, gray hand in a fist. "You set me up, didn't you?" He looked around the room. "You took my clothes! Turned off my alarm!"

Cole reached for him before he could hurt himself. "Grandpa, stop!"

"Don't lie to me!" His grandpa's sharp voice rattled through the room. "You set me up. Gonna get me fired!" Then he twisted hard out of Cole's grip, pushing him.

And Cole was the boy in the corner. The switch had flipped, just like the night he left. He stepped away, but there it was, all the hurt and confusion, littering the space between them. Casualties of alcoholism and loss decimating the landscape.

His grandfather leaned in. "You good-for-nothing—" His grandfather let out a slew of foul words. "You think you can come in here and take what's mine, don't you? I won't lose what's mine—"

Two nurses rushed in and Cole backed away, listened to his thundering heart and the buzzing in his ears.

"Edgar, I found your clothes right here." The nurse lifted a cotton shirt from the side table.

"Give me those." He did his best to snatch the clothes away, as much as a weak, feeble man could.

"Have you looked outside this morning?" The nurse Cole had met earlier went to the window and opened the curtains, letting light flood the space. "We put out a new bird feeder and it's been getting quite a bit of traffic."

His grandfather collapsed, breathing hard, starting to sob. "I won't let them take what's mine. Where's Cole? Where's my grandson?"

The nurse turned to Cole, put a hand on his shoulder. "Can you wait outside? Let us calm him down?"

Cole nodded, stepped out into the hallway where the smell of old age and disinfectant made it hard to breathe. A light in the hallway flickered, incessant buzzing adding to the noise in Cole's head.

Somehow, in his lost mind, the man was searching for *Cole*. And the sadness of that fact soaked in, pressed down on Cole's chest.

Clearly he'd completely forgotten why they'd had to take him away.

He wandered back to the main entry area, uncertain if he should stay or go.

"Mr. Barrett?" the receptionist called to him.

He stopped. Looked at her.

"You are Edgar Barrett's grandson, right?" She stood at the desk.

"Yes. Yes, ma'am."

"Ms. Chase wanted to speak with you. She thought maybe you'd already left town." The woman gave him an apologetic look as Ms. Chase, the case manager, stepped from her office carrying a folder. She laid it out on the raised reception desk.

"So, originally, we thought that billing had been completed through the end of February, but during the financial audit yesterday, an error was discovered and billing had only been completed through January. I'm so sorry. Your grandfather's account is actually due."

"What does that mean?"

"It means that we'll have to transfer him next week to Duluth." She paused. "Unless he has funds to pay off the bill. I have the transfer orders here."

Oh.

And suddenly he saw himself walking through the house with Nathan, pointing out all the defects. No wonder his real estate agent had looked at him like he'd been kicked in the teeth.

Cole had run away perfectly good buyers—buyers ready with cash in hand. And why?

Because he hadn't been ready to say goodbye to Megan. The truth dug in and squeezed.

Because he didn't want to leave Deep Haven.

But what choice did he have? His grandfather needed the money—and it was his house, after all. Cole should call Nathan back. Apologize—he owed him that anyway. And maybe, by some chance, the people might still be interested.

It was the only viable solution, really, because...despite all that his grandfather had done, he was still his grandfather. And deep in his core, he believed family still mattered.

"No," he said quietly. "He stays."

She looked up from the clipboard, her pen frozen midword.

"Excuse me?" She leaned in. "Did you say something?"

"He stays. I'll get you the payment."

Her brow raised. "Okay—you understand we'll need it by close of business next Friday?" She gave him a pained look. "Unfortunately, our parent company has really buckled down on these things. Our hands are tied."

"Yes, ma'am. I'll get it to you."

"Okay then. We're glad to hear he'll be staying." She gave him a smile. "Do you know when you're leaving town?"

He blinked. "No." He swallowed. "Not yet." He gave her a nod and walked away.

Shoot. He didn't know when his math had stopped computing—he'd known all along he'd have to sell the house to pay for his grandfather's care. Somewhere along the line, he started thinking that he'd come up with a better solution.

Clearly, he wasn't supposed to stay.

He hadn't realized he'd taken a wrong turn until he reached a dead end. An emergency door with an alarm on it.

The last room in the hall had a small placard next to the open door.

CHAPEL

Purple, blue, and orange blocks of color lit the floor, cast from within.

He had no idea why, but he stepped inside.

It was only twelve feet or so wide, with a stained glass cross sitting at the front of the small space, lit from behind. A wood railing spanned the width of the room with a step for kneeling, and three rows of four upholstered chairs sat on each side of the center aisle.

Cole slid into the back row and stared at the cross. He'd have rather had a gym than a chapel. Somewhere he could yell and scream and hit and throw things. Somewhere he could vent all the frustration and confusion boiling inside him.

Better might even be a shooting range.

Footsteps in the hall and a light knock on the open door drew his attention.

"Hey—I'd about given up on finding you." Darek stood in the doorway, pulled his knit cap from his head.

Cole leaned back, interlocked his fingers together in his lap. "What are you doing here?"

"I had to drop off some prayer shawls my mom made and saw your Jeep in the lot. I've been driving around with this application and thought I'd hand it off to you."

"Application?"

"For the vacant deputy position."

Cole let out a sharp laugh. "I thought I told you you've got the wrong guy."

"What if I don't?" Darek slid into the seat across the makeshift aisle and held up the packet in his hands.

"I have to sell the house. Like ASAP." He looked back at the doorway to the hall. "You know about my past with my grandfather?"

Darek nodded.

"He's a mess today. Yelling and screaming at me—that I'm going to take things away from him. I'm the bad guy." Cole stood and walked to the altar rail, ran his hand down the smooth wood. "And then he started crying and talking about losing his grandchild—me."

"I'm sorry."

Cole shook his head. "You know, I don't expect—or want—to be best friends with the guy. But I'd like to be able to air it all out. Maybe, for once, have him admit what he did was wrong."

Darek leaned forward, his hands clasped over the back of the chair in front of him. "You want an apology?"

"For starters. I don't know how we'll ever move forward until he asks for forgiveness. I think he owes me that much." Cole balled his fists. "I mean, I hear people talk about him quitting alcohol, returning to God. Except, after I left, I never heard from him again. If he was so sorry, then it seems the least he could do is own up to it."

"What if he can't apologize? What if you can't get the closure you want?"

"I don't know."

Darek sat back up in his chair. "You know, I got married really young to a local girl named Felicity. I was a terrible husband. Young and selfish."

Cole stayed silent.

"One day, she was hit by a car while out running."

Oh. Wow. "I'm sorry."

"One of the hardest things I had to deal with was never being able to apologize. To never be able to rectify the wrongs I'd done. It's the other side of the same coin."

"What do you do with that?"

"I wish I had a pat answer. Some ten-step solution." Darek shook his head. "But I did have to find a way to forgive myself if

I wanted to move on. And I had to forgive others. Let go of my anger. Forgiveness isn't about justice. It's about freedom."

"Justice is important to me."

"I get that. Forgiveness doesn't negate justice. It simply puts it in the hands of God, where it belongs. Allows you the ability to move on."

Or stay. Cole picked up the application and stared at the first page job description and salary. "When does this close?"

Megan stared at the remnants of the homemade pizza and cheesy bread that lay before her on Cole's dining room table. Her gaze shifted to Cole, who looked entirely too delicious in his white T-shirt and jeans as he stood to clear plates.

Even though she couldn't eat another bite, she didn't want the meal to end. Because now, she had to find the right way to tell him she was moving out. That she'd made that sacrifice so he could pursue his dreams and take care of his grandfather.

Because that's what love did. It sacrificed. And she was in the position to help. To fix the problem.

Especially after she'd heard about what went down at the care center yesterday. The altercation with Cole's grandfather. And the announcement delivered to him in a very public reception center. Information she'd grilled her friend Rhino, a nurse in the care home, about when he'd made a passing comment of concern about Mr. Barrett's predicament.

Cole had to sell the house—he had no choice. And according to Rhino, they'd even talked about him leaving town. So maybe he didn't want to.

But he had no choice.

Because love sacrificed.

Maybe, however, her announcement could wait for a bit. Until after she'd soaked in all the comfort of a family dinner around the table. The banter of easy conversation. Because once he knew she could move out, the house sale could be fast-tracked, and she wasn't quite ready to face the inevitable. Wasn't quite ready to tell Josh to pack up.

Happy endings were for other people.

When Cole had invited her and Josh to join him for dinner, she wasn't sure exactly what to expect. They hadn't been able to spend time together since they'd kissed.

Yeah, the memory of that kiss—that long, lingering, delicious kiss—still made her toes curl.

But Cole said nothing about it and instead set them to work when they arrived, throwing aprons on Josh and her. He helped Josh press the dough out and slather sauce across the crusts while she assembled their toppings.

There was corn meal, flour, and cheese littering the countertops, and it'd been hard not to stop working just to watch them. The way Josh wrinkled his nose at the olives and Cole's tactics to get him to try something new. Josh was so eager to please and Cole seemed to delight in sharing the experience with him.

So much so, it hurt her heart to know it couldn't last. To know Josh would have to say goodbye to all of this too.

Sooner was better than later. She was doing the right thing by moving out. Helping Cole say goodbye.

"Dessert?" Cole's voice snatched her back to the present.

Somehow that question brought up images of their kiss, again, and heat rushed her cheeks.

He set a large cake on the table in front of them, this one from the bakery.

"Wow. What's the occasion?"

"It seemed like a good day for a celebration."

Maybe that meant Nathan's buyers hadn't been chased off by Cole's absurd sabotage. Which was a good thing, despite it causing a small ache in her chest.

"Yes!" Josh jumped up and down.

"I thought treats were bad for your PT test." Megan raised a brow.

"I didn't say *I* was having any." He quirked her a smile and hefted a too-large piece of cake onto Josh's plate.

"Don't feel like there's any competition to finish that whole thing." Megan wrinkled her nose. "I'm all for cake, but that's a lot of cake."

"Will you come to my tournament next Saturday?" Josh asked, taking a large bite of chocolate cake. "The doctor said my wrist should be fine by then."

Cole looked at her, a question in his eyes. "Well, Blades, that would be up to your mom."

Oh.

"Please, Mom?" Josh gave her one of his wicked, gap-toothed smiles. The ones that made her want to snatch him up and squeeze him like he was still her little boy. Every time he lost a baby tooth, it gave him a hockey-player grin.

"But while you're thinking about it and Josh is enjoying his cake, why don't you let me show you a few things." He held out his hand.

Oh, dear. Because getting alone with him just might involve more clandestine kissing.

He led her to the front of the house and pointed to the ceiling. "I was thinking I could tear down those broken sections of crown molding and get a contractor to make me custom pieces to match."

What? The man stood in the middle of the room like the host of some house-flip show. Only more rugged and dangerous.

Worse, his focused attention on her always made her feel so…wanted. Remembered. Special.

How was she going to leave this man? Or…let him leave her?

"Follow me." He led her up the stairs to the second floor.

There was no doubt with the work he'd already done and the work he planned to finish—the house would sell, and fast.

Yep. Moving out was the right thing to do and having the Huestons' place available afforded them both the easy exit required.

"Take a look at this." He tugged a sheet off a heap on the master bedroom floor. A tarnished brass chandelier with chains lay in a pile on the carpet. He lifted it from the floor. The fixture had five metal light shades, each with different colored glass insets hanging from heavy chains that sprouted at various lengths from a fleur-de-lis-shaped ceiling fixture. "I found it in the attic. I think it's from the 1940s. Do you like it?"

The worst of Art Nouveau meets Gothic Victorian. Even if age had treated it better, it was ghastly.

"It's...it's...hideous." She covered her mouth with her hand.

He opened his mouth in shock. "You don't think it will go with my modern Victorian theme?"

"You can't hang that thing. Friends don't let friends hang ugly lamps. Not if you ever want to sell this house." Her wedding business put her in the same circles as several designers, and modern Victorian design had been a hot market for several seasons. Drop a freshly remodeled house into an upscale North Shore town and, yeah. It would sell fast. Unless the light said anything about his final plans.

His soft laughter, warm and full, filled the space. "So I should definitely hang it then."

"Stop. You can't hang it." She paused, his words soaking in. She met his eyes. Mischief lit the bright blue. "What exactly do you mean by that, Ranger? Are you—are you talking about *staying* here?"

He blew out a long breath. "I don't know." His eyes met hers. "Maybe?"

Her mouth went dry.

"But, your grandpa? And the Deputy Marshal job? You want

that. David's expecting you in Washington. He's counting on you, right?"

"I do. It's a great job and I'm sure I'd be hired." He bit his lip. "And, yeah, David and I would need to talk."

"I don't understand."

She started to turn away, but he caught her, drew her close.

"There's this other possibility, though."

She pressed her hands against his chest, let the warmth of him chase away the sudden chill in her bones.

He caught her wrists up with his hands, let his fingers glide down the length of her forearms, and stepped closer. So close his body heated her from head to toe.

She swallowed. "Um, yeah? What's that?"

"It seems there's a deputy sheriff position that's open."

What? Wait—

"So, what do you think? Would I make a good deputy?"

The only thing more devastating than Cole Barrett himself would be Cole Barrett in a uniform. Walking around Deep Haven. Her town. Staying.

She needed to get space between them before she did something really stupid, like, yes, kiss him again. Why had he given Josh such a big piece of cake?

Her phone buzzed in her pocket. "I should check that." She stepped out of his arms and farther into the room, drawing her phone out to read the text.

Ingrid Christiansen's name scrolled across the banner.

Thanks again for house sitting. The Huestons said they'll pay you $1k for your trouble.

Almost enough money to make up the rest of her down payment for the Black Spruce. She started to shove her phone back into her pocket when it vibrated again. This time, she saw Trevor's name on the screen. She swiped it to ignore the call. He had no business interrupting her life now.

Cole leaned against the wall. "Are you done?" He quirked a brow at her.

Even that was irresistible.

"Well—"

"Because I haven't told you the best part."

"You haven't, huh?" She swallowed, bolstered her courage. "I need to tell—"

He held up his hand. "Wait." He closed the gap. "Then you can finish." He stood so close she had to tilt her head up to look him in the eye. "I was thinking how ideal it is to have you and Josh in the garage apartment."

Huh? She wasn't entirely sure she was tracking what he meant. Why in the world would that be ideal? "You mean you might stay? What about your grandpa's care?"

"I crunched some numbers and the rent you pay on the apartment will help cover some of his bills. I don't have all the answers about money or about my plans with David. But..."

And, as if she still didn't fully understand what he meant, he pulled her close, ran his fingers through her hair, and kissed her. And her brain pretty much exploded.

He tasted amazing, his arms strong, and she lost herself in his kiss. Oh, the man could kiss. And frankly, she always knew it, always dreamed of—

"Mom?"

Somewhere between devastating delirium and common sense, her brain registered the voice.

Oops.

Cole stepped away, grimacing, and mouthed the word *Sorry*.

But maybe he didn't have to apologize because Josh stood in the doorway watching them, a wild grin on his face.

"So, that's a yes about going to my game?"

CHAPTER 12

*C*ole's entire future was riding on the application and job description in his hands. He stood in the mayor's office, rubbed his hands on his jeans. He'd decided he'd better find out more about what he might be applying for.

Seb leaned forward in his desk chair. "So, you *are* interested in the job?" The City Hall office looked like it might enjoy a minimalist makeover. A stack of files created a formidable Monday workload to Seb's right, and a collection of coffee mugs and Deep Haven souvenirs lined the bookshelf behind him.

"Yes, sir."

"Outstanding." He made a note on his memo pad. "You've read through the job announcement?" He picked up a file folder from his desk and thumbed through it, pulling out a document and sliding it over to Cole.

Cole skimmed the page. He checked all the boxes for qualifications. And then some. "Yes, sir."

"And we'd tack onto that the collateral duties—the CRT." He gave a pensive smile. "You know, *if* you get the job. We can't guarantee it until all the applications are reviewed."

"Yes, sir." It seemed unlikely that a North Woods deputy position could provide the level of activity Cole was accustomed to as a Ranger. And yet, somehow, when he thought of dinners at home—like the one he'd shared with Megan and Josh—the adrenaline rush didn't seem quite so important. "I understand, though, no guarantees, of course." Cole rubbed his hand on his thigh.

Jensen knocked lightly on the open door. He stood with a man in uniform whom Cole recognized as Kyle Hueston, the sheriff. "Excuse me." He entered with a smile and both men offered a handshake. "We heard a rumor about an applicant stopping by today."

"It's true." Seb sat back in his chair.

"It'd be great to have you," Kyle said. "I can't tell you how badly we're in need of someone to set up a real Crisis Response Team."

Cole remembered Kyle from childhood. He'd been one of the older teens around town, had played with a band at some of the local events. He was tall with an approachable demeanor. Unlike many small-town cops Cole had met, Kyle didn't act like a man who had anything to prove.

"You saw only a small fraction of the issues we run into up here," Jensen said. "There's nothing in place for emergency management and response."

"I've heard that." And it was still difficult to believe since Cole's entire military career had centered on being ready for fast action.

Kyle nodded. "We've got unique geography here. This county alone is over three thousand square miles. Add in the three national protected areas, the Boundary Waters, the seasonal weather extremes. It's literally a lot to cover."

Cole checked his watch. "I'm looking forward to hearing more about it." He paused at the door. "I'd better get going. I need to pick up Josh from practice. Thank you for your time."

"Sure. Feel free to stop by my office. I'd be happy to answer any questions you have about the department," Kyle said.

Jensen gave him a nod. "Hey—thanks for sending the glass repairman. My contractor let me know he came today."

Cole laughed. "You're welcome. It was the least I could do." He held up his application packet. "I'll get back to you on this."

With a job secured, maybe he'd be able to live in his grandfather's house and pay for his care.

What if he can't apologize?

Darek's words still gnawed at Cole's heart. He'd even dug out his Bible still sitting on the shelf in his old room. He hadn't had much to say to God since Rebecca left him. If he were honest, he hadn't had much to say to God since his parents died.

He slid into his Jeep, grabbed his phone.

He didn't want to let David down. He punched in the number, almost hoping it'd go to voicemail. Instead, David answered on the first ring.

"Hey, what's up?" A sports announcer called out a play-by-play in the background.

"Do you have a few minutes?" Cole cleared his throat.

"Sure, one sec." The background noise silenced. "Okay, talk to me."

"I'm still in Deep Haven."

"That many repairs? Geez."

Cole stared at the deputy paperwork in his hands. "There are a lot. But the problem is, I'm not sure I want to leave."

"Whoa. What?"

Cole cringed. "I know. We had a plan."

"Have a plan. You're a shoo-in for the position. What's going on? Is that tenant still giving you trouble?"

She was trouble, all right, just not exactly the kind David was thinking. Holding her. Kissing her. Talking about a future. The soft little moan she'd made when she'd surrendered into his arms and met his kisses with the same desire.

"I—uh—" Cole cleared his throat. Tried to summon a rational explanation.

"Are you kidding me? You've fallen for her." Frustration wove through David's accusation. "How many weeks has it been this time?"

Ouch. Cole probably deserved that one.

"It's not like that. I told you she's the one I used to talk about. The girl I grew up with."

"Do you know how much time I've put into talking you up? I've got a place rented out for us."

"I get it. I'm sorry."

David let out a long breath. "So, what's next? What do you want me to do?"

"Nothing yet. There's a position here. I'd like to apply with the sheriff's department, but I wanted to talk to you first. And maybe I won't even get it." Cole gritted his teeth. "Can you wait for me? See what pans out for me here?"

"Okay." David paused. "I'm good to go for another month before I'll need to dig in and look for a new roommate if you're not coming."

"Thanks, man, you're the best."

"You're welcome. You know I'd do anything I can for you."

"I know." Because David was the kind of man who'd sacrifice his life for another. Whose heart was filled with duty.

"But Cole?" David paused a beat, his tone serious. "Be smart this time."

Cole closed his eyes. "I will."

"Seriously," David added. "You've been gone a long time. People change. Watch your six."

"I get it." He couldn't expect David to know anything different.

"Keep me posted. If she's as great as you think she is, I'm looking forward to meeting her."

"Thanks, David."

Cole parked at the rink, tossed his phone on the seat before walking over to watch the action. The team was still focused on their drills. He stood along the wall with the other parents waiting for practice to end, an assortment of hockey moms and dads, with a few grandparents thrown in. And him.

He could get used to being part of a normal life. Josh asking him to go to the tournament had nearly taken him apart. He was so eager to bring Cole into his world.

Cole swallowed. Watched Josh zip across the ice and it warmed his heart. He'd never spent time around kids. But Josh made it easy—he was so much like his mother.

"How's it going?" Darek asked. He approached from the lot and took a spot next to Cole. He wore his standard Evergreen uniform—jeans and an Evergreen Lodge jacket.

"Pretty good."

"It's good to see Josh back on the ice."

"Yeah, it really is. Tiger's been a huge help, encouraging him."

Darek watched the boys set up cones on the ice for a drill. "How's the Crawford wedding coming along?"

Cole laughed. "You know, I'll be honest. I volunteered because I'm a big fan and I knew Megan needed it, but—man, the things we're having to do to pull it together. Unreal."

"Because of the short turnaround?"

"Because of the crazy ideas they—actually, I think mostly the bride—have about what their wedding must entail." He cupped his hands around his mouth. "Nice shot, Josh!" He turned back to Darek. "So, they apparently met at a summer street fair. They have a whole carnival theme going for their reception, which isn't easy with several feet of snow on the ground."

Darek laughed. "Why didn't they plan for a summer wedding?"

Cole shrugged. "That's a question beyond my pay grade."

"It sounds like Megan will be the big winner when it's all said and done."

"And that's exactly the reason we're jumping through ridiculous hoops to get everything they want. Except the dunk tank. We told them no one was going to take a polar plunge at their reception. And the ice cream truck has proven to be a tough find."

"Casper said your repairs are looking good."

"Yeah, I think so. It's a good thing my buddy roped me into helping him remodel his parents' house every time we were stateside, though, or I'd be in real trouble. Your brother's handy with drywall. He jumped in to help me last night when he stopped by."

"He's full of surprises." Darek let out a good-natured laugh. "I'll have to put him to work more at Evergreen."

"Don't tell him you heard it from me."

"Never. That reminds me—my mom wanted me to let Megan know she can use the Evergreen truck to move out if she needs it."

"Move out?" Cole shook his head, frowning. "She's not moving out."

Darek's brow furrowed and he looked away.

Cole swallowed. Took a slow breath in an attempt to unfurl the knot in his gut.

"I'm sorry, man. I assumed you knew." Darek shoved his hands into his pockets. "She's moving into the Huestons' so you can sell the house."

The twist in Cole's gut cinched down.

"That's what you've wanted, right? Or were you putting in for the local position?"

"Yeah. Sure. No, that's true. Need to sell." But his voice emerged tight. "Don't worry about it. See you later. Looks like Josh is heading this way." He gave Darek a nod and walked away, his throat dry and his heart thundering in his chest.

Moving out? Cole had spent his morning making plans, actually considering *staying* in this town. Had started thinking of ways to share the possibility with Megan, only held himself back because he hadn't known what to do about his commitment to David.

Why would Megan be moving out now? Why hadn't she said anything?

People change. Watch your six.

He wanted to confront her, but maybe it would be better to wait. Give her a chance to explain herself. And if she didn't… then he'd know exactly where he stood.

"I'm ready." Josh came around the rink carrying his gear bag.

They climbed into Cole's Jeep, and Darek's words continued to churn in Cole's mind. He resisted the urge to ask Josh if he knew what was going on. He didn't need to drag Josh into the middle of a conversation that was probably about bigger issues. Like his future.

Maybe he'd gotten the wrong read on the relationship. Wouldn't be the first time.

His phone began ringing and he pressed the speakerphone.

"Hello?"

"Is this Cole Barrett?"

"It is."

"I'm Jennifer Smith with the Human Resources Department at the U.S. Marshals Service office in Washington, DC. I'm calling to set up your—"

He popped in his earpiece. The phone switched off speaker.

"—interview with Richard Watkins. Interviews for the region will be held in Minneapolis at the Federal Building on Third Avenue South this Saturday. Would a nine-o-clock appointment work for you?"

The same day as Josh's tournament. Except, Megan hadn't told him about moving out. Moving on. And he hadn't a clue why. He glanced at Josh in the rearview mirror. An ache pressed in on his heart. Time for a contingency plan.

"Sure. That would be perfect."

~

Megan had almost finished packing a box of her old clothes—no she probably didn't need that U of MN sweatshirt anymore— when her cell phone buzzed. She pulled it out and groaned. Trevor again. But maybe she should find out what he wanted, just so he'd leave them alone.

"What do you want, Trevor?" She slid down onto the couch.

"Hello to you too, Megan."

Her skin prickled at the sound of his voice, her pulse pounding in her ears. "Sorry. Hello. Now, what do you want?"

"I've been trying to reach you for a while. If you're going to keep dodging me, maybe it's time I get a judge involved—"

"Don't go there." Please. Let it be a bluff. She dropped the sweatshirt into the box. The last thing she needed was a custody battle with Trevor. Not when her housing future was in limbo. From what she'd heard, the man was lethal in the courtroom.

"They did a write up about the teams going to play in the Peewee Meltdown in Minneapolis. I saw Josh's name."

Megan gripped the armrest with her free hand, her throat tight. "And?"

"I want to go. I want to be there for him."

"He doesn't need you there." She didn't need him there. Didn't want him there. Not after the years it took to stop pretending he'd ever come back. Ever want her.

"He's my son."

"No, he's not—you made that clear when you left. You wanted no part of our lives."

"But he is. I was wrong." He paused, continued with a softer voice. "Please?"

"Why, after all these years, do you decide this?" The shake in her voice betrayed her.

"Some things happened in my life this past year. I was…" He took a long pause. She could imagine him, his blue eyes looking at her. The way he rubbed his temple when he was thinking. He blew out a breath. "I was diagnosed with cancer a year ago."

The news had the unfortunate effect of gripping her heart. "I'm sorry to hear that."

"I've been through treatment and I'm cancer free now."

"That's good." Because she cared. As much as she didn't want to, she still cared. Because this was the man she'd once planned to spend the rest of her life with.

"But those days battling it made me reflect on everything. On the choices I made. Our relationship. On Josh. It made me want to be a better man."

The better man she'd always wanted him to be? The man she thought he was when she fell in love with him?

She closed her eyes. Thought of all the times Josh had waited for Trevor to show up. The few times he actually had.

"I don't know. I don't want him to have expectations. The last time—"

"I know. I blew it. That was before—" He paused. "Let me be there for him."

She swallowed, stayed silent. Because while her heart was screaming all the reasons to tell him no, her mind was telling her all the reasons she had to say yes. Because, legally, he had a right to see his son, no matter how she felt about it.

"Facing death changed me. Please, Megan. No strings. I just want to be there. Watch him play. Show my support."

"I only have two tickets for the family section and they're spoken for."

"By who? Is there someone in your life?"

"Yes." At least, she hoped so.

"I think I should have a right to know who is taking my place."

"Your place? You don't have a place in Josh's life. You've been a no-show for the better part of the last nine years."

He drew in a breath. "I'd like one." The earnest tones of his voice raked the old wounds open. "Please let me be there for him. Let me have a ticket."

Shoot.

"Fine. I can get a regular ticket for you, but, really—I don't know about this."

"Okay. Have them hold it for me at the gate."

"Trevor?"

"Yeah?"

"Please don't mess this up."

"I won't, Megan. This time, you can count on me."

She hung up. The last person she wanted to count on was Trevor.

She carried another box to her stack by the doorway. Why did her life suddenly feel like it was spiraling toward disaster?

Josh blasted through the doorway. She held out a hand to steady the precarious box stack.

"Whoa there, look out for the boxes."

"Sorry—I'm late to meet up with Ethan to do our history project." He dumped his gear bag on the floor and grabbed his backpack. "I'll be at his house."

He clopped back down the stairs and she looked up to find Cole standing in the doorway.

"Hey, thanks for picking him up."

He closed the door. Stood, trouble worrying his brow, which didn't bode well for the conversation she needed to have.

"So, how are the plans for our eccentric celebrity couple going?" Megan hoped his dark mood didn't have anything to do with the list of arrangements being made for Cameron and Mariah's wedding. Most couples didn't want a popcorn machine, carnival games, or an ice cream truck for their wedding reception, but who was she to judge?

"Fine." He stood there in his boots and coat, unmoving.

He was stewing on something and it had successfully tied a

large knot of worry in the pit of her stomach. "Do you...uh...
want a cup of coffee?"

"No," he answered.

"A Coke?"

"No."

Awkward silence hung between them until she couldn't take
it anymore. "Is everything okay?"

"Where are you taking those?" He stared down at the boxes
on the floor like target acquisition.

She slid in front of him, into his line of sight. "The boxes?"

"Yeah." He paused, his face stern. "Are you moving out?"

Oh. "That's—that's actually a funny story."

He wasn't laughing. In fact, he looked...dismantled. Not his
all together, charge-into-the-storm-Ranger self. No. Utterly
dismantled.

As if she'd...*hurt* him? Her explanation rushed out of her,
messy and muddled. "A few days ago, I thought you still needed
to sell the house." She nodded, trying to get him to acknowledge
it. He stared down at her, his jaw tight. "So, after you left church
on Sunday, I found out the Huestons needed a house sitter. I
thought I'd be helping you out so I agreed to move into their
house."

"So, you *are* moving out?"

"Cole, I was trying to help. I wanted to fix it."

"Then that's a yes. That's not how you fix something—not
when we've—I've—"

"Hey—you're the one who told me I needed to move out."
She held out a hand. "Let me finish."

"Why didn't you say something?" He shook his head. "It feels
like you were hiding it from me."

"I was going to tell you, and then—I didn't because it meant you
could leave, and I was trying to work up the courage. Honestly, I
wasn't looking forward to practically pushing you right out of
Deep Haven with a golden path of opportunity. But then you told

me you might find a way to stay—" She swallowed. "And I thought I shouldn't move out, but I'd already committed. And you still haven't solved how to pay for your grandpa's care. They were going to pay me one thousand dollars to live there. You know that would really help." She sighed. "It's taken me two days of calling everyone I could think of, but I finally found someone else who can do it if I can't. So, no, I'm *not* moving out. That is, if you're still thinking of staying. If you want me—us—to stay. The boxes are donations."

His face grew unreadable. "I had a call from the U.S. Marshals Service for an interview."

Of course he did. The news shouldn't rattle her, but now she sunk down on top of one of the boxes stacked by the door.

Leaving. She didn't know why she'd thought differently. Worse, she'd given up the house to move into and the extra funds it would have come with.

He stared at her for a long time, as if running through his plan A, plan B kind of Ranger scenarios. Contingency plans for everyday life.

He reached out, wove his fingers into hers. His Adam's apple bobbed. "Stay." He plucked a box from the stack, dropped it on the floor, and sat down facing her. He wore a strange look in his blue eyes. "I don't think I'm going to take the job." He paused. "If they offer it."

"No?"

"No." He smiled down at her.

"And you're sure about that? Have you talked to David?"

"We've talked a bit."

He leaned forward, let his forehead touch hers. And the simplicity of the movement, the stillness of him so close to her, as if suddenly they were of one mind...it wove a deep, unexpected hope through her.

He was staying.

"I kind of feel like I do need to show up for the interview, though. I owe David that much." He leaned back, looked her in the eyes. "But maybe I can cancel it."

Yeah. Her life suddenly felt very complicated. She nodded. "Okay, well…" She let go of his hand and wrung both of hers in her lap. "There's something else you need to know too."

"What?"

"Josh's dad has called me a few times."

Cole's expression darkened. "What does that mean, exactly? Why didn't you mention it before?"

"I haven't answered his recent calls or texts until today." She reached for his hand, curled her fingers into his. "Remember, I told you that he's stayed in contact on and off over the years? But mostly off?" Despite her best attempts in the early years to find a path to reconciliation.

"Yeah, so, why did he call now?"

"He wants to come to Josh's game. He says he's had a change of heart."

Cole's jaw tightened. "A change of heart?" He pulled away from her.

"It's not like that. He just wants to watch him play." She reached out again, touched his hand. "Honestly, I'll be really surprised if he shows up. We've heard it before. I'm not even going to tell Josh. It's set him up for disappointment too many times."

He nodded. "But I—I still get to sit with you?"

And, oh, the vulnerability in his blue eyes. The fearless Army Ranger. Courageously holding out his heart to her in his hands. She sucked in a breath. "Of course. I wouldn't let him back into our lives. He'd never take your place."

He stood, drew her up against himself. She let herself soak in the heat and comfort of his body.

Finally, he let her go. "I should get going. I need to run some errands."

He gave her a kiss goodbye that was too quick and left her wishing for more.

She couldn't stop thinking about Cole, however, and his words. *I don't think I'm going to take the job.* It wasn't exactly a marriage proposal, and he'd said he didn't *think*...but there was something in his eyes. And the plea in his own voice. *Stay.*

Yes, the man was finally coming home.

CHAPTER 13

*C*ole glanced in the rearview mirror. He looked like a bona fide hockey dad when they pulled onto Highway 61 for Minneapolis in his Jeep. He'd donned team colors and had even gone so far as to order a jersey with Josh's name and number on it—a surprise he'd unveil at tomorrow's game. And no one, especially not Trevor McAllister, would stand in their way.

Excitement vibrated through the steering wheel. The blue in the sky held the promise of a memorable weekend. He'd even been able to drop off a payment he'd scraped together from his grandfather's accounts. At least it would put things with the care facility on hold. For now. Buy himself more time to figure out exactly what he was doing with his life. Maybe even time to get the position with the sheriff's department. If he wanted it.

Who was he kidding? He wanted it.

He wanted all of it. The job, the home, the family.

Megan sat in the seat next to him, her jeans and pale blue cashmere sweater hugging her curves. Between her feet, she'd stuffed her enormous mystery mom tote. He'd learned such a bag was nearly as handy as his own rucksack. From the depths

SUSAN MAY WARREN & RACHEL D. RUSSELL

of the bright teal and yellow fabric, she held all kinds of survival gear.

Fruit snacks, apple slices, granola bars, water bottles. And at the first rest stop, he'd discovered tweezers, a pocket knife, notepad, and Chapstick.

Maybe she had a little Ranger in her blood. There was something appealing about a girl who knew how to be prepared.

And then she broke out into "Life Is a Highway" and Josh joined in.

Cole swallowed, his heart filled with the memory of his mother belting out songs on family trips, making up lyrics whenever she forgot them. He glanced over at Megan. She was using two Fruit Roll-Ups as drumsticks, jamming on the dashboard and door like she was a rock star.

He loved her. Amazing, wonderful, giving, Mae. He *loved* her.

And he wasn't even jolted, rocked, or unraveled by that realization. Maybe because, deep inside, he'd *always* loved her. And now her son too.

Nope, he wasn't going anywhere.

She started in on the second verse and he joined her. Let the words speak to his heart. Because he did love her now like he loved her then. And more.

By the time they took the exit off Highway 35 and pulled into the Bear Creek Resort, his cheeks hurt from smiling and his throat had gone dry from singing. Megan's voice was a little raspy, but the joy hadn't left her face.

"We're going straight into the water park," Josh announced.

"Whoa, Blades, slow down." Cole held out a hand.

"Are you kidding? Do you know how much I've wanted to go to a water park?" Josh hefted his duffel from the Jeep. The kid was on a mission.

Cole could think of fifteen places he'd rather go than a water park and the list even included some foreign deserts he'd spent time in. His grimace must have shown.

"You look like we're heading into a funeral," Megan said, clearly sizing him up.

"Cesspools of germs." He shivered. "Water parks gross me out."

She raised a brow at him. "Really, Ranger? You're tougher than that." She lugged her small, silver suitcase from the back.

"I'm serious. I'm not sure all my Army vaccinations will cover me for this place." He took her suitcase from her.

"Josh is going to have a blast with the team. It'll be fine." She took a few steps toward him, leaned in, and gave him a sweet smile. "I'll take care of you."

Oh.

And those five words were exactly the reason he found himself donning snow globe swim trunks from the hotel gift shop forty-five minutes later and plummeting down a plastic tube slide behind Josh. They landed in a splash and Cole picked Josh up, tossed him into the deeper pool.

The whistle blew and a lifeguard picked up his megaphone, pointed at Josh as Cole came up out of the water. "Hey, kid—tell your dad not to do that."

Josh grinned. "Don't do that, *Dad!*" And he shrieked with laughter before diving into the lazy river.

But any response stuck in Cole's throat. He blinked, wiped the water from his face. His gaze landed on Megan standing at the side of the pool. She returned his smile with her own. Josh dove at him for another tag, and he couldn't stop the laughter that bubbled from his chest before he jumped back in.

An hour later, they'd changed for dinner and made their way down to the hotel restaurant. Megan slid into the booth next to Cole. Josh sat across from them, his eyes scanning the oversized menu.

"I'm starving," he said.

"Let's make sure your eyes aren't bigger than your stomach," Megan said.

"Where's the fun in that?" Cole asked.

"Unless you want to be on stomachache watch all evening, you'd better trust me on this one."

The restaurant catered to the hockey crowd, with auto-graphed photos and jerseys hung on the walls. He savored the meal, not only for the best mozzarella sticks but for the company. Between Josh's giggles and Megan's soft laughter.

She'd even managed to work information out of the waitress —newly engaged. No definitive plans yet. And by the end of the conversation, the waitress was practically begging for Megan's business card and thinking Deep Haven was probably the best place in the world to tie the knot. Yet it never came across as a sales pitch. Megan's genuine care led the petite redhead to ask questions and listen to the answers in between soda refills and table checks and plate removals.

He walked them to their room with reluctance. They were two floors below him, and Josh headed straight to one of the queen beds and flopped.

Megan stood in the doorway and he wanted so much to kiss her goodnight. He reached out to her, slid his hand around hers.

"Thank you for allowing me to come."

"Of course. You belong here." She looked up at him, and the urge to kiss her nearly made him lean in. Except, Josh was right there, sitting in the room. Nope. This time, he'd follow Megan's lead.

She didn't help when her gaze flicked from his lips to his eyes as if she were thinking the same thing. "We'll see you at breakfast?"

"Yes, ma'am. I'll be down at seven." He rubbed his thumb across the back of her hand, gave it a squeeze before letting it go. And forced himself to stop staring at the soft curve of her lips.

"I should get inside." She nodded her head toward the room.

"Yes, ma'am."

Neither one of them moved. Megan chewed on her lower lip.

He'd never wanted to linger in a hotel hallway longer.

"Can we play cards?" Josh squeezed into the space between Megan and the partially open door like a splash of cold water.

"Yeah. Sure, hon." Megan took a step backward into the room, not breaking her eye contact. "Why don't you start shuffling the deck? The cards are in my tote bag."

Josh disappeared.

"Okay. I'd better, uh, go. Now," Cole said.

She wrinkled her nose but nodded and stepped inside the room, the door latching behind her.

He returned to his room and punched in the number for the U.S. Marshals Service. Voicemail. Again. He'd been trying to reach someone for twenty-four hours, hoping to cancel his interview.

No such luck. He sat on the bed and tossed the phone down next to him before picking up his notes. He looked through the papers and tournament schedule. He had enough time to meet the interviewer and then get back to the arena in time. It'd be close, but really, he didn't see any other way. As he stared at his paperwork, doubt edged his thoughts.

Was he really going to bail on the plans he'd made with David? He punched in David's number.

David answered, his voice a little groggy. "Hey, how's it going?"

"Good. I'm in Minneapolis—I'm supposed to have that interview tomorrow."

"Excellent. I'll be flying back to DC tomorrow. I'm glad you decided to follow through with it."

Cole stood up and looked at his reflection in the window. He'd put on a little weight since returning to Deep Haven. All those family meals. Maybe he'd been a little too thin before. He took a breath. "Actually, I was thinking of canceling it."

SUSAN MAY WARREN & RACHEL D. RUSSELL

"Because of the girl?"

"Yeah." Cole began pacing through the hotel room.

"Dude. Are you ready to give up the job for a girl?"

And he didn't know why David's tone irked him, but, "She's not just any girl." Not any girl at all. Megan turned every dark, dismal day into joy. Laughter. Family. "You know I've known Megan practically my entire life, David. She's the one."

It felt good, something soul cleansing to say that.

"You know, Cole, you're like a brother to me. I don't begrudge you any happiness. It's just—don't you think you should at least show up for the interview?"

Cole ran a hand through his hair. "I don't know. Why?"

"Listen. I've been talking you up every chance I get. I went out on a limb for you, assured them you were worth waiting for. Can't you have this girl *and* this job? Why does it have to be one or the other?"

"I appreciate that, I really do—but she'd never leave Deep Haven."

"My advice? Show up. It doesn't hurt to have the discussion. It's a great opportunity for you and we'd get to work together again. It'll give you options. Don't close the door. You never know..."

David didn't finish. He didn't have to. *You never know when your relationship is going to fall apart.* Like his last one—his marriage to Rebecca.

Cole let out a breath. "I'll think about it. Thanks for everything, bro." He wouldn't even venture to explain the whole Trevor issue. David would be certain Cole had lost his mind.

"Let me know how it goes." David hung up. Cole studied the schedule one more time. It might be too late to cancel his interview, but he *could* show up for David's sake. Let them know his plans had changed. Maybe he could be on standby.

But he'd hustle through the interview and hightail it to the game. Because the more he thought about the sound of Josh's laughter and Megan's song, the more he knew that was the only place he wanted to be.

~

Cole was late. Really late.

Popcorn, hotdogs, and soft pretzels permeated the Xcel Energy Center arena. The place buzzed. Megan scanned the stairway entrances again, searching for Cole.

He'd come to breakfast wearing his suit and when she'd given him a raised brow, he'd told her he needed to run to the interview—that he hadn't been able to cancel. She'd handed him his ticket and reminded him what time the opening face-off would be. And then she'd pressed him and said what maybe she should have left unsaid.

You really should follow through on the interview. This was your plan.

When he'd paused just a little too long, she'd actually torn out her own heart and encouraged him.

Go on, see it through. I don't want you to have any regrets. You'll have plenty of time to get to the game.

But he'd assured her he wouldn't have any regrets. Promised he'd be here for the face-off and would help her with the post-game pizza party order she'd signed them up for. For sure.

And yet, his seat next to her remained vacant.

Parents, families, friends, and other tournament teams flooded the arena, packing the family section.

Why hadn't she told him she needed him? That she wanted him to stay and be part of their lives?

Because, really, deep down, she wanted him to want her—them—without being asked. She wanted, for once, to be chosen. Remembered. *Treasured.*

Maybe he was having second thoughts. Maybe she'd misread the look on his face when the lifeguard had referred to him as

Josh's dad. Maybe he *had* decided his commitment to David was more important.

She stood up in her seat next to Ivy when the team took the ice to be introduced, cupping her hands around her mouth and cheering for Josh.

"Want some cotton candy?" Ivy asked. She offered Megan a tuft from Joy's ball of sugar confection.

"No, thanks."

Ivy nodded to the empty seat. "Where's Cole?"

"He had to follow up on something. He'll be here." He had to be.

She'd already sent him two text messages. Still, she punched in his number. Let it ring until it went to voicemail.

Debated, then, "Hey—it's me. Wondering where you're at. Wanted to make sure everything was okay."

She disconnected. Slipped her phone into her pocket, trying not to worry.

Josh skated up to the edge of the ice and she could read the question in his eyes.

She shook her head and mouthed, "Not yet."

He gave her a nod and skated back across the ice to finish the warm-up.

The crowd had swelled, far larger than a typical tournament crowd due to the Blue Ox players' participation throughout the weekend, including special appearances, photo ops, and an exhibition game.

The first period started, and no Cole. Megan checked her phone a couple times. Nothing.

When the first period ended, Ivy leaned toward her. "Have you heard from him?"

Megan checked her phone again. "No. Nothing. And he didn't answer my text."

"Cole sure looked cute with Josh last night."

Megan smiled. "Yeah. They had a good time together."

"So, what about the Hueston place? Are you still moving in to house-sit?"

"No."

Ivy raised an eyebrow.

"I was able to find someone else to do it—one of the ladies from church whose house needs new insulation put in."

Megan scanned the crowd again for any sign of Cole.

"Maybe I shouldn't have encouraged him to talk to the interviewer. Shoot. It is his dream job. He'd be back working with his Ranger buddy."

"You and Josh are his dream."

She made a face.

"Really, Megan. Cole is crazy about you," Ivy said.

Darek leaned forward. "Do you want me to check outside? See if something happened to his ticket?"

Megan looked at the game clock. "I don't want you to miss anything. He'll be here." Really.

"Maybe his phone went dead."

Movement caught her eye and she let out a breath. A man was coming down the stairs and standing at the end of their aisle.

Finally. She turned to Cole.

"I was wor—" Except, not Cole. Trevor. Still painfully handsome. Still drawing looks from those around them. Still grinning at her with a smile that could turn a woman weak.

A different woman. Not her, not anymore.

He wore a blue-and-gold jersey with his dark wash jeans, his dark hair freshly trimmed.

Trevor slid into the seat next to her like he belonged there.

"You can't stay here. This seat is taken." Never, ever, did she really expect him to show up. She hadn't even warned Josh.

"No one's in the seat, Megan. I've watched through the entire first period and no one's been sitting here."

"You don't belong here."

He cocked his head at her. "C'mon. Let me be part of this. I'm his fa —"

"Fine." She cut off his words. "Sit. For now."

A few parents turned their heads at the disruption.

"Please, don't make a scene. Don't ruin this for Josh."

"I won't." He reached out, placed a hand on her arm, his blue eyes oddly soft. He leaned in close and spoke against her ear. "Thanks, Meggie. We're going to have fun. Trust me."

"You'll have to move when my friend arrives."

Trevor lifted a shoulder.

Ivy leaned in on her other side. "That isn't...?"

"Yes." Megan gave her a look. "It is."

Ivy raised an eyebrow, but the cheering started with the buzzer for the second period.

Trevor rose to his feet and cheered for Josh, and it cut away a small piece of her heart as she stood next to him. Listening to him cheer for his son. How many times had she hoped for exactly that? For him to show up in Josh's life?

Except, what would Cole say when he showed up?

Only, he didn't. Halfway through the second period, and no Cole.

Trevor leaned toward her during a timeout, smiled. "You look good, Megan."

She managed a smile. "Thank you."

She sneaked a peek at him while his eyes returned to the game. He'd lost weight and his dark hair had been cut short.

And yet, there was nothing in her heart for him. Nothing that stirred her.

Nothing, no part of Trevor, could compare to Cole. Sure he was handsome, but he didn't have Cole's heart. Cole's dedication.

Cole had been more of a father to Josh in a few weeks than Trevor had been in nine years.

She snagged her phone from her pocket and punched in his number again. It went straight to voicemail. Again.

During the second intermission, Megan felt compelled to introduce Trevor to Darek and Ivy, who graciously greeted him. He was standing there, cheering for Josh like his life depended on it as the team fought against the opposing team's early lead. She rubbed her hand against her chest.

In the third period, the Huskies made a stunning comeback and Megan was pretty sure she'd be hoarse from cheering. Down by one, with seconds left on the clock, Josh got the puck.

He skated around the net, back out, playing with the puck. Passed it off and skated near the net to receive the pass back.

He pulled the puck back, around a couple charging defenders. *Oh, no!* He was going to lose it.

The defenders had locked on, committed. Any second they'd slam Josh into the boards.

He dodged them. Feigned. Flicked the puck to his backhand. And in a second—Josh slapped the puck in.

The siren sounded just as the buzzer went off.

The crowd erupted and Trevor jumped into the air next to her, arms stretched overhead. "That's our boy!"

Our boy.

Cole, where are you?

Then Trevor picked her up, hugging her tight in celebration. The movement so took her by surprise she didn't even resist. He put her back down, ending with a side hug before letting her go.

Okay, that felt way too weird.

The crowd began moving en masse toward the aisles, some of the parents running out on the ice.

She wasn't sure where to go, when Ivy tugged Megan's sleeve. "Will you need a ride back? We need to get Joy back to the hotel. She isn't feeling well."

"Too much cotton candy?"

"Probably." Ivy scooped up her bag. Darek was making his way out to the ice via the other aisle, Joy gripping his hand.

Megan directed Trevor out into the aisle and turned back to Ivy. "Josh and I can catch a ride with one of the other parents if Cole isn't here somewhere."

Ivy nodded, and Megan made her way down to the ice to Josh. Trevor followed behind her.

Megan turned to Trevor. "He isn't expecting you."

"You didn't tell him?"

She swallowed, shook her head. "I wasn't sure you'd show."

Trevor raised a brow, pinned her with a glare. "I see."

She expected more pushback. Instead, he followed her, remained quiet.

Josh charged her on the ice, throwing his arms around her. She pulled him into a hug.

"Great job! You were spectacular!"

"Did Cole see that? He taught me that move!" He was looking past her, toward the stands. Right past Trevor.

"Sorry, bud, no. He couldn't make it." And it occurred to her that here she was making the same excuse for Cole that she always had to for Trevor.

His eyes settled on her companion. "Dad?"

"Hey, Josh, great job." Trevor stepped forward and began lifting his arms, dropped them. Instead, he held out a fist.

"Thanks." Josh gave him a lackluster bump, the excitement gone from his face. And everything around Megan began sinking. Josh looked so baffled and disappointed. Her mistake was clearly written in the uncertainty clouding his face. She should have said something. But, really, she never thought Trevor would actually show up.

He scanned the stands.

The crowds had cleared out of the arena, leaving only a few families reliving the highlights. "Your mom tells me you've just recovered from a sprained wrist."

Josh directed his attention back to Trevor. "Yes, sir." He looked back across the ice. "Um, I gotta get in the locker room with the guys."

"We'll wait for you by the entrance." She only realized her words after he'd skated away.

We. As in her and Trevor. His father.

Nope. She spotted Lucy Brewster, the goalie's mom, and called out to her. "Lucy! Can we catch a ride with you?"

Lucy waved her hand, shaking her head. "I'm sorry, my van is full."

"I can give you a ride back," Trevor said.

She gave him a look.

"I'm going to wait for Josh," she said. Maybe Cole was waiting near the entrance.

But when she got there, joining a few of the other families, there was no sign of Cole.

And when Josh appeared, showered and toting his gear, she turned to Trevor. "Okay." They piled Josh's gear into his Mercedes SUV.

"So, that law degree worked out for you?" she said as he closed the hatch.

He shrugged. "Company car." Right. One more reason the small-town girl never measured up for him. Because a high-powered attorney needed a high-powered wife. Not a small-town nobody.

Josh climbed into the back seat, a little too quiet. He picked up the remote to the overhead video screen.

Megan pursed her lips as she slid into the front. "We're staying at the Bear Creek Resort."

"Fun place." He glanced in the rearview mirror. "It was great to see you play, Josh."

"Thanks." He was scrolling through the shows available. But he looked at her when she turned back, and she could see him blinking back his confusion. Underneath his polite reply, he was wondering the same thing she was. *Why had Trevor shown up and not Cole?*

They pulled into the hotel lot and Megan gathered her bag. "Thanks for the lift."

Josh unbuckled, looked at Trevor. "Are you staying?"

"I don't think he can stay," Megan answered.

"We have a team party," Josh said.

Oh, no. The party. And she'd signed them up to bring the pizzas. With Cole. She unbuckled her seat belt. "Yeah. We need to hustle."

"I should get going. Maybe I can come watch you again some time. Or visit."

Josh looked away and it squeezed her heart. How did she cause the entire day to go so wrong?

Megan slipped out of the SUV and walked to the back hatch. "Glad you made it."

She glanced back at Trevor. Saw his Adam's apple bob and when he blinked back moisture in his eyes, it nearly gutted her. She had to say something.

"Actually, do you—do you want to come to the team party? I could use some help grabbing the pizzas."

"Sure. I'd be happy to. If that's okay with Josh."

Josh nodded, climbed back into the vehicle.

It wasn't until Trevor steered the Mercedes out of the parking lot and onto the main drive that she finally glimpsed Cole's Jeep sitting in the hotel parking lot. She tugged out her phone to check for a message. Nothing. And she couldn't stop the fear that had begun unraveling her entire day.

CHAPTER 14

It had probably been too much to hope that the game had been delayed and that he'd have made it to Megan in time. Cole had glanced at his GPS. Three miles to go to get to the Xcel arena. When he'd heard the interviewer's plane would be late, he'd thought of bailing then—only to learn from the receptionist that the traffic on 35E and surrounding routes were backed up due to several accidents.

There was no way he'd have made it to the game on time.

The Federal Building on Third Avenue had been nearly empty. Not surprising for a Saturday. It reminded him of the older buildings at Fort Benning. Slightly stale, with the ostentatious design of decades past.

And then, Richard Watkins had arrived straight from the airport. A lean man with dark hair and the bearing of a soldier. His gray-green eyes had taken in everything, and Cole immediately felt a kinship with the man. They'd sat down in an empty conference room.

"I know you're in a bit of a rush due to my flight delay," he'd said. "So, here's what I can tell you. You'd be perfect for the job. A high level of skill and integrity. David's talked a lot about you

215

and you're exactly the kind of person we're looking to hire." He'd flipped through the pages of Cole's application. Asked about his time in the Army. "If you're heading to DC to visit David, why don't you stop in at our headquarters? I can give you a tour and we can discuss the position more."

It made complete sense. Exactly what he'd been hoping and planning for. What he'd committed to with David. Instead, the words spilled out. "No. Thank you, but I can't accept the position."

The man leaned back in his chair, nodded, and pulled a business card from his suit pocket. "Here. Take this. In case you change your mind."

Cole had shoved the card into his back pocket and shook the man's hand. "I appreciate your time, but I have somewhere I need to be."

He bypassed the elevator and took the stairs two at a time, blasting through the stairwell door into the lobby. "Don't forget your phone," the receptionist had called to him and held out his phone. "Security said you left it at the metal detector."

He hadn't even taken the time to listen to the messages. All he could think about was getting to the arena. To Megan and Josh.

He'd pulled into the arena parking, wedged his Jeep into a narrow spot against a pillar, and raced inside.

The electricity of the crowds buzzed through the gates when Cole entered. He glanced at his ticket and headed through the arena doors. The entire crowd was standing on their feet, the sound raucous, less than five seconds left on the board.

He spotted Josh's number. He was skating toward the goal, two defenders racing in on him. And just like he'd taught him, Josh waited for them to lock in, commit to it, then he feigned, brought the puck through to his backhand. Tight. Perfect execution. And with one well-timed slap, it flew under the goalie's pads. The cheering of the crowd nearly drowned out the final buzzer. Josh threw his hands into the air, his teammates rushing him.

Cole found Megan in the crowd, a dark-haired man standing next to her, shouting, with his arms stretched overhead. And he turned to Megan, threw his arms around her, and lifted her off her feet. And when he set her down, he left his arm around her a moment too long.

What in the world?

His throat went dry, his fists balled. The guy was wearing a jersey with Josh's number, and Cole did the quick math.

Trevor. Josh's dad. At the game. In *his* seat. Except maybe it wasn't his seat—not really. Her words pierced him. *I'd always hoped for redemption—hoped he'd come for us. Even prayed for it.*

He couldn't watch a moment longer. Cole crumpled the ticket and walked away.

Don't jump to conclusions. He repeated the words to himself a half dozen times while he drove back to the hotel to wait for Megan. There had to be a plausible reason.

From his hotel window, he watched the parking lot as each family returned. And, finally, Darek, Ivy, Joy, and Tiger. But no Megan. No Josh.

He tried calling Megan. It went to voicemail.

He texted Darek, who sent a prompt reply.

She said they'd get a ride back. Is everything okay? Missed you at the game.

A ride back. He didn't want to know. A Chevy and a Mercedes pulled into the lot, taking two of the last spaces.

Cole's heart nearly stopped when Josh jumped out the back door of the Mercedes.

Moments later, Megan had stepped out of the passenger side and…Trevor from the driver's side.

What—?

Then as they'd stood at the back and talked, he'd watched his hopes die. They'd all climbed back into the Mercedes. Driven away.

And now, twenty minutes later, Cole paced his room, took some deep breaths, and watched out the window. Waited another five minutes until the Mercedes returned to the lot and Megan hopped out carrying a stack of pizzas.

The party. How could he have forgotten the party?

He ran down the stairwell to the lobby and approached the information desk. "I'm looking for Megan Carter, with the Deep Haven Huskies team. We're supposed to have a room reserved for a party."

"Sure, let me look that up." She punched the keys on her keyboard. "Okay, it looks like they're in our Sunrise conference room. If you head down this hall here, it's the second room on the right."

"Thank you."

Cole stepped away, turned down the hall

"Hey, I heard you asking for Megan."

Cole turned. The guy from the arena. Trevor. Oh, yeah, Cole wanted to tear him apart. From his shiny leather shoes to the smug smile on his face.

Trevor stepped in front of him. "You must be Megan's friend she mentioned."

Cole gave a noncommittal shrug. He didn't owe this guy anything.

"You don't belong here. This is my time with my family."

"They aren't your family." Cole ground his jaw.

"Yeah? I'm pretty sure Josh's birth certificate says otherwise. He doesn't need you and neither does Megan."

The anger broke loose and Cole couldn't stop himself. He reached out, shoved Trevor against the glass windows, his voice a low growl. "How dare you—"

"Cole—stop!"

Cole turned, his fists still full of Trevor's jacket collar. Megan was standing with her eyes wide, Josh right next to her, his mouth open. "Let him go." She stepped closer, her eyes bright with moisture. "Let him go."

"He shouldn't be here." Cole released Trevor, straightened his own jacket.

Trevor squared himself off. "This? *This* is the guy you're allowing around my son?"

Darek stepped out into the hallway, with Ivy tucked behind him. "Is everything okay out here?"

Trevor leveled a look at Cole, then at Megan.

Yeah, well, the joke's on you, creep. Cole stepped back, let Megan have her space to tell the guy exactly what she thought of him.

Except, she turned to Cole. Her voice held a steel he'd never heard before. "You need to go."

"What?"

"You need to go."

Josh blinked, his eyes reddened.

Nice. Cole turned away. He wanted to destroy something.

And that was it. He didn't say another word. Just walked away. Straight to his room and began shoving everything into his duffel bag. Including his ridiculous jersey. What had he been thinking?

A knock at the door jolted him moments later and he opened it, expecting Darek.

Megan stood there, alone, her eyes wet with tears.

"I—I had to, Cole." She tried to step toward him, but he put out his hand. Backed away. The more distance the better.

"No." Bitterness clipped his words. "No, you didn't. Why did *I* have to leave?"

"Because you were making things worse!"

"Worse? Excuse me—he started it. Why is he even here?"

"I was trying to fix it—I had to let him come."

"Maybe you should stop trying to fix things—because you just destroyed everything."

She flinched at the words. "Cole?"

"I saw you *with* him. I saw you at the game with Trevor." And sheesh, he knew he sounded unreasonable, but frankly, it was Rebecca all over again. "But I knew everything would be okay. I trusted you."

What a fool he was.

"You gave up my spot to him. After you told me he'd never take my place." He zipped up his duffel. "And then you left me—"

"You didn't show up. You—you broke your promise."

"You talk a lot about promises—which promise is this? To come back to Deep Haven?"

"No. The one to be in our lives. To be here for us."

"I tried to be here—I couldn't help it. But maybe it's a good thing. I got to see who you really are now."

"I should have known better. I'm sorry I ever relied on you."

"I'm sorry I ever came back to Deep Haven."

She wiped tears from her eyes. "You didn't even show up to get the pizzas for Josh's party. And you were *here*. Do you know what that did to him?"

"You're the one that roped me into helping you with this. If I'd have known you had your own contingency plan, I would have stayed at the interview." He took another step back and wasn't sure he cared that the door was open, their argument streaming out into the hallway. "Is that why you encouraged me to stay for my interview? So you could *explore your other options*?" He shook his head.

Her mouth gaped, but he couldn't seem to stop himself. "I saw how he looked at you. I should have known—you tried to tell me how much you hoped to make your relationship with him work." His voice turned ragged. "Clearly, I was too dense to listen to what you were saying."

Her voice trembled. "No, Cole. I want you. How can you say that? Why can't we talk this through?"

"Because, Becca, I have nothing else to say to you."

Megan's hand covered her mouth, she hiccupped, shook her head. Her lips moved, but nothing came from them. She looked…shattered.

He might actually be ill.

He walked back to the doorway, put his hand on the door. "You need to go."

She hadn't walked inside and now he just closed the door.

Just closed it on her protest, on her open mouth. On her wrecked expression, her hazel eyes spilling over with tears.

Closed the future, the family, the home.

Closed it all. He pressed his hand over the door. And refused to open it even as her words filtered through the door.

"I love *you*, Cole."

Whatever. He'd been there before. And he should know better.

He sat back on the bed, the noise in his head roaring like a C-130.

His phone rang. David. The man who'd seen him through the worst of his divorce. The man who'd put in a good word for him with Richard Watkins. The man who'd warned him.

"Now's not a great time."

"Interview went that badly?" David laughed. "My flight just landed. Wanted to check in."

Cole said nothing. Couldn't say anything.

"Cole?"

"Yeah. I'm here." He swallowed, his voice ragged.

"What's going on?"

"You were right. I can't believe you were right." Shoot. He blinked back the moisture that slicked his eyes. "About Megan." He glanced at the closed door. *I love* you, *Cole.* "Hey, man, I need to go. I'll catch you another time. I've got to get out of here."

"Whoa. No way. I'm not letting you drop that and leave." Cole could imagine David waiting at his airport gate, his blond hair grown out into unruly waves and his gray eyes taking in everything around him. No one would suspect the towering man had nearly bled out after a roadside bomb had mangled their vehicle. "Are you still in Minneapolis?"

"Yeah."

"I just landed in Chicago on my way to DC tonight after some training in Seattle. I can be to Minneapolis in..." Cole heard a rustling noise through the phone. "It looks like there's a flight to Minneapolis in an hour. I can be there in a little over three hours."

"No. I...I'm okay." Hardly, but he'd managed to figure out his life last time, and this hadn't gone nearly as far. At least he hadn't proposed. Hadn't gotten married. Maybe this was a last-minute divine rescue. Although it didn't feel like it. Still. Keep moving. Cole tugged the business card from his pocket. "How about I meet you in DC tonight? I need somewhere to clear my head."

"Sure. I have a car at Dulles. Go to Arrival Door Five and call me when you're ready."

Cole grabbed his bag. The sooner he got on the road, the better. By the looks of it, Megan had her return ride covered by Mr. Mercedes.

"Got it."

"Hey—Cole, you okay? Really?"

No. Nothing would be okay until he'd put Deep Haven in his rearview mirror once and for all.

Megan swiped back a tear and scrubbed a rust stain from the sink. How could Cole possibly accuse her—*her*—of being unfaithful? Wouldn't even let her explain. Because all she could think of when she saw him in the hall with Trevor was custody battle.

Trevor knew the law. And he'd threatened to take her to court. She just couldn't risk it. Her house was crazy clean after two days of frenzied, anger-laced scrubbing. It would be ready for whoever decided to buy the house.

She was moving out, as soon as she could find a place.

She didn't need Cole Barrett. Not as her landlord, not as her business assistant, and definitely not as her husband, let alone Josh's father. She'd always known happy endings were for someone else. Her entire business model was based on it. Well, she'd put her life back together before and she'd do it again. Alone.

She turned on the water to rinse the rust and it bounced off the bottom of the sink and sprayed her face.

Whatever. Grabbing a towel, she wiped her face. Stared at her reflection in the mirror. Aw, she looked like a wreck.

Again. Not unlike when Cole had left her the last time. She didn't even know where he was. He'd checked out and left them behind like forgotten baggage on the curb. Left her to beg a ride off Darek and Ivy.

She dropped the towel, bent, and scooped up Puck, burying her face in the cat's soft fur.

Calm down. She'd been fine before Cole had landed back in her life. And she and Josh would be just fine now.

"Can we make pancakes?" Josh slid onto a stool at the kitchen peninsula.

She put down the cat and washed her hands. "Sure, hon, but you can't be late for school."

She turned on the burner and began heating the pan. "Are we making them super-sized today?"

"Yes, please."

She pulled out the mix, haphazardly dumping the powder into a bowl before adding water.

SUSAN MAY WARREN & RACHEL D. RUSSELL

She still had to find somewhere to move in to. If only she hadn't turned down the Huestons. And how in the world would she pull off two weddings at once?

Josh padded over to the window in his bare feet. "Do you know where Cole is? Has he come back?"

Megan poured batter into the pan. "I don't know. Are you all packed up for school? I put your lunch in your backpack." She went back to scrubbing the sink.

"He still hasn't called?"

"No." The rust stain was almost gone. Just one tiny smudge she couldn't seem to get rid of.

Josh hadn't stopped asking about Cole since they'd said their brief goodbye to Trevor after the team party. Yeah, some party. After she'd politely declined Trevor's request for a date and climbed onto the hotel bed with Josh. Had tucked him into her arms while he cried, ripping out so many pieces of her heart.

All she'd wanted was to keep the peace with Trevor. Show him she and Josh were fine without him. Satisfy his need to drop in on their lives. Yeah, except, Cole hadn't cared to hear the truth from her, which meant exactly one thing. Deep down, he didn't actually love her.

"I think it's best that you don't count on Cole. I really don't want to talk about him anymore." The words came out tight.

"But—he—"

"Josh!" Her raised voice filled the small apartment. "I *don't* want to talk about him. You have to stop asking about him. He's gone and he's not coming back." She sucked in a deep breath. Smoke. "The pancakes!" It registered in her mind the same time Josh shouted.

Acrid black billowed from the pan.

She swiped the pan from the burner and turned off the stove. A piercing blare blasted through the apartment. The smoke detectors had been hardwired and all three of them erupted in quick succession. Even on its highest setting, the stove vent did little to pull any smoke from the room. Megan grabbed a towel and waved it at the smoke detector with zero success.

"No! No-no-no!" She hauled a dining room chair into the kitchen and stood on it, flailing the towel until the electronic blasts ceased.

"Hey, Megs, are you okay?" Ivy opened the apartment door and let herself in. "Oh, Megan…" Ivy's eyes went from the blackened pancakes to Megan's bare feet on the chair.

Yeah, Megan probably looked pathetic. She'd donned her rattiest clothes and put barely a thought into pulling her hair back. Nothing said I-don't-care like chipped toenail polish, greasy hair, and an eight-year-old torn T-shirt.

"I hope you weren't coming for breakfast. Unless you like blackened pancakes and bad company."

"No, no thanks." Ivy dropped her satchel and opened the window, letting in the cold, early-February air.

"Breakfast is going to have to be fend-for-yourself, Josh."

He nodded, avoided looking at her. She wanted to reach out, hold him. But she couldn't stand the thought of him pulling away. He tugged on his socks and shoes.

"Unfortunately, we don't have much because I still need to go shopping."

"However," Ivy interjected, "I've brought you half a dozen of World's Best, so, donuts for the win!" She set the box onto the countertop in front of Josh and flipped open the lid. "I'll bet you can find something you like in here. Grab it fast before it tastes like it came from a smokehouse."

He nodded and snagged the chocolate-filled Long John. "Thank you." He hitched his backpack onto his shoulder. "I'd better go wait for my ride. Bye."

No hug goodbye today. Well, she probably didn't deserve one.

"Goodbye." The words caught in Megan's throat. "I love you."

The door snapped closed.

Megan turned to Ivy. "I'm a terrible mother."

"Everyone burns the food sometimes."

"No. I got mad at Josh. He wouldn't quit asking about Cole and I yelled at him." She dumped the frying pan into the sink and filled it with water. "I just wish I hadn't dragged Josh into the middle of it."

"Are you ready to talk about what happened?"

"Not really." Megan gave the pan a furious scrubbing.

"It isn't over, right? I mean—you two are crazy about each other."

"Crazy sums it all up. Because you heard me tell him to go." She could still see the wrecked look in his eyes. As if she had wholly decimated him. The memory carved out her heart and she wanted to weep. And then... Oh, her heart still ached. Her voice dropped to a whisper. "And when I went to find him, to explain, he called me Becca. And then, he told *me* to go."

Ivy sucked in a breath. "Megs." She set down her maple Long John and folded Megan into her arms. "I'm sorry."

And all the emotions Megan had tried to hold together broke free in sobs. "How could I let him into our lives? He knows me. He should know I'd never do that to hurt him."

"You used to talk about getting back together with Trevor. And Cole's got a wounded heart too. It's hard to trust when you've been betrayed so many times."

"But Trevor and I are over. Way over." She pulled away, wiped her nose with a tissue, and threw it into the trash. "It doesn't matter that he's had a turnaround in his life. I thought Cole was the one who'd keep his promises. The one who might love me—might see me as...enough."

"I think he does love you." Ivy went to the sink and dumped a generous amount of powdered cleanser into the pan and began scrubbing. "Cole does want you. Or, he did."

And Megan couldn't escape the memory of the rejection on

his face when she'd told him he needed to go. Like she'd crushed him with those four words.

"If that were enough, then he would have listened when I tried to explain. Instead, he shut me out. Ignored all the promises he made, and then he abandoned us. Just left us there. He said he was sorry he ever came back to Deep Haven."

Which meant sorry he'd come back to her. He didn't even have to say the words.

"Pain says ugly things."

"Don't do that, Ivy." Megan bit her lip and blinked back tears. "Don't defend what he said to me."

"Megan, I'm not."

"Ivy, my parents left me. Trevor left me. And now, Cole. I tried so hard to do what's right—fill their needs."

"We can't earn anyone's love any more than we can earn God's love."

Megan let out a sharp laugh. "If God loves me as much as I try to believe, then why does my life feel so empty?"

Ivy frowned. "Is it really empty?"

Josh's gear bag leaning against the door caught Megan's eye. She could almost hear his laughter fill the space. She wiped the tears that fell. And Ivy, standing there washing her pan.

"No." Her voice cracked, jagged with emotion.

"God is enough. You don't have to be—you can't be, in the deepest sense of it all." Ivy grabbed the towel and began drying the pan. "We are all wholly inadequate. That's exactly why we need our Savior. We sin, no matter how hard we desire not to. We hurt each other." She set the clean pan down on the stove. "And yet, He loves us."

Megan covered her face in her hands. "I can't escape the feeling that I should have done more. He didn't ask me for anything—maybe that's where I failed."

"I understand how you feel. I wanted desperately to fix Darek's problems, but I ended up having to take away his son on behalf of the court!" Ivy closed her eyes. "Let me tell you—that was a nightmare for someone who prides themselves on fixing things." She turned on the burner. "He felt betrayed, of course."

Megan blew her nose again, wiped her eyes on her shirt sleeve. "What happened?"

"God took care of it in ways I never would have guessed or imagined. Far better than I could have." Ivy poured batter into the pan. "Darek had to choose forgiveness—but he had to find his own path there."

"I don't think there's any way I can make Cole forgive me."

"Stop trying, Megan. That's what I had to learn. I had to let God do His work and accept whatever His answer was. I realized it wasn't up to me to fix it." She set down the bowl of batter. "And it isn't up to you. You can't depend on earning Cole's love." She looked at Megan. "I would never be enough to earn Darek's love, to put it in your terms. I'm going to fail."

Megan leaned into the words. Except, Cole had chosen *not* to love her.

And never would. And she wasn't sure how she'd come to peace with that. "I heard from Seb that Cole was hired by the U.S. Marshals Service," Megan said. "I have two weddings to do by myself." She gave Ivy a look. "Cole emailed me the spreadsheet file he created for the Crawford-Lee wedding. I couldn't even make myself open it."

Ivy plated a small stack of pancakes and slid them in front of Megan. "Trust God."

"I was going to eat the donuts." Megan gave her a half smile.

"I don't recommend putting yourself into a sugar coma. You're going to need clear thinking to pull off two weddings. I'll talk to Raina and we'll see what we can do to help you out." She reached out and placed a hand on Megan's arm. "You're going to get through this. Remember, none of this surprises God."

"Thank you—but you really don't have to do that. I'll figure it out." She shivered against the cold air and slammed the window closed.

"You don't have to figure it out on your own. That's what I'm trying to get through your head." Ivy grabbed her coat. "I need to get going. I'll connect with you later, okay?" She reached forward, squeezed Megan's shoulder before drawing her into another hug. "Really. You're going to get through this."

Megan closed the door behind her, the silence assaulting her senses.

Just like it had when Trevor walked out, leaving her heaving on the bathroom floor with morning sickness. Just like it had when her parents left town, without even a thought of her and Josh.

Alone.

Except... *But even the hairs of your head are all numbered. Fear not, therefore; you are of more value than many sparrows.*

She watched Ivy's car pull away. Cole's Jeep still wasn't at his house, but Nathan had stopped by and shoved a For Sale sign into the snow. So, the house was officially on the market.

And apparently, so was she.

Trust God.

CHAPTER 15

*T*hree nights in DC hadn't done anything to still the restlessness in Cole's heart, and his return to Deep Haven to finish packing up the house only made it worse. The VFW had become his hiding place and he sat at the bar, staring at his untouched drink.

He'd avoided Megan since he'd returned to town.

He could still see her face that night at the hotel. The hurt, shock, and anger. But he knew what he saw. She didn't even deny it.

She hadn't called. Not that he expected it. If he'd been wrong, then he couldn't imagine she'd have much to say to him. Okay, maybe she'd have a lot to say. And if he'd been right, then what was left to say?

He just didn't come back from betrayal. *We can work this out. We can rebuild our marriage.* Rebecca's voice, right before he walked out on her. But she'd left him first, right?

And at the time, his anger felt justified. Even satisfying.

Not this time.

By the time his plane had landed in DC, he didn't know what to believe even after two hours of pacing and ranting across the over-priced, six-hundred-square-foot span of David's apartment. Cole had stared at the nearly vacant two-bedroom. A crash pad for a nomad. No more a home than the sandy tents they'd slept in halfway around the world.

Home.

David had handed him a bottle of water and told him to sit down. Then he'd surprised Cole.

What are you doing here, man? You've never been this worked up over a girl—not even Rebecca. Go home. He'd reached out and placed a hand on Cole's shoulder. *Work it out. Find a way. I'm kicking you off my couch.*

He'd tried to shake off David's words. They'd driven him back to Deep Haven. Cole told himself it was to pack. Let Nathan sell his place. He could send Cole the papers.

Except, he'd barely packed half a box before making his way back here to his new stool at the bar where he'd spent the past two nights.

Darek slid onto the stool next to him, followed by Casper on the opposite side.

"Why does this feel like an ambush?"

Darek clapped him on the shoulder. "We're here as the brothers you never had. You know, brothers have a way of telling you how it is."

"Come on, guys, really? Both of you?"

"Don't make us take this outside. There's two of us, Ranger." Casper ordered a Coke. "Even at your best, I don't know that you could beat the both of us."

Darek nodded. "Lucky for you, we aren't here to fight. We're actually here to meet with Seb and Jensen about starting a team and decided we'd swing over to see how you are."

Cole stared at his drink. "Good luck with that—the team."

"Dude—I heard a rumor that you're bailing on us. What gives?" Casper took his Coke from the bartender.

"I was wrong."

Casper snagged a pretzel from the bowl on the counter. "About what?"

"Megan."

Darek leaned in. "Yeah, I'm still waiting to hear what in the world happened in Minneapolis."

"She lied to me, that's what happened. Just like my ex-wife."

Casper frowned. "That doesn't sound like Megan."

"I would agree with you except I saw it all happen." Even as he said the words, they'd lost their venom. She'd looked...devastated by his accusations. Not guilty or caught. And then she'd gotten angry. Maybe the kind of angry that comes from being wrongly vilified.

He'd hurt her.

Darek's brows drew together. "Sometimes what we see isn't an accurate representation of the truth."

"Even still—it would be better for her to marry Josh's dad." He'd missed Josh's game. Left the kid hanging without even a goodbye. And, oh, the way Josh's face crumpled when he came out the door, saw Cole with Trevor pressed up against the wall. Geez, he was just like his grandfather. Josh deserved better.

Casper put a hand on his shoulder. "That couldn't be farther from the truth. You know my story about Layla. I can't even believe it, but I once thought something along the lines of what you're saying. I even tried to get Owen to marry Raina. I can't begin to tell you how wrong that would have been for every single one of us."

"I saw her with her ex. They looked pretty friendly." Cole tried to push the image from his mind. How easily he'd been replaced. "And then, she chose him over me. Right there, in the middle of the party." He gestured toward Darek. "You saw it."

"Don't be dense, Cole. You know, for an Army Ranger, you're sure obtuse." Casper took a drink of his Coke.

"Has it ever occurred to you that she was terrified Trevor would engage her in a custody battle? That maybe she was trying to keep you from getting an assault charge?" Darek narrowed a look at him. "Do you really think taking the Deputy Marshal job will solve your problems?"

"Or are you willing to stay and fight for the woman you love?" Casper said.

"Are you willing to find forgiveness?" Darek still held his eyes on him.

"And going to quit letting anger fuel your decisions?" Casper added.

"Admit you were wrong?"

"Quit pushing people away?" Casper set down his drink like a gavel.

"Take a breath. Sheesh." Cole swallowed. "Custody?"

"He's a lawyer, dude. A high-powered lawyer with far deeper pockets and legal skills than Megan has."

Megan was the kind of person who might feel pressured to say yes to the needs of others. To, yes, fix the problem herself.

Cole grimaced.

He heard his terrible words to her. *I'm sorry I ever came back to Deep Haven.*

And the look on her face...stripped. Because he might as well have said he was sorry he'd ever come back to *her.*

"Don't let your pride stop you from working through this with Megan," Casper said. "The truth is you walked out on her the same way your grandfather emotionally checked out on you. And you may not have left any physical marks on her, but I'm sure the emotional beating you gave her left a few open wounds."

Cole tightened his grip on the glass, the thought turning his gut. He hadn't meant to hurt her. Or maybe he had.

Or maybe he was just tired of being hurt and fired back without thinking. Because, yeah. He'd learned to act first. Protect himself. Whether that meant lashing out or leaving. And he'd done both.

Darek and Casper stood to go as Seb, Kyle, and Jensen entered the VFW together. "Looks like our meeting is about to start." Darek paused. "Listen, Cole. There will always be pain in this life. Always be people we care about who hurt us. But you can't abandon them or push them away every single time, or you'll always end up alone. Relationships are hard...but they're worth it. Forgiveness is worth it." He looked at Casper. "Take it from a couple hardheaded, happily married brothers. Take a risk."

Casper nodded. "Take some time to think about what you really want your life to be before you leave town. Okay?"

He nodded halfheartedly, but the words soaked into Cole as he sat there surrounded by the sounds of the men discussing the potential for a local Crisis Response Team and the niggling sense that he should be part of it.

He left the VFW, climbed into his Jeep, and drove toward the house.

But he couldn't stop there. It stood dark. Vacant, like his days since he'd left Megan and Josh. He kept driving until he reached the memory care facility.

Restore us.

God does not waste our suffering. And then Pastor Dan had added the words that Cole still didn't quite know what to do with. *If we never suffer, how do we ever realize we need more?*

More. Like Christ in his life. Not a token Bible in his bedroom, but an integral part of his life. And...forgiveness?

What if he can't apologize?

Cole had determined he'd never become like his grandfather. Never lash out at those closest to him. Protect the vulnerable.

The truth is you walked out on her the same way your grandfather emotionally checked out on you.

The words seeped into him, permeating to the marrow of his bones.

He could do better—he *was* better, right?

Or maybe not. Maybe, despite his efforts, he was exactly the same as his grandpa. Broken, mourning, and alone.

After being buzzed in, he went to his grandfather's room.

Empty.

The bed was stripped. The room cleaned. The smell of pine cleaner and disinfectant permeated the air.

What?

"Mr. Barrett? I'm so sorry—we tried to reach you." Ms. Chase, the case manager, was walking down the hall.

"Where's my grandfather?"

She stilled. "I'm so sorry. He's gone."

Gone. His grandfather was gone? No. He'd expected to have more time to wrestle with forgiveness. To feel *ready* for it. The overwhelming sense that he was too late poured over him. He put a hand on the doorframe and blinked back the moisture in his eyes. "When did he pass?"

Her brows raised and she sucked in a gasp. "Goodness, no, he didn't die."

Cole stood, faced her. "I don't understand. Where is he then?"

"Our understanding had been that you were going to pay your grandfather's bill before our next medical transport to Duluth. That's why we tried to call you on Friday. We couldn't get through."

Friday. When he was on his way to the tournament. "I *did* pay it—dropped it off Thursday afternoon." They'd *moved* him. Cole could imagine how confused the already jumbled mind of his grandpa must be.

"I don't have record of it in the books." She scanned the documents in her clipboard.

"Where's my grandfather?"

She shook her head. "I'm—I'm not sure."

"What do you mean, *you're not sure?*"

"He was on the transport list—but now, I'm not seeing his name on the final roster." She pursed her lips together.

"How do you lose a patient?"

She grew flushed. "I don't mean he's *lost*. I just don't know where he is right now. I'm wearing a few different hats right now—"

"That sounds an awful lot like *lost* to me."

"I'll find him." She tucked a lock of hair behind her ear and pressed the call button on the wall. "Jeannie, can you tell me where Mr. Barrett is? His room is stripped down and he isn't on the final transport roster."

A voice came over the speaker. "He's currently in a physical therapy session. His room was moved to 110 because of a plumbing issue in 73."

"Thanks." She turned to Cole. "See, he's fine."

Cole's mouth tightened.

"Okay, now that we've located him, I'm going to go look into the payment issue. His therapy session will probably be running another fifteen minutes. You're welcome to watch from the observation window outside the therapy room."

She pointed down the corridor and Cole stopped in front of the interior window. Several patients worked with staff in the large, rubber-matted room. His grandfather walked slowly between two parallel bars as the therapist stood behind him holding on to a support band around his waist.

"Are you Mr. Barrett's grandson?" A male nurse approached from the main corridor. A big man, sporting a dark beard and tattoos.

Cole nodded.

"When we were preparing to move him for transport, we found this box of personal effects." The man handed a shoebox to Cole. "Ms. Chase asked me to give it to you."

The man gave him a nod and disappeared, leaving Cole

alone in the long hallway. He remained at the window, watching his grandfather.

So frail. So lost. *Restore us.* Cole placed a hand against the window pane.

Forgiveness is worth it.

Oh, God. He'd clung to his anger. Fed it for so many years. Because that was what kept him safe. Or so he thought. But now? Now, he couldn't escape the sense that he'd made a mess of it all.

His grandfather stumbled forward and Cole's breath snagged. The therapist held the waistband firm. Kept him from falling.

And inside, something began to shake free. Anger maybe. Or the sense of betrayal.

The therapist eased his grandfather down into the wheelchair at the end of the parallel bars. The old man shook, but settled in, exhausted.

Were those...tears?

He swallowed the thick emotion caught in his throat. His grandfather hadn't even cried when Cole's parents died.

God does not waste our suffering.

Cole leaned his head against the cool glass. Somewhere, buried inside the shell of a man, was the one he once loved. Trusted. He let his whisper fill the empty space. "I forgive you." He took a breath, undone suddenly. But maybe, right now, he could find his way back, and he repeated the words. "I forgive you, Grandpa."

And he let that soak into him, uncertain what it could mean to him to not carry the burden anymore.

He walked back down the corridor, carrying the box with him.

The clerk at the reception desk looked up. "Mr. Barrett, I spoke with Ms. Chase and she wanted me to let you know that they had found the missing payment and that's why the transport roster had been changed. The paperwork just hadn't been entered into the system. Everything is good to go now. We're very sorry for the mix-up."

"Thank you." He nodded, ignored the scrape in his voice, and kept walking, straight out the door. Let the full force of the cool air wash over him.

He climbed into his Jeep. Stared at the box in his hands and lifted off the lid. Inside, he found assorted notes. Random shopping lists, paperclips, a broken pencil, voided checks. The strangest, most useless pile of trash for a man to pack around with him.

He lifted one of the notes and took a closer look. *Milk. Bread. Spaghetti sauce...* Cole sucked in a breath. Blinked back the moisture in his eyes and dug through the rest of the items. It wasn't a box of junk.

Oh, Grandpa.

The realization hollowed him out. Each note was written in Grandma's delicate cursive. Her shopping lists. Her honey-do lists. Cole lifted the broken pencil from the box. It was covered in telltale teeth marks.

I see you chew your pencils too. Your dad used to drive me bananas when he was younger, chewing up all my pencils.

Cole had laughed at the time and apparently left it behind. Maybe one summer. Maybe before he left town.

And Grandpa had held on to it in the same box as his treasured reminders of everyday life with his wife, the one he'd still called his bride after decades of marriage. The love his ravaged mind didn't even remember anymore.

Oh, shoot. Cole sniffed, wiped his nose. These were the reminders Grandpa had packed up. Carried with him, *in hopes he wouldn't forget.*

He dug deeper into the loose paper, and his fingers snagged the corner of an envelope. He lifted it out of the box and stared at the address.

The sealed envelope was addressed to Cole in care of one of his foster homes with an *Undeliverable* return stamp from the postal service.

Are you going to quit letting anger fuel your decisions?

Yeah. Maybe. Cole slid his finger under the edge of the flap, tearing it open and lifting the pages.

He thought he was ready. Ready for excuses. Ready for an explanation. Instead, the words broke through his protective wall, brick by brick.

Dear Cole,

I've stopped drinking with the help of a veterans' group. They talk straight with people like me. Don't let me get away with anything. Hold me accountable. It's good for me. Good for my relationship with God.

I have many regrets. The parts I remember. The parts I don't. I know there's a lot that only you know. That's more than anyone should have to bear. I'm sorry.

I hope to be a better man every single day. If you ever want to come back home, I want you to know that.

Love, Grandpa

If. If he ever wanted to come back home. If he could win her back. If he hadn't destroyed every piece of the relationship they'd built.

By the time Cole returned to the VFW, Kyle and Seb were paying their tab and the others were standing to leave. All eyes turned to him when he approached the table.

He took a breath and then executed his op. "I'm looking for a team to help me pull off a rescue. Who's in?"

The dark clouds in the east were backlit with bright sunshine and Megan couldn't help but hope it was God's sign. He heard her. He saw her. She mattered.

And He'd do his part and hold off the storm.

Trust God.

Cole. It seemed he was using every Ranger skill he possessed for covert operations to avoid her. She hadn't actually seen him since he'd returned, despite every attempt to catch sight of him coming or going from the house.

She knew he'd been by. But, oh, the Sold sign in the yard said all there was to say, and when she called Nathan about a rental, he had one just coming on the market.

Perfect. As perfect of an ending as she could have. And that was okay-ish. But see, God could fix this.

Even if it wasn't how she'd hoped.

She finished setting up wedding number one for the day at the Art Colony. Helpers had come out of the woodwork. Even Kyle had stopped by to see if there was anything he could do to help, and she'd never had Mayor Seb Brewster stop in to unload floral arrangements before.

Ivy and Darek had gone to the Atwoods' Pine Acres Resort to get things set up, and Casper was keeping Josh busy with some project at Evergreen Lodge.

The last thing Megan wanted was a pity party. She tried to send them away, but every one of them refused and assured her they wanted to help.

They were probably all hoping for a sneak peek at Cameron Crawford or one of the many other Blue Ox players who'd arrived in town. She didn't really blame them. Having celebrities wandering around town had everyone on alert, and if she could convince any of the other eligible bachelors on the team to come to town for their nuptials, all the better.

"All set?" Megan took a peek at her bride. Hannah Swanson stood in the makeshift dressing room, elegant and vibrant, her graying hair swept into a twist.

"I can't believe I'm finally marrying Erik."

Megan smiled. "It's been a long time coming, hasn't it?"

Hannah nodded. "I thought we'd have married at eighteen but, you know, life took us in different directions. Careers. Marriage. Illness. Being widowed." She turned to Megan, her blue eyes bright and clear. "I wouldn't trade my life for anything, though. I wouldn't be who I am."

Megan let the words fill her, pressed away the pang of sadness.

Hannah placed a hand on Megan's arm. "Sometimes life surprises you. God surprises you."

Raina slipped through the door, charged with excitement. "I forgot how much I enjoy weddings," she said. "I've got this, Megan. You can head up to the lake."

Megan turned to her bride. "You're all set, Hannah?"

"I am." She smoothed her hands over her simple satin gown.

"You met my assistant, Raina, last night at the rehearsal. She's is going to take things from here, like we planned."

Megan picked up the uncomplicated bouquet of pink peonies tied with a deep purple ribbon and placed it into Hannah's hands.

"Perfect. Thank you." She leaned in and gave Megan a squeeze. "You're the best."

Megan did a final walk-through on her way out. The string quartet played in the main hall while the family and friends took their seats.

She blew out a breath. She still wasn't sure she'd done enough to win Mariah's favor when it came to the North Woods Premier Wedding Planners list despite the hours she'd spent working on it with Cole.

Oh, Cole.

She pressed away thoughts of him. Avoided the tangle of memories that couldn't be unraveled. Nope. She had to stay focused today.

By the time Megan arrived at Pine Acres, Ivy and Claire already had everything set for the ceremony.

Ivy greeted her at the door. "Mariah should be ready for you to help her finish dressing."

It was hard to believe that three weeks ago, there'd still been flooring, sawdust, and plastic across the floor.

It hurt a little to admit what an incredible job Cole had done with the vintage carnival theme. Truly Pinterest worthy and executed to perfection.

Red-and-white striped canvas covered each chair, reminiscent of carnival tents. The twinkle lights had been arranged in a canopy over the room. Megan peeked in the kitchen at the caramel apples, doughy pretzels, and—was that a rearing elephant ice sculpture?

Ivy nudged her. "Amazing," she whispered. "Did you see the High Striker outside?"

"High Striker?"

"You know, the ring-the-bell carnival game with the big hammer? I can't wait to see all the players take a go at it. They had to clear the snow to set it in place." She squeezed Megan's arm. "Looks like a happy ending to me. Someone's getting everything they wanted."

Right. She remembered Cole telling her he'd find one of those. Megan wrinkled her nose. "Yeah. Almost a happy ending. It's enough, though. I'll have the Black Spruce after this." And Cole would have the career he wanted.

Everything ending how it was supposed to end. Yep. *Almost* a happy ending.

Ivy gave her a look, a hint of a smile on her lips. "Don't ever give up on a happy ending or what God might do in your life, Megan. You just don't know how God can surprise you in unexpected ways."

"You're the second person today to say that to me."

"Huh. That's funny. Must be a sign."

The only sign she'd seen was the one Nathan had parked right outside her apartment door. She blew out a long breath.

She'd have to trust that God had a plan for her. One she couldn't earn.

Claire approached. "I've never seen this kind of planning for a wedding before."

"The carnival?"

Claire turned her tablet. "Yes, but I specifically meant these files you sent me. How did you create all this? It's incredible. Made it so easy for Ivy and me to get everyone and everything organized. And it's been a lot."

"I didn't." Megan frowned, stared at the spreadsheet. "Cole did." Before the end of the world as she knew it. A detailed operational mission executed with military precision. Tabs across the bottom organized all the vendors, their contact information, the day-of schedule. A backup plan. All the display layouts.

Claire gave her a half smile. "Well, it's great. We've been able to focus on making sure everyone is ready. Mariah's in the master bedroom finishing getting dressed. Here's her bouquet."

Megan took the bouquet of roses—white on the bottom of each petal with deep red on the inside. "Wow."

"Those are one of my favorites." Claire picked up three smaller bouquets. "I'm going to take these to the bridesmaids. Pictures are scheduled to start in ten minutes."

Megan carried the bridal flowers down the hall and knocked on the door. "Mariah? It's Megan."

"Come in."

She pushed open the door and Mariah sat in a chair with the stylists finishing her hair and makeup. She wore long, false lashes and her smile beneath the pale pink lipstick was photo-white. Her platinum hair was woven into an intricate twist.

"All set? I have your bouquet."

"Yes. I'm ready for the dress."

Megan perused the spreadsheet. "I'm so sorry we weren't able to get the ice cream truck."

"You still couldn't?" Disappointment filled her voice. "It's just...just...I know it's silly, but the first thing he bought me was a two-scoop cone." Her smile relaxed with the memory. "It felt so normal. Here was this big hockey player who could buy anything he wanted and go anywhere he pleased... And he chose a small-town celebration. And ice cream."

"I'm so sorry—"

"I know." The words rang with dismissal.

Megan cringed. She hadn't delivered everything her bride had desired. And it looked like she might actually lose her Premier Wedding Planners slot because of two scoops of ice cream. Despite peanuts, popcorn, ice elephants, and...twinkle lights.

Trust God.

Somehow, over the past day, she'd started to believe Ivy's words. God could fix this. Somehow. She just had to stop trying to fix everything herself and trust Him, right? She'd even stood in her kitchen this morning and said the words. *God, please fix this. I'm choosing to trust You. I'm choosing to believe that You love me.*

She'd live without the registry—it would just mean a harder grind to market the Black Spruce as part of her wedding business.

Mariah reached out and took her hand for balance. Then she stepped into her gown and Megan zipped it up.

The Vera Wang gown was cut in an A-line with a lace-and-crystal overlay across the bodice and extending in ornate swirls down onto the lower skirt. Elegant. Her hair had been topped with a tiara, and diamonds—Megan was pretty sure they were the real thing—sparkled from her ears and around her neck. She looked like she was ready for a *Brides Today* magazine photoshoot.

"You look gorgeous."

"Thank you."

The door opened and three more bridal party members came in. The women, all wearing deep red gowns, carried their bouquets.

Ivy leaned in the door behind them. "They're ready for pictures."

Megan looked at her watch. "Okay, we've got one hour and fifteen minutes for photos, then we'll bring you all back here before guests begin arriving." She handed off the bridal bouquet and let the ladies out to the great room where the men were already waiting.

Cameron wore a black tuxedo, his long, dark hair in slightly wild waves. The Blue Ox center was even more imposing in person. He stood near the tall windows, his blue eyes watching for his bride's entrance.

One would think Megan would have shaken out all her fangirl jitters during rehearsal the day before. But, nope. They resurged when she saw Wyatt Marshall, the team's goaltender, standing nearby with his wife, Coco, on his arm.

Coco's gray-green eyes connected with Megan's, and she gave Megan a supportive smile.

Megan stepped aside and watched for that magical look the groom always gave the bride when he saw her for the first time, when he stood breathless and a little goofy faced.

Yeah, that look got her every time.

The photographer set about posing them, and Megan turned her attention to helping Claire and Ivy with the finishing touches.

By the time Megan returned to the main living space, the chairs had filled with guests and Ivy had tucked Mariah away with her bridesmaids. Even though she'd seen the guest list, she was still a little starstruck too. She recognized two of the Christiansen sisters, Grace and Eden, sitting with their hockey-player husbands among the guests.

The sunlight broke through the clouds, bathing the frozen lake with golden light.

A perfect happily-ever-after. No, *almost* perfect. Despite her best efforts, the ice cream truck had become her Achilles' heel. The one thing she couldn't deliver.

And she couldn't fix it.

She looked around the room. Ivy, Darek, Claire—they'd all shown up to help her. And Raina. And Casper. Even Cole, in his absence. He'd delivered on this wedding. Over-delivered.

No, she wasn't alone. God had placed each of these people in her life.

And if her parents hadn't left, she never would have set her sights on the Black Spruce. She would have continued in her role, trying to earn their favor, trying to be enough.

But she didn't have to be enough.

Trust God.

Oh, Cole. She could see him standing in the hotel hallway, overwhelmed by the sense that she'd chosen Trevor over him. Not understanding her fears because she'd never let him in. She'd kept things hidden out of fear. Fear she didn't actually have the control of her life that she desired.

Fear because she hadn't ever let go and trusted God.

Fear that she wouldn't know what to do if God's plans didn't look like hers.

I should have asked You for help.

She blinked back tears, letting the warped beliefs she'd clung to shake free.

But even the hairs of your head are all numbered. Fear not, therefore; you are of more value than many sparrows.

The couple's pastor from Minneapolis stood up front to officiate and Cameron took his place next to him.

Megan stood at the back, timing the entrance of each bridal party member, then took a seat at the back with Claire and Ivy.

"This is magnificent," Ivy said.

Megan nodded. As usual, she got a little weepy eyed with the romance of the I-dos.

And maybe, okay, this time it hurt a little bit more.

The ceremony ended and the bride and groom made their exit to the foyer while the caterers changed out the room for the reception. Megan took the bride's bouquet from Mariah as she and Cameron stepped into a private room for a moment alone.

Casper blasted through the front door. "Megan, you're going to have to come out front. There's an unexpected guest in the driveway."

Nope. Not today. Not when everything was riding on this wedding.

"Here." She shoved the bride's bouquet into Ivy's hands. "I'll be right back."

Megan ran out the front door and froze at the tinkling chimes of an—ice cream truck?

It was the size of a parking patrol vehicle. Three-wheeled. Diminutive.

With Cole. She swallowed.

He'd squeezed himself into the driver's seat. Well, the only seat. He wore his suit and an old-fashioned soda fountain hat and he looked positively ridiculous.

Wedding guests had followed her out. She caught Eden tucking behind her extremely large husband, covering her laughter.

Megan stood on the doorstep as he pulled up.

"I heard you needed an ice cream truck." He smiled, but something of worry seemed to linger in his eyes. He unfolded himself and climbed out of the truck and stood in front of her. "We have seven delicious flavors."

Oh, she bet he did.

Casper stepped forward, popped the hat off Cole's head and put it on his own. "Ice cream, anyone?"

Mariah came out the door with Cameron. "What?" she

shrieked. "Are you kidding me? You got the ice cream truck? Megan—you really are the best!" She threw her arms around Megan.

"I live to serve," she said lamely.

Mariah let her go and headed toward the truck.

Cole walked to Megan.

"You look like a clown in that car." She wrapped her arms around her waist.

He stood there, a hint of whiskers across his chin, and she focused her eyes on the lake. Looking at him still hurt too much.

"I know I don't deserve a second chance."

She drew away from the crowd, his footsteps following. She turned, faced him. "What are you doing here? You disappeared. Just...left." She shook her head. "You didn't even say goodbye to Josh. Broke your promise and left us. And then you show up in a —a—in an ice cream truck?" She gestured toward the crowd.

He reached out, his fingers brushing the tangle of hair that had blown across her face. "I know, Mae. I'm so sorry for the awful things I said. For the accusations. For leaving."

Oh.

She stared at him, standing there holding out his heart to her. She swallowed and lifted her hand toward the miniature vehicle. "That really makes a statement. I think it beats the minivan."

"I hope it's the statement that says I'm sorry. I was a terrible, rotten idiot." He stepped closer, until she could smell him, feel the heat of his body. "I wish I could take back the things I said. I wish I hadn't left."

Megan closed her eyes, stepped away. Let the words soak into her soul.

"Mae?" He called out to her, soft and sweet and low. "I hope it says I love you."

She faced him. Took in all that the future might mean. Yeah, not how she'd hoped God would fix it. Because loving Cole meant leaving Deep Haven. Following him to his new job.

But maybe she felt like she was ready to trust. Ready to take that leap of faith.

"I love you too, Cole."

He wrapped her in his arms, held her close.

"I'm sorry too. I didn't know how to handle Trevor's calls. And then, I felt stuck. If I turned him down, I was afraid he'd come after me legally—but then, I didn't maintain the right boundaries either."

"I understand now."

Laughter trailed out the front door of Pine Acres behind the family and friends beginning to head back inside. "Oh, no! The reception—I'm—"

"Shh. It's okay." He pointed over his shoulder at Casper. "You're special to a lot of people, Megan. Ivy and Claire have it covered inside."

"How did you find the ice cream truck?" She gestured toward the cart where Casper waited to fill orders.

"With a lot of help. Casper, Darek, Kyle—"

"You got the sheriff in on this?"

"Yes, ma'am. Found it at a resale shop and Josh helped me paint it at Evergreen." He winked and a smile tipped his lips.

"Josh?"

"Yeah. When I asked for his forgiveness, he made me fight for it. He challenged me to a push-up battle."

"Really?"

"I think he let me win." He drew his fingers along her cheek and took a deep breath, as if he might be preparing for a jump. "Ever since the first time you climbed my grandfather's back fence to get your Frisbee—"

"You remember that?" She smiled, slid her hand into his. "You know, I threw it over on purpose. I wasn't even playing

SUSAN MAY WARREN & RACHEL D. RUSSELL

with it… I just wanted to get a better look at Mr. Barrett's cute grandson." She wiped tears from her face.

"I remember all of it. I've always remembered you." His eyes held hers. "You've always been the one." He reached for her and she stepped into his embrace. He wrapped her in his arms. "I love you, Mae."

"I love you, too, Ranger."

"I have this nice little apartment available while I'm fixing up my house."

"Your house? Maybe you didn't notice, but it's sold—but you know what? I'll follow you to Minneapolis. To DC. Wherever they assign you, Josh and I will go."

"Right. That." He grinned at her. "I hear the buyer dickered quite a bit, but he's a tough former Ranger—"

She sucked in a breath. "You bought your own house?"

"I bought my grandfather's house. So I could make it our home."

She pressed her hands to his face and met his eyes. "It's about time."

CHAPTER 16

*M*egan stood facing Cole. She was right. It was about time. He wrapped his arms around her and kissed her.

A kiss of longing, of youthful dreams realized. A kiss that said he'd never leave her.

A kiss that meant home.

When she shivered, though, he let her go, tugged off his jacket and wrapped her in it.

Most of the guests had filtered back inside to the reception, now set up. But Megan led him downstairs to the quiet corner where he'd thawed her out.

Or maybe she'd done the thawing.

He saw a tinge of blush on her cheeks, too, when they sat down.

Laughter rose from the crowd on the upper level. Ivy appeared at the top of the stairs, holding a bouquet of flowers.

"Sorry to interrupt—but if you two are ready to join the party, there's a bride who's raving about the amazing day."

"Yes, soon," Megan answered.

SUSAN MAY WARREN & RACHEL D. RUSSELL

Ivy looked from Megan to Cole. "Right. We won't be holding our breath."

"I kind of feel like a wedding crasher." Cole rubbed the back of his fingers down her cheek.

"You're a wedding crasher of the best sort. Besides, you did help plan it with military precision."

"Looks like you'll be named to the North Woods Premier Wedding Planners list." He gave her a wink.

"Looks like it."

"And you have the cash to buy the Black Spruce."

"What are you going to do?"

"I've applied to the sheriff's department. Seems they could use a guy like me."

"*I* could use a guy like you." She waggled her brows at him.

"Yeah?" He reached out and tucked a loose lock behind her ear.

"Definitely."

"Have I mentioned how sorry I am?" He squeezed her hand. "There isn't a lot that scares me, but that—the thought of losing you—I should have known better. Trusted." He shook his head, swallowed. "I know you better than that."

"When you didn't show up, Trevor moved down and...I've never been good at telling people no. Didn't want to create a scene." She looked up at him. "And then, when you didn't show up, didn't call—at first, I was worried. But then I saw your Jeep at the hotel and I knew you'd chosen to not come."

He nodded. "I was letting anger fuel my decisions. And then, once I'd convinced myself I was wrong, I went downstairs to find you—"

"Only to have me tell you to leave."

"Yeah." He let out a breath. "It's best that you did. That isn't the way I want to handle things."

"He probably had it coming." She rubbed her soft fingertips across his hand.

"Still. Fighting isn't what I do unless it's necessary. But I can promise you I won't let him hurt you or Josh. And if he ever tries to misuse the law to take Josh away, we're in it together."

"Yeah?"

"Yes, ma'am."

She tugged gently on his tie, drawing him closer.

He traced the curve of her jaw with his fingers and she leaned into his hand. He lifted her chin, let her golden eyes hold his, and kissed her. Right there on the couch, with an entire room full of wedding guests upstairs. Only this time, no one would interrupt them.

She molded her body against his, wrapping her hands around his neck. It was more exciting than jumping out of any airplane. Better than any successful mission. She tasted like sweet comfort, trust. Safety.

Yeah, he always knew it. She tasted like home.

The sunshine descended on Deep Haven three weeks later, warming Megan to her soul when she climbed out of her Subaru. The Sold sign had been pulled from the front yard and the snow had turned slushy, squishing beneath her boots. There was an ever so faint hum of spring in the air. The promise of a new beginning.

Josh bailed from the car and began running to the house.

"Hey—don't forget your project supplies," she called to him.

"My what?" He paused. "Oh. Yeah." He ran back to the car and tugged the bag from the back seat.

"You're unusually energized for a Saturday morning."

"Let's stop in and see Cole," Josh said, bypassing the apartment door and heading straight to the house.

Megan smiled. She'd had an opportunity to sit down with

SUSAN MAY WARREN & RACHEL D. RUSSELL

Josh and talk about Trevor. What his place in Josh's life might be
—and that Josh would be involved in those decisions.

Cole sat in the remodeled front room, the smell of fresh
paint permeating the air.

"Hi," he said. "I have some exciting news."

"You do?" She turned to close the door and realized Josh was
gone. "Where did—"

"Must have had to go take care of something." A smile
hitched the side of his face. Completely mischievous.

"So, what's the big news?"

"Say hello to the newest addition to Deep Haven's finest." He
held up his official job offer.

"Excellent! When do you start?" She wrapped her arms
around his waist, inhaling his rich, masculine scent.

"Monday." He took her hand. "And there's something I want
to show you."

"Okay. Where are we going?"

He led her out the front door and across the soggy yard to
the Black Spruce and pushed open the door.

The entire first floor glowed with twinkle lights.

"I've gotten pretty good at decorating."

"Yes." Not only was the great room filled with warm light,
but several large floral arrangements filled with red roses and
white lilies had been added.

She sucked in a breath. "What is all this?" Her stomach did a
little flip-flop.

He tugged her inside her latest acquisition. They'd already
repainted the interior and she'd selected several new furniture
pieces.

"So, you like what I've done with the place?"

"What are you up to?" A giddy excitement started swirling in
her stomach—like each summer when she saw him step out of
his parents' car.

He got down on one knee, tugged a ring from his pocket.

"Megan Rae Carter, will you marry me?"

Megan nodded, let the tears flow, half laughing, half crying. "Yes. Absolutely, I'll marry you."

He slid the ring onto her hand, stood, and wrapped his arms around her. He leaned down, his smooth-shaved cheek against hers, and he kissed her. He tasted like laughter and friendship and the future.

She pulled back and wiped the tears from her cheeks. "Wait a minute—was Josh in on this?"

Cole nodded. "He was. I had to make sure…"

He'd put his heart in the hands of a nine-year-old.

"So, he approved?"

"Yes, ma'am."

Realization washed over her. "Did he really need supplies for a school project?"

"We might have planned a diversion for you."

"Yeah. I thought something seemed fishy when he ambled around and couldn't even tell me what he needed, then decided on a binder and some markers." She let the comfort and warmth of his body press against her and looked up at the canopy over them. "You've got mad skills with the twinkle lights."

"You like those, huh?"

"I do."

"I like hearing you say that."

She loved him so much it ached in her chest. Left her a little breathless.

She placed her palms flat against his chest, feeling his heartbeat beneath her fingertips. "You know, there will be times I need to talk to Trevor."

Cole nodded, his blue eyes soft and bright. "Yes, ma'am, I understand." He placed his hands over hers and gave a soft squeeze. "Thank you."

"For what?"

"For knowing my weaknesses and loving me anyway."

"Ranger, from the moment you stole my Frisbee, you stole my heart."

He smiled, and there it was. The excitement and adventure of the boy she knew.

She rubbed her fingers against his. "So, tell me about this team I keep hearing about."

"It's been impressed upon me that the region is in need of an organized team to respond to community crises, search and rescue needs, and remote injuries."

"Definitely."

"So Kyle is tasking me as the team coordinator and sheriff's department liaison in the newly established Crisis Response Team. We're looking through the skills volunteers already have. The equipment we have access to—I can't even believe there isn't a helicopter available."

Megan nodded. "Yeah, I still think about Josh and Tiger— what happens when people are farther out into the Boundary Waters?"

"Exactly. I'll be working to create an implementation plan. Getting things geared up, ensuring every one of the volunteers and paid staff have up-to-date training. And we'll need funding for all that, but I think we'll find a way to get it done. I don't know how yet—it's pretty ambitious."

"If anyone can do it, it's you, Ranger."

Josh appeared in the kitchen doorway. "Did she say yes?"

Cole gave him a thumbs-up.

"Of course I did. You're okay with that, right?"

"Yes!" Josh threw his hands over his head. He ran back into the kitchen and the back door creaked. "She said yes!"

She heard the bustling of footsteps and voices entering from the back door.

What in the world? "Are you kidding me? You invited a houseful of people over?" She cut him a look. "You've had half this town in on everything between the wedding and this."

"It was a calculated risk," he said. "And I didn't have a contingency plan."

"You're pretty courageous."

They all spilled in—Ivy, Tiger, Darek, Casper, Raina, Seb, Jensen, and Claire.

And Josh, who was smiling and laughing and running around the place.

"I think this calls for a celebration." Cole turned to the group.

"Congratulations," Ivy said. She waggled her brows at Megan. "I guess all those hours baking paid off."

"You're hilarious."

"I knew it was all a matter of time." Ivy slid her arm into Darek's.

"Just so we're clear, this is going to be a very short engagement." Megan leaned in and kissed Cole. "I think we've waited long enough, and I have some connections in the industry."

"I agree. How about an April or May wedding? We can keep it small."

"Sounds good to me."

"And I think we should have it here—the first official event at the newly renovated Black Spruce."

"Sounds perfect."

She felt like she glowed even beyond the twinkle lights that filled the space. They'd worked hard since she'd finalized the purchase of the Black Spruce. Cleaning. Planning. Cole had already set to work on repairs. She had no doubt it would, in fact, become the event center she'd dreamed of. A place for happily-ever-afters.

Starting with theirs.

CONNECT WITH SUNRISE

Thank you so much for reading *Still the One*. We hope you enjoyed the story. If you did, would you be willing to do us a favor and leave a review? It doesn't have to be long—just a few words to help other readers know what they're getting. (But no spoilers! We don't want to wreck the fun!) Thank you again for reading!

We'd love to hear from you—not only about this story, but about any characters or stories you'd like to read in the future. Contact us at www.sunrisepublishing.com/contact.

We also have a monthly update that contains sneak peeks, reviews, upcoming releases, and fun stuff for our reader friends.

As a treat for signing up, we'll send you a free novella written by Susan May Warren that kicks off the new Deep Haven Collection! Sign up at www.sunrisepublishing.com/free-prequel.

You're the One That I Want

For other books by Susan May Warren, visit her website at
http://www.susanmaywarren.com.

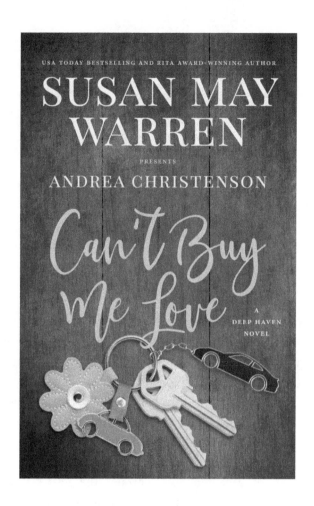

Turn the page for a sneak peek of the next Deep Haven novel,
Can't Buy Me Love ...

SNEAK PEEK

CAN'T BUY ME LOVE

These shoes were going to be the death of her.

Ella wiggled her toes and waited for the elevator to arrive, refusing another glance at her watch. Yes, she was late, but what did they say about being fashionably late?

Just down the hall and through the lobby, music spilled out of the bar area of the Century Hotel in downtown Minneapolis. Elegance dripped from the high-hanging chandelier of the foyer, the deep blue and gold carpets, and the massive floral arrangement on a center table. Through the glass ceiling that arched over the lobby expanse, the night sky had turned to diamonds, while just below it the breath of the underworld pumped out of the massive vents in the sidewalks like a dragon aslumber.

It was a fairytale night.

A fairytale she didn't belong in. Ella *should* be at home in Deep Haven in her flannel pajamas instead of freezing to death in this skimpy ice-blue satin dress. Colleen Decker, her former college roommate, had loaned her the dress, an ankle-length ball gown that hugged Ella's slim curves before flaring out at the knees. The neckline dropped to just below her collarbone in the front and just below her shoulder blades in the back. The shoes —Manolo Blahnik stilettos that Colleen had found on eBay— would probably cut off all feeling from her toes by the end of the night. She should have worn her pink Converse.

The price she paid for her dreams.

She inventoried the contents of her tiny handbag for the third time in as many minutes. Lip gloss? *Check.* The 3x5 notecards for her pitch? *Check.* Thumb drive with a backup copy of her pitch? *Check.* Shareholders' Gala invitation with "Ella Nicole Bradley" embossed in gold across the front? *Check.*

She squeezed the clasp back together. If only Colleen would have let her bring her own normal-sized purse along. That bag had been relegated to the same pile as the flannel and jeans. But she probably wouldn't need the Kleenex, sewing kit, hand sanitizer, Band-Aids, granola bar, and other supplies she usually kept fully stocked in her oversized purse.

Probably.

Ella adjusted the white faux mink stole Colleen had thrown across her shoulders at the last moment.

"You're going to need something warm," her friend had said earlier that evening. "It may be nice outside now, but it's still winter in Minnesota. The weatherman said we may get a late-March snow tonight."

"No way." Her conversation with Colleen drifted back to her as she watched the elevator lights crawl down from the twenty-first floor. "That dress is way out of my comfort zone." She turned to look at the back of the borrowed dress in the mirror.

"Nonsense. This color is perfect with your blonde hair, and it will bring out the blue in your eyes. You want to knock 'em dead tonight. After all, you might meet the devastatingly handsome and irredeemably rakish Adrian Vassos." Colleen had given her a wink. "Did you hear he drove his car into the nearly frozen Lake Kellogg a month ago? Silly man. He should know that the ice wasn't going to be thick enough this late in the winter. He's lived there all his life. Good thing that boy is hot. He can get away with things like that." Colleen fanned her face with her hand, pretending to swoon at the thought of Adrian Vassos.

Adrian Vassos was the last person on Ella's mind tonight. He could drive into as many lakes as he wanted, woo any girl he came across, as long as he stayed out of her way. He might be the son of the owner, but her goal was a face-to-face with the man at the top of the food chain.

Her last chance to salvage the life she hoped to create.

The lights dinged at floor fourteen.

"A good pair of shoes make all the difference." Colleen had reached to the back of the closet and pulled out a shoebox. Nestled under the lid inside a few sheets of tissue paper lay a pair of pale blue slingback heels with tiny crystals sewn in a star pattern across the toes.

If only they fit. Her feet screamed, even after only ten minutes. Why hadn't she stuck to her Converse sneakers?

"Over my dead body! Girl! You don't wear Chucks to the party of the year."

So, yes, she'd tried on the shoes, a little mesmerized. Maybe these shoes would bring the confidence she so desperately needed.

"Fine, I'll wear them, but if I fall on my face and die, I'm coming back to haunt you."

Colleen had grinned at her. "Haunt me all you want. I'm on your side. Want to practice your pitch one more time?"

"Let's just get going. Wouldn't want to be late to the party of the year."

The drive from Colleen's apartment in Robbinsdale to the newly built Century Hotel in downtown Minneapolis passed more quickly than Ella would have liked.

"I don't think I can do this," she'd confessed as they pulled up.

Colleen had waved her words away. "Nonsense. You can and you will. You have months of research under your belt. No one could be more prepared than you."

"They will know I don't belong here. They'll know I'm just pretending."

"Why do you hold so tightly to the idea that you don't belong? The party is for shareholders, and *you are a shareholder.*"

"Colleen, I have one half of a share. *One half.*" Ella's palms grew damp. She clutched the edges of her seat to keep from wiping her hands on the satin of her dress. "They'll see right through me the second I walk through that door. I'm just a housekeeper, a glorified maid."

Colleen pulled up to the valet stand and put her car in park. "Ella, look at me. No, look me in the eyes. Ella Girl, you are the daughter of a King, and no one can look down on you."

"I *used* to be the daughter of a king." It was true. Her dad had been Michael Bradley, the King of Clean, owner of the Helping Hands cleaning empire. But all that came to a screeching halt when he died two years ago.

"That's not what I'm talking about. Do you believe you are a child of God? He's the king I mean. You are every bit as worthy as the people inside this hotel. Not because you have half a share or a thousand, not because of your job or anything in your bank account." Colleen had been so earnest, Ella couldn't stop herself from nodding.

Besides, Colleen was right—she *had* studied for months, practicing and perfecting her formulas as well as her sales pitch. It was time to take Essentially Ella to the next level. All she needed to do now was convince Mr. Vassos to listen to her for five minutes. Surely he'd give that much time to the daughter of an old friend. And then, hopefully, he'd love her idea.

"You got this. Go in and knock 'em dead."

Right.

Now, Ella shifted again in her too-small shoes as the elevator dinged to the lobby.

"I can do this," Ella murmured. "I am prepared. I am ready. *I can do this.*"

The doors slid open.

Oh no.

The curving back of the tiny elevator was a clear pane of glass, a window to the world. Supposedly these glass elevators were elegant and classy, offering riders a view of the sprawling city below...but the open look across the high vista of downtown Minneapolis sent a shiver down Ella's spine. It was easier to pretend she wasn't up so high when she didn't have a constant reminder of the distance. The elevator seemed to be designed to make passengers feel like they were soaring into the clouds.

Maybe she should take the stairs instead.

She took a step back and nearly stumbled. Nope. In these shoes the elevator was the only real option.

Ella wobbled inside, grabbed onto the brass handrail, and hit the button for the twentieth floor. She would just face forward, breathe deeply, keep her eyes on the wall panel, and watch the numbers go up as she rose higher and higher. She would be fine.

Probably.

After all, the odds of plummeting to death in a catastrophic elevator incident were about one in 10.5 million.

Above the number panel was a poster for a charity event happening tonight on the twenty-first floor. Buy-in was listed at three thousand dollars. Apparently it was an opportunity for rich people to prove to their rich friends how charitable they all were.

Checking her reflection in the mirrored surface of the elevator wall, Ella noticed one of her blonde curls escaping the updo she and Colleen had labored over earlier. She reached a hand up to re-pin the wayward piece of hair. This whole outfit was beginning to feel like a costume, a mask that Ella put on to accomplish her goal.

Her stomach grumbled, lunch with Colleen a distant memory. See—she *did* need her regular purse. At least then she'd have snacks.

This had to be the slowest elevator in the world.

The doors finally started to slide shut when she heard a shout.

"Hold the door!"

Ella rolled her eyes but stuck her hand against the door to keep it open. A tuxedoed man slid in, bringing the spicy scent of cologne. The delicious, heady fragrance washed hints of pine and summer rain over her. He carried a purple stole in his hands.

One of the upper crust, heading to the upstairs party. She knew the type.

"Thank you. Floor twenty-one, please," Tuxedo said as he stood slightly to the left.

Yep. She hit the button, stole a glance sideways.

Goodness. The man was possibly the most handsome human being she'd ever shared a small space with. His tuxedo stretched across broad shoulders, and dark, wavy hair skimmed the back of his neck, nearly to his collar. His green eyes sat over a Grecian nose. Suddenly the heights weren't the only thing making her blood zing through her veins.

Oh brother. She hadn't come to the party to swoon over the men.

Focus, Ella, focus. You have one night to make this happen. One night to change lives.

No distractions allowed.

She risked another glance at him.

ACKNOWLEDGMENTS

I listened with rapt attention to Susan May Warren's announcement with Lindsay Harrel in the fall of 2019. I had no idea how their call for applications to Sunrise Publishing's inaugural year would drastically change my life. How *Still the One* would take shape from an idea in my head to a story on the page—nor, truly, how many incredible people would help me bring it to life.

This novel has been an opportunity and exercise of spiritual growth for me. Gratitude and praise for my Lord and Savior, Jesus Christ.

Not a word could have been written without the endless support of my husband, Brian, and our sons. Thank you for giving me the courage and support to pursue this calling. For giving me the endless hours required to write, feeding me, cheering me on, and providing invaluable feedback. I could not have done this without you. Thank you for believing in me and telling me, "We know you can do this."

My mom, who has been my longtime cheerleader. Thank you for encouraging my writing at an early age, for chasing down every author who would speak to me at the elementary school programs, and for sharing in my excitement. A special thank you to each of my siblings who shared in my enthusiasm and prayed for me throughout this process.

Susan May Warren, whose tireless guidance, mentoring, prayer, and friendship has made me a better writer and person. I'm grateful beyond words. Thank you for believing in me long before I believed in myself. Your expert gentle redirection (aka constructive criticism) and genuine passion for teaching are gifts, and I treasure being a recipient of your generous and faithful ministry. I would not be the writer I am today without your instruction through Novel Academy, classes at Oregon Christian Writer's, and the mentorship of this past year. Thank you for sharing your world of Deep Haven and the beloved characters with me.

Lindsay Harrel, who was willing to ask the hard plot and detail questions. Thank you for pushing me to chase down answers to those niggling questions a reader would have. For every email that started with, "One more thing—," thank you.

For my Season One Deep Haven writing partners—Andrea Christenson and Michelle Sass Aleckson. I can't imagine doing this without you. You've made this experience so much richer and transformative. I'm honored to work with you. Thank you for sharing prayers laughter, and tears. For responding to every "SOS" writing emergency I had. The endless hours of brain-storming, rewriting, and editing would not have been nearly as much fun (rewriting is fun, right?) without you. Your GIFs, emojis, and writer memes are the best.

Barbara Curtis, my editor. What an amazing gift you have! Thank you for helping me hone the story, finessing it to completion. You've helped me smooth out the muddled bits and polish the best of it all to make the story shine.

Rel Mollet, whose passion for books translates to expert proofreading and marketing skills. I appreciate your attention to detail with the eyes of not just a reader, but a true bibliophile.

Tari Faris, who never hesitated to jump on the phone and spitball a scene. Thank you for sharing your insights. You have no idea how many times you talked me down from the angst, strife, and turmoil of being an author working under a deadline.

For members of the My Book Therapy huddles who have supported me, I am grateful. Barbara, Deanna, Gracie, Heidi, Jenni, Kristi, Mandy, Nancy, Suzy, and Tari, thank you for your prayers and encouragement. How many times did your prayers seem to go directly to God's ears and show up for me when I needed it most?

For the ladies of CCM: Audra, Beth, Bethany J., Bethany L., Heather, Jordan, Keli, Michele, and Patty. I'm ever grateful that God brought us together. Your prayers, friendship, encouragement, and excitement for me have filled my heart.

Thank you for my local writing critique group: April, Danika, Julie, Kendy, Kelly, Linda, Melinda, Melody, and Sandra. You have helped me grow through your prayer, feedback, edits, and encouragement. Thank you for pushing me to go deeper, cut out the fluff, choose great verbs, and show the story on the page.

Amie and Kim, who listened to me endlessly wax on and on about my fictional friends, who read my earliest writings years ago (the really awful ones!), and still believed in me. Thank you for every word of encouragement and feedback you gave me when all I had was a dream and a scene.

For the Thursday night Novel Academy peptalk crew. Thank you for showing up every Thursday night. I've learned so much being a part of such a talented and diverse group of writers.

My greatest fear as I write this is that I will leave someone out—if that's you, know that it's with zero intent! I have been overwhelmed by the amount of support for this novel. My heartfelt thanks to each and every person who has been on this journey with me.

ABOUT THE AUTHORS

USA Today bestselling, RITA, Christy and Carol award winning novelist **Susan May Warren** is the author of over 80 novels with nearly 2 million books sold, most of them contemporary romance with a touch of suspense. One of her strongest selling series has been the Deep Haven series, a collection of books set in Northern Minnesota, off the shore of Lake Superior. Visit her at www.susanmaywarren.com.

Rachel D. Russell is a member of Oregon Christian Writers, My Book Therapy's Novel Academy, and is a regular contributor to the Learn How to Write a Novel blog. When Rachel's not cheering on one of her two teens at sporting events, she's often interrogating her husband on his own military and law enforcement experience to craft believable heroes in uniform. The rest of her time is spent cantering her horse down the Oregon trails and redirecting her three keyboard-hogging cats. Visit her at www.racheldrussell.com.

Still the One: A Deep Haven Novel

Published by Sunrise Media Group LLC

Scripture quotations are taken from the King James Version of the Bible.

Scripture quotations are also taken from the Holy Bible, New International Version®, NIV®. Copyright© 1973, 1978, 1984, 2011 by Biblica, Inc®. Used by permission of Zondervan. All rights reserved worldwide.

For more information about Rachel D. Russell and Susan May Warren, please access the authors' websites at the following respective addresses: www.racheldrussell.com and www.susanmaywarren.com.

Published in the United States of America.

Cover Design: Jenny at Seedlings Designs

Editing: Barbara Curtis

CPSIA information can be obtained
at www.ICGtesting.com
Printed in the USA
LVHW031653180121
676812LV00024B/196